WICKED CAPTOR

BOSTON MAFIA DONS

BIANCA COLE

CONTENTS

1

SIENA

The breath from my lungs escapes as I watch the magical winter scene rush past the window. Glistening, glass-like ice encases the leaves on the trees lining the boulevard, and soft snow lies on the sidewalk, covering everything and filling the air with a sense of alluring magic.

The Christmas spirit hits me harder than ever before. The scenes outside the car remind me of the Christmas movies you watch on television, but I never imagined it would be this awe-inspiring in person.

Snow rarely appears in Palermo and never like this. Mount Etna has snow in the winter, but the trek up the mountain isn't pleasant in the cold weather. I'm not a fan of the cold. However, wrapped up in the warmth of my faux-fur winter coat in the heated cab, the wintery scenes rushing past cause an oddly warming sensation.

My first impression of Boston is that it's a sprawling

concrete jungle, so different from the cities in Italy. Rome is a similarly large city but steeped in stone buildings and an archaic history that few places on earth can match. There's history here, but it's more modern.

My phone buzzes, and I dig it out of my purse. Aida's name flashes on the front.

Are you here yet?!

I smile at her infectious enthusiasm and type back.

Yes, I'm in the cab. See you soon.

The past four months have been crazy since Gia and Fabio's secret was revealed. My initial reaction was anger since Gia had been lying to my face for months. The argument we had the day after she visited Aida was monumental, and I was so angry that I couldn't forgive her right away. Unfortunately, we both said things we regret.

For a month, I gave her the cold shoulder and didn't return her calls. However, life in Sicily was lonely without either of my best friends. After a month, I gave her the chance to grovel and explain herself. It's not been easy, but our relationship is on the mend.

I can't imagine how Aida felt learning about her best friend and father. Out of the two of us, she is the one who has the right to hate Gia forever.

Everything has changed so fast. Gia is no longer my roommate and is heavily pregnant. It's been strange living alone above the shop, but I still see her every day when she comes to work.

I think back to the times Gia would wind Aida up about how hot her father was. Never in a million years would I have thought she'd marry him. Aida didn't speak to Gia for a couple of months, so Gia flew out with me for her birthday, hoping that Aida might listen to her.

I'll give it to Gia, she groveled. After a few days, the tension settled, and Aida forgave her. Deep down, we both knew that Gia didn't want to hurt anyone, no matter how selfish her actions were. After seeing her with Fabio frequently, it's clear they are truly in love.

Nothing will ever be the same again, though, as Gia's lies did damage that will exist between the three of us for the rest of our lives. It surprised me when Aida told me she had invited Gia and Fabio for Christmas, as Aida hadn't spoken to her father since before he sent her to Boston.

This Christmas could be interesting. I shake my head and try not to dwell on the inevitable awkwardness surrounding my two best friends' relationship.

This year will be the first I'm not spending Christmas in Rome with my family. My father had business to attend to in Hong Kong, so they stayed for Christmas as it's such a long way. They invited me to fly out, but I opted for Christmas in Boston, mainly because Aida begged me, as she can't face her father and Gia alone. I've never been to America and have always wanted to visit.

The driver curses as he hits more traffic then glances at me in the rear-view mirror. "I'm sorry, but we're going to take longer than I expected."

I smile at him, shaking my head. "No worries. I'm not in a rush."

He nods. "Where are you from?"

"Sicily. I'm here on vacation to spend Christmas with my best friend."

"Nice. It's colder here than Sicily, I'd imagine," he says as the traffic begins to move more freely.

"Yes, far colder. I'm not used to the cold."

"No, but it's nice weather for Christmas." He falls silent again as we travel through the city toward Aida and Milo's home. From the pictures Aida sent me, it's more of a mansion than even Fabio's modern villa on the coast of Sicily.

After another twenty minutes, the man pulls up a driveway, and the house comes into view.

"Wow, your friend must be rich," the cab driver says.

"Her husband is," I reply, digging into my purse in search of thirty dollars to pay the fare. "Here you go." I pass him the money before slipping out of the car.

He gets out too and helps me with my bag. "All set. Have a great Christmas."

"Thanks, and you too," I say, glancing at the imposing mansion as he gets back into his car and drives away.

A squeal from the doorway tells me Aida's already there to greet me before I make it up the porch. She doesn't even wait for me to move, rushing down the steps and charging into me.

I laugh as I hug her tightly. "You'd think we hadn't seen each other in years."

Aida tuts. "We haven't."

"You are so dramatic. I saw you two months ago."

Gia appears behind her, smiling. "Hey, Siena." Gia

arrived a few days earlier as Fabio has business meetings to attend with Milo. She walks down the steps and greets me, pulling me in for a hug. "How was your flight?"

I sigh. "Long. I'm glad I'm here at last."

Gia takes one of my bags. "Let me take that." She turns back to the house to carry it inside.

"Come on," Aida says, leading me up the grand stairs to the porch of the mansion she calls home. "I want you to meet some people." She leads me through the door, and my mouth drops open.

The size of the Christmas tree is ridiculous. The tree has to stretch about twenty feet high, standing proudly at the center landing of an imperial staircase that sweeps up either side. "Wow." It's the only word I can find. The sheer luxury of Milo's home is awe-inspiring.

Aida smiles and links her arm with mine. "Leave your luggage here, and the staff will take it to your room." She leads me away from the front entrance, down a wide corridor, and into a vast library where ten people gather, chatting. Aida glances at me. "Milo will be pleased to see you again."

I jerk her to a stop. "The man hates me, Aida. If you can't see that, then you are blind."

She tuts and waves her hand. "Nonsense. Milo doesn't hate you, Siena. He is like that with everyone."

I sigh as she drags me over to her grump of a husband. "Hey, Milo, how are you?" I say, making an effort.

Milo looks at me with an ice-cold stare that could

frighten anyone. "I'm fine, Siena. How are you?" His jaw clenches just asking me that question.

"I'm good, thanks. A lovely house you've got here." I gesture at the room.

He takes a sip of his drink. "Indeed."

That kills the conversation. Aida is speaking to a man next to Milo, so I nudge her slightly to signal that I want to get away from Milo. She doesn't read the signal. Instead, she introduces me to the man she's talking to. "Oh, how rude of me. Siena, this is Piero."

She smiles at Piero. "Piero, this is Siena, who is one of my best friends."

I hold my hand out to him to shake hands, but he brings the back of it to his mouth and kisses it. "Pleasure to meet you, Siena."

I reclaim my hand and nod. "Yeah, good to meet you." I cross my arms over my chest, feeling uneasy at his intense gaze.

"How was the weather in Sicily when you left?" he asks, trying to make polite conversation.

I shrug. "It was warmer than here but gray and overcast. The snow and ice here are much more magical even if it's freezing."

Piero laughs. "I agree, although the Sicilian coastline was magical in the summer when I visited last." His brow furrows. "I don't remember meeting you on my visit."

I shake my head. "No, I don't think we met." I notice Gia to one side with Fabio and decide to leave. "If you will excuse me."

He nods. "Of course."

As Fabio talks to some man I don't recognize, I walk over to Gia, who is sipping an orange juice. "Hey, I had to get away from Aida's husband. He isn't friendly."

Gia smiles. "He's like that with everyone. You get used to it, in the end."

Fabio finishes talking to the man and turns back to his fiance. "Hello, Siena," he says, holding out his hand to me.

I shake his hand, keeping things civil. It's not the first time I've spent time with them as a couple, but I can't help the anger I harbor for him. The man knew us when we were kids and should have known better than to go near Aida's best friend. Despite knowing they are in love, a part of me thinks it's wrong.

"How are you?" I ask.

He smiles, unlike Milo. "I'm well. How is everything with you? Real estate picking up yet?"

I shake my head. "No, it's still tough." My brow furrows. "I thought you would know that since you run Sicily."

He shrugs. "I had heard that things were picking up, but perhaps that was wrong."

I wish it were picking up, but unfortunately, work is slow. It's why I've decided to make the drastic move to Rome as there are so many more opportunities.

Life in Sicily has changed so much, and I accept there is nothing there for me anymore. I'm a firm believer that everyone makes their luck in life, and sitting stagnant on an island with no prospects is getting me nowhere.

"I haven't noticed it yet. Maybe soon," I say. Guilt

coils through my gut since I intend to keep my new job a secret until after Christmas.

For Aida, it won't be such a big deal. Rome is easier to get to from Boston. But it will upset Gia that I'm leaving the island since we see each other all the time.

It's a decision I had to make for myself. I'm going to start a new, exciting chapter in my life, even if it is scary.

2

MIKHAIL

"I want collateral, do you understand?" I ask, glaring at my sovietnik, Lev. "Andrei is going to visit in one month, and I need to make progress before then."

Lev nods. "I understand." His brow pulls together. "Do you mean Mrs. Mazzeo?"

I grind my teeth, frustrated by the ineptitude of the men who work for me. "Yes. Who else would I mean, Lev?" I walk to the counter on the left-hand side and pour myself a shot of vodka, knocking it back in one. "I want her here within twenty-four hours, or there will be hell to pay."

Lev pales and nods. "Of course, sir. I'll get on it right away." Lev leaves me alone with my chaotic thoughts.

I can't allow Milo to sign the merger with Bionantechnic Group, which he is due to do just after Christmas. It will give him too much legitimate power in the city. It's bad enough that he's entered politics, landing himself a seat on the city council. The man is gunning to control the city, but I won't stand aside while he snatches it.

I have left Milo unchecked for too long. His war with the Irish is waning, but it's about time I shake things up. I can't allow him to get off so easily. According to the rumors, Milo has one weakness now: his wife. She is his world, and I intend to snuff that light from his life and leave him in a state of panic.

Of course, I don't intend to harm her. All I will do is hold her to ransom and blackmail Milo into complying with my demands. I may have to knock her about a bit to get what I want, which may lead to war, but that is life. The Italians are no match for me, even with his pathetic alliance with Fabio Alteri.

"Got a minute, Boss?"

I turn to face Milan, the spy for our bratva. "What is it?"

He shuffles the papers in his hand. "I've got the inside information on Andrei you requested."

I clench my jaw and nod, beckoning him inside my office. "Have a seat."

He shuts the door behind him and sits down opposite me, placing the paper down on my desk. "This is all the dirt I found on him, as requested."

Andrei may be my ally for now, but I don't trust easily. Our partnership has been longstanding, but lately, he's made moves on other cities in the states that concern me. The man is power-hungry, and I won't blindly ignore the moves he makes and wait for him to do the same to me. I have more intelligence than to sit back and wait for him to strike.

"Anything of note?" I ask, knowing that Milan has a good eye for this kind of thing. It's why he's my spy in the bratva.

He nods and shuffles about the papers. "Did you know he is in talks with Spartak Volkov?"

I clench my jaw, shaking my head. "That's news to me."

Spartak, who runs the Volkov bratva of Chicago, is one of my longstanding enemies.

"What talks?" I ask.

Milan shrugs. "I couldn't find out exactly, but I can only assume he wants to join forces. The Volkov bratva is almost as powerful as his."

I run a hand across the back of my neck, shutting my eyes. The past was so much simpler. Ten years ago, when my father died, none of these inter-alliances between cities existed, and Pakhans kept to their turf and avoided each other. Now, Andrei Petrov, the young, inexperienced New York City Bratva leader, has changed everything. He's intelligent but too fucking ambitious.

"Thank you. Keep a vigilant eye on him and try to find out what the talks with Spartak are about." I pick the papers up off the desk. "I will read through the rest of your findings."

Milan stands. "Sir." He bows his head. "Any news on stopping the Italian merger?" he asks since he was the one to bring me news of it.

"I have a plan in place, which Lev is carrying out as we speak."

Milan makes a face. "Are you sure he is the right person to be your sovietnik?"

It's a question I keep asking myself, but I don't appreciate being questioned about my choices. "Are you questioning my decision, Milan?"

He shakes his head. "Of course not. I'm merely voicing my uncertainty over his capabilities."

I narrow my eyes at my spy. "If you were in my shoes, who would you choose?" None of my men, in my eyes, can compete with Aleksander. I wish I could have convinced him to stay, but after thirty-five years of loyal service to the Gurin Bratva, I had to let him retire in peace.

Milan rubs a hand across the back of his neck, looking uncertain about answering the question. "Have you considered Timur?"

I raise a brow. Timur is a young Boyevik who has been with the bratva for only a few years. He's loyal and a great warrior, but I never considered him for the position of sovietnik. "He's too young."

Milan shakes his head. "He is wise beyond his years and far more intelligent than Lev." He holds his hands. "No disrespect meant."

I nod in response. "If Lev fucks up, I'll consider him for the position. Is there anything else?"

Milan straightens, shaking his head. "No, sir. I believe we've covered everything." He runs a hand through his long, dark hair. "Do you want me to continue digging on Andrei?"

I regard my spy, wondering if it's a good idea. Andrei isn't the kind of man who accepts spying amongst allies. "No, I think we have all we need for now. Just find out why he's meeting with Volkov."

Milan nods. "Sir." He walks out of my office.

I stand, pacing over to the dresser on the far wall. I pour myself a double of vodka and knock it back. The hot, fiery liquid takes the edge off. I loosen my tie and then pour myself another, walking over to the couch in my office and slumping down on it.

If it's not one thing, it's another. My life as pakhan of the Gurin Bratva is exhausting. When my father died ten years ago, it forced me to rise to this position earlier than I expected. I had been only twenty-one years old when the Italians killed him in a feud over real estate.

My father cared about nothing more than his family, and he treated me well and taught me how to be a powerful leader. I miss him every day, even if I don't allow myself to dwell on it too much. Grief is cancer that can destroy you from the inside out, and it's why anger became my mantel.

His death tore apart our family. My mother couldn't stand living in the city anymore and moved back to Russia. She rarely visits, unhappy with my decision to take on the role as pakhan. My eldest sister, Yana, lives in Mexico with her husband, Alex, and won't speak to me anymore. My youngest sister, Natalya, lives with me during vacations and attends a private boarding school in Maine.

Natalya's the heir to all of this since Yana wants nothing to do with the family business anymore. My mother didn't agree with Natalya's decision to stay with me, but Natalya begged me to win custody from my mother as she has only ever known life in America. She didn't want to be ripped from it and taken to Russia.

I thought Natalya remaining here would have been enough to convince my mother to stay, but nothing could.

The Syndicate Academy is the perfect place for her to learn everything she needs to know. It's an academy for heirs of powerful families, and Natalya has attended since she was eight years old. In just seven months, she will graduate and take her place by my side as the heir to the Gurin Bratva.

I am looking forward to her return for Christmas vacation in two days.

A child of my own has never been in the cards for me, and I don't trust others, so the burden falls on my baby sister. Until she returns from the academy, I won't know whether she truly has what it takes. Natalya can be ruthless, and her teachers confirm she's one of the strongest pupils in the entire academy.

I'm confident she will reign with an iron fist once I'm no longer here, even if it will take some change for the bratva since it has always been a patriarchal organization. At only thirty-one years old, I intend to continue as the pakhan for many more years to come.

However, if there is one painfully tough lesson I've had

to learn since my father's death, it's the life never turns out the way you expect. He would have still been here, running the bratva and teaching me the ropes, if it hadn't been for Vincenzo Mazzeo, Milo Mazzeo's father.

My phone buzzes, and I dig it out of my pocket. My mother is due to arrive in three days to spend Christmas with us, and it will be the first time she has returned to America for three years.

Somehow, my mother convinced Yana to visit with her husband for the first time in ten years. A few years ago, I went down to Mexico to visit them and make some deals with our suppliers, which didn't go down too well with her. We haven't spoken since then.

I land at three o'clock in the afternoon. Be there to collect me.

As always, she's short and to the point. Her anger over my decision still haunts our tenuous relationship, especially as she blames me for Natalya staying, too.

I sigh heavily and stow my cell phone back in my inside pocket, rubbing my temples. Christmas is the worst time of the year for me, and family events only dredge up the gaping hole my father left in our lives ten years ago.

I can't wait for the holiday season to be over, so we can return to being estranged. Life is easier when the family isn't around to complicate it.

3

SIENA

I sit in the back of the car, glancing out at the magical scenes that pass us. Milo wasn't too happy about the idea of allowing his wife out with Gia and me only. However, Fabio convinced him we'd be fine, especially since we have Aida's bodyguard, Carlo.

I get the sense that Fabio is trying any way he can to make amends with Aida. She's stubborn with him, and I don't blame her. Fabio should never have sent Aida off the way he did nor slept with Gia, as he should have known better.

"Where is it we are going, then?" I ask, glancing over at Aida.

She smiles. "Milo's bar, La Mura."

I raise a brow. "I can't believe you are married to a millionaire."

Aida clears her throat. "Billionaire."

I roll my eyes. "That's fucking ridiculous."

Aida and Gia laugh. "Now we just need to find you your millionaire or billionaire," Gia says, glancing at Aida. "What did you think of Piero?"

My brow furrows, and I shake my head. "You can't be serious?"

Aida shrugs. "You are single, and he's single. Why not?"

"Because he's a criminal."

Both Gia and Aida look a little offended by the blatantly obvious truth. "What's your point? So is my husband," Aida asks.

I shake my head. "Yeah, and your father forced you to marry him. I have a choice in the matter, so no, thank you."

Gia laughs. "Fair enough. I guess she doesn't understand because she's never had a criminal of her own."

Aida glances at Gia, giving her a warning glare. "Please don't talk about having my father, Gia."

Gia swallows, and her cheeks turn red. "I didn't mean it like that." She shakes her head. "I'm sorry."

An awkward silence floods the back of the car for the rest of the journey. I sense this entire Christmas is going to have way too many awkward moments like this. Aida isn't on board with the whole Gia becoming her step-mom and marrying her father thing yet, and rightly so. It wouldn't have surprised me if she had never wanted to see either of them again. However, Aida's heart has always been too big, and she can't stay mad at Gia.

When we finally get out of the car, the mood lightens

again. "I am going to have non-alcoholic drinks since you both can't drink."

Aida and Gia shake their heads. "You don't have to do that."

I raise a brow. "Well, I don't want to be the only drunk one tonight, do I?"

We walk into the bar, and Aida is instantly greeted, then ushered to the VIP area of the bar and given a booth.

"It's like you are a celebrity," I say as I sit in the plush velvet seat around the booth.

Aida laughs. "No, just the owner's wife."

The bodyguard tailing us stands nearby, watching. It's not unusual that Aida has a bodyguard, as she had one the entire time she lived in Sicily.

"What can I get you, Mrs. Mazzeo?" the server asks.

"Two non-alcoholic cocktails for Gia and me." Aida glances at me. "And, what do you want, Siena?"

"I'll have the same, please."

Aida's brow furrows. "Surely you want a drink since you can?"

I shake my head. "I'll be supportive and stay dry tonight."

Gia laughs. "Don't worry, we're not alcoholics, just pregnant."

We all laugh at that. "So, three mocktails?" the server confirms.

I nod. "Yes, please."

The server writes the order on a notepad and leaves.

Gia shakes her head. "I never expected to see the day when Siena ordered anything other than Pinot Grigio at a bar."

Aida and I laugh as the atmosphere lightens. Even if we're not drinking, we need this time, just the three of us, to clear the air.

The server brings our mocktails and sets them down on the table. Once she walks away, I lift my glass. "A toast to friends," I say.

Aida and Gia both exchange uncertain glances before lifting theirs, too.

"To forgiveness," I say, tapping my glass against each of theirs. "It's time to put our differences aside and get hypothetically drunk."

Aida laughs. "I agree. It's been too long since I had a girls' night out."

Gia smiles at Aida. "Agreed."

Awkward silence pulses between us as Gia and Aida sip their non-alcoholic drinks.

"How have you been, Aida?" I ask since it's been a couple of months since I last saw her.

She shrugs. "As well as expected. The feud with the Irish isn't settled yet, but the intensity is waning at last." Her brow furrows. "Can you both keep a secret?"

I exchange glances with Gia. "Of course we can," I say.

Aida glances at Gia. "From my father too."

Gia nods. "I promise."

"I've been meeting with Malachy's wife, Scarlett." She

runs her fingers through her hair anxiously. "We're trying to work out a way to get Milo and Malachy to agree to a truce."

My eyes widen at her admittance of getting involved in such dangerous affairs. "Is that wise, Aida?" I shake my head. "Couldn't you and Scarlett end up dead?" I ask.

Gia stares at Aida thoughtfully. "It is dangerous, but if you guys can pull it off, it will end a lot of grief and suffering for Milo and your father."

The mention of Fabio changes the atmosphere as Aida sits up straighter. "Well, I don't intend to do it for him." Her anger toward her father is unwavering.

"No, but all I'm saying is if you two could team up and get them to drop the war, it would be beneficial for everyone." Gia takes a long sip of her mocktail as if it will ease the tension in the air. When your friends are pregnant, that's the problem: alcohol isn't an option to diffuse the tension.

"It all sounds risky to me, but what do I know?"

When we were little at school, we knew Aida's father was a dangerous man. Everyone on the island knew what kind of shit her family was into, but it didn't change our relationship with Aida. It's hard to believe that both Aida and Gia are entangled in such a dangerous situation because of the men they love.

"Enough about that. Tell me what you've been up to in Sicily, Siena," Aida says, her attention moving to me.

My life ever since Aida moved away and Gia fell for Fabio has been a little boring. "Not much. You know me, same old, same old." I pick up my glass and knock back the rest of my mocktail, wishing I hadn't been so supportive and had instead opted for the strong stuff. "How are you both feeling about becoming mothers?"

Aida sighs heavily, placing her hand on her belly. "Right now, I'm just fed up with carrying this urchin around."

I laugh. "Yeah, I can imagine it's not fun." I've always wanted kids, but I never expected Aida and Gia to have them so early. We're only nineteen, which is seriously young to start a family.

"I hate that I'm always craving peanut butter, even though I'm allergic and hate the stuff," Gia says, leaning back in the cozy bar chair.

"Seriously? Have you been tempted by it even though you are allergic?"

She shakes her head. "No, I don't have a death wish, but the cravings are so weird."

We all laugh at that as the atmosphere lightens. The three of us can't stay mad at each other for long.

"I'll be right back. I need to use the restroom," I say, standing.

Aida smiles. "Sure, it's at the back on the right." It's crazy that her husband owns this swanky bar, as well as a few other establishments in the city. Part of me is jealous that she has such a rich and successful husband, not to mention that he's also gorgeous. My two best friends are married to rich, powerful men, and I'm left alone and scratching to make ends meet with a real estate job that is suffering as sales dry up.

For a while now, I've thought it's time for a change. Gia won't be so upset now that she's got her life with Fabio when I break the news that I've accepted a job in Rome.

I enter the ladies' bathroom and walk up to the mirror, checking my appearance. Part of me forgot what it's like to be around Aida and Gia since everything changed. Their lives have moved on, and they are different people, whereas I'm stuck in the same rut. All I can hope is that moving to Rome will change that.

I turn around and head into a cubicle, locking the door. As I get up and flush the toilet, I reach for the door.

The door to the ladies' bathroom shuts, and I hear someone turn the lock.

My brow furrows as I move my hand from the door, reconsidering stepping out.

Why the hell would someone lock the door?

I can't understand why a sense of unease sweeps over me as heavy footsteps thud slowly outside of the door. They stop in front of my door, making my breathing hitch.

"Come out, little girl," a foreign male voice calls.

I swallow hard, wondering if he is talking to me. "What do you want?" I ask, reaching into my purse to grab my cell phone.

My heart sinks when I can't find it, realizing I left it at the table.

Fuck.

"I just want to talk." From the sound of this man's accent, he's Eastern European.

I stare at the door, too afraid to move.

He bangs on the door, making me jump. "I haven't got all day."

I glance up above the stall and see a small window, which I'd probably just fit through. Whoever this man is, he's bad news. I put the toilet lid down and stand on it, forcing open the window.

"What the fuck are you doing?" the man asks, his tone turning angry.

He attempts to break down the door, slamming his body into it hard.

I make quick work of unfastening the window and slide it open, going head-first out of it. I wriggle, trying to get through the compact space.

"Fuck," I say as my dress snags on something.

The sound of the door breaking open behind me instills a sickening fear in me. A hand grabs hold of my ankle, but instead of pulling me back, he pushes me out of the window. I tumble to the concrete beneath, thumping my head on the floor. "Fuck," I say.

Why the fuck did he throw me out the window?

The thud of nearby footsteps answers my question. Another man approaches me, and he kneels next to me. "There is no escape from us," he says, pulling a syringe out of his jacket pocket.

Adrenaline rushes through my veins as I try to get to my feet. My head swims as I do, and I barely take two steps before the man yanks me back. I scream, hoping someone will hear me in this back alley behind the restaurant.

He places a hand over my mouth quickly, stifling my

screams. Then he thrusts the needle into my neck forcefully, releasing the drug into my system. I instantly feel woozy as another man approaches, speaking in a foreign language to the guy holding me.

The other man walks up to me and slams his elbow into the side of my head, plunging me into darkness.

4

MIKHAIL

I circle the pretty little Italian woman my men picked up, wondering who she is. They got the wrong woman, as the woman sitting slumped in the chair is not Aida Mazzeo.

Again, I'm left in awe at the ineptitude of my sovietnik. Perhaps Milan is right to question me, as I'm questioning myself. He's been in the position for three months now, and all I get from him is one mistake after another.

When I don't say a word, Lev moves closer. "Is there something wrong, sir?" Lev asks, still blissfully unaware that the woman he snatched is not the intended target.

Idiot.

I turn around and face him, narrowing my eyes. "Who did I tell you to bring me?"

His face pales at the tone of my voice. "Mrs. Mazzeo, sir." He shuffles from one foot to the other, proving how intimidated he is by me.

I nod. "Correct. And, who is this?"

His brow furrows as realization kicks in. "I'm going to assume it's not Mrs. Mazzeo."

Anger coils through me as I walk slowly toward him, grabbing the lapel of his suit jacket hard. "You assumed correct," I growl as my rage takes on a life of its own. He fucked up such a simple job, which makes me wonder why I ever chose him. "How the fuck did you make such a rooky mistake?"

Lev pales and shakes his head. "I'm sorry, sir. The men believed she was Aida."

I glare at my sovietnik, fed up with his constant excuses. "Find out who this woman is now and if I can use her to my advantage before I kill you for being a fucking idiot."

Lev bows his head as I let go of his lapel. "Of course, right away, sir." He's shuddering as he turns to walk away. I appointed a cowardly idiot to the position of sovietnik. As a boyevik, he proved talented, but he can't take the pressure of such a high-level position.

I turn to face the unconscious young woman, wondering if she can be of any use to me. Aida Mazzeo was the perfect target for leverage, but the botched kidnap has revealed our intent. After this, Milo will keep his wife under lock and key, meaning we have little chance of getting her.

There's an angelic beauty about the woman as she sleeps in the chair. Her dainty features are perfect, as though an artist sculpted them. I want to see her eyes and whether they are as breathtaking as the rest of her.

I move toward her and run my fingertips gently

through her sun-kissed golden brown hair, enjoying the softness of it. Her scent is intoxicatingly sweet, and it drives my senses wild as my cock hardens in my pants. "Kukolka," I murmur, knowing it's the perfect word to describe her. A little doll, as she is as flawless as one.

Dirty and dark thoughts flood my mind at the thought of using her in any way I see fit. I tighten my grip in her hair as the thought of taking her right now while unconscious is almost impossible to ignore. I grit my teeth together, knowing that there's something desperately wrong with me for having such thoughts.

I move my hand from her hair and run my finger down her cheek before pressing my thumb to her plump bottom lip. "Who are you?" I murmur, wanting the answer right now.

Lev will bring me the answer, but it will take too long. She is a friend of Aida Mazzeo, so I hope Milo's wife will want her friend back. The question is, how much sway does Aida have over her husband to stop this merger?

Either way, I intend to use this beauty any way I want. Right now, I want to use her in the most primitive and primal way. I move my hand back into her hair and tighten it, pulling her head back to study her face in more detail, memorizing every blemish and freckle.

Her lips part on a soft groan, and I feel my cock harden, but it pulls me back to my senses. I don't wish to be here when she wakes, even if a part of me longs to gaze into her eyes. First, I must learn whether we can use her. I can't reveal to her that my men fucked up and took the wrong woman, as it will make us look inept and less intimidating.

After one last lingering glance at her beautiful, serene face, I let go of her hair. I march away from temptation, forcing myself not to glance back as I exit the door to the basement. I shut it and rest my back against the door, steadying my erratic breathing. Whoever she is, her beauty has an intoxicating effect on me.

I adjust myself in my boxer briefs and collect my thoughts before ascending the stairs back into my home.

Polina almost walks straight into me, stopping just in time. "Oh, I'm so sorry, sir. I didn't see you." She clears her throat and walks around me, continuing to dust the pictures and ornaments in the hallway.

I grunt and carry on down the hallway toward my study. Lev better find me my answer fast before I hurt someone. The violence inside me is rising to the surface, and I can sense my control over the situation slipping.

I won't hesitate to kill Lev if he doesn't straighten this out. There is no room for mistakes in this world, and Lev has made too many already.

I RUB MY EYES, feeling unrested after a night of tossing and turning.

The Italian woman I know nothing about haunted my thoughts and dreams any time I drifted off. All morning I've struggled to focus on my work due to lack of sleep and all-consuming thoughts of the mystery woman.

The crunch of gravel under tires draws my attention to my office window. I stand and glance out of it, thankful to see Lev's car. That fucking idiot better have answers for me. I still need to punish one of the men involved in the kidnapping for such a monumental mistake. Who will pay for the mistake remains to be seen.

My eagerness to find out who the woman is driving me toward the front door, as I'm too impatient to wait for him to come to me. After I left her yesterday evening, I haven't dared return. First, I need to learn who I'm dealing with and her affiliation with Milo Mazzeo.

The front door opens. Lev pales when he notices me marching toward him.

"Any news?" I ask.

He swallows, his Adam's apple bobbing. "Yes, and she is one of Aida's friends visiting from Sicily."

My stomach twists as I wonder if she is the one Fabio Alteri has gotten engaged to. It was all over the Sicilian news when it broke that Aida's father was having an affair with his daughter's friend. "The one engaged to Fabio?"

Lev shakes his head. "No, a different one."

Oddly, I am relieved to hear that. Milo won't care what happens to Aida's friend, though. "How close is she to Aida?"

Lev shuffles on the spot. "They're best friends and grew up together in Sicily."

I pace the breadth of the hallway, contemplating how this is going to work. Milo loves his wife. That much was clear as day when I met them together at his casino night. I'm uncertain whether he would break off the merger to save her friend. "We have no choice but to work with it. Milan has confirmed that Milo has yet to let Aida out of his sight since the incident. He knows we want her and fucked up." I glare at my sovietnik. "One more mistake, and I will have to demote you, or worse."

The fear in Lev's eyes is clear as he nods. "I won't let you down again." His brow furrows. "Do you wish to know her name?"

"Yes," I say.

"Her name is Siena Giuiusa. She was born in Rome." He hands me a file on her. "This is all the information I could dig up on her."

I tighten my grip on the file, feeling an unsettling sensation twist in my gut. "Thank you." I wave my other hand in dismissal.

Lev gets the hint and walks out of my house.

I glance down at the file, oddly desperate to learn more about the beauty I have enslaved in my basement. Impatience drives me back to my office as I sit down at my desk, placing the folder on it.

Siena.

Ever since I set eyes on her earlier, I can't stop thinking about how beautiful she is. Normally, when I capture leverage, the intention is to rough them up and threaten the target with death if they don't comply with my demands. Although I have no problem roughing her up, I want to do it in an erotic capacity, which is not standard procedure.

The folder Lev bought me includes a copy of her passport, CV, and lots of other personal information. I move one sheet of paper and notice a photo beneath. When I lift the photo, I groan.

It's a photo of her on the beach dressed skimpily in a bikini. A flood of envy takes hold as I wonder who took this sexy photo of her. Siena is utterly stunning in a burgundy two-piece that complements her tanned, golden skin. It's hard to believe how angelic this woman is.

My cock hardens in my boxer briefs as I take in every dip and curve of her flawless figure. Her large breasts are perfect and round in the tight bikini top. I've never desired a woman the way I desire Siena. Trust Lev to bring such a tempting and delicious woman into my hands by mistake.

The urges inside of me are untamable. I unzip my pants and free my cock from my boxers, fisting it roughly in my hands. Siena is the epitome of temptation, and she is tied up in my basement, exactly how I like my women; restrained.

Lev fucked up and brought me a woman who isn't married to my sworn enemy, meaning she's available in every sense of the word. I don't care if she has a husband or boyfriend at home.

Precum leaks into my boxer briefs as I think about shoving every inch cock deep inside of her. The need inside of me grows as I continue to fist myself. A bang outside of my office door breaks my attention, and I clench my jaw, feeling like a pathetic teenage boy.

I'm the pakhan of my bratva and a man who takes what he wants. I don't jerk off like a teenager over a photo when what I want is tied in my basement. I take what I want, and I want her.

I put my painfully hard cock back into my boxer briefs, zipping up my pants. Siena is going to meet the devil. I can't wait to look into her eyes when I tell her she's mine. Now that I know who the woman is, nothing can stop me.

Siena is going to be my slave in every sense of the word. I can't wait to hear her scream when I take her like the animal that I am.

5

SIENA

The day before…

The thud of footsteps grows further away. The slam of a door brings me out of my state of unconsciousness.

I open my eyes, squinting through the darkness. It takes a short while for them to adjust, but once they do panic slams into me. I'm in a basement.

I groan, trying to lift a hand to my aching head.

And when I try to move, I notice the restraints tying my hands down to the arms of the chair I'm sitting on. My heart pounds so hard in my chest it makes me nauseous. I try to rack my brain and remember what happened, but everything is hazy and unclear.

Flashbacks from being locked in my grandparent's basement when I was little hit me. I tense, my breathing coming in sharp, erratic rasps. My entire world is caving in on me as I try desperately to get enough air into my lungs, as the lack of oxygen makes it even harder to clear my mind.

I bite my lip hard enough to draw blood, knowing the only way to stop this panic attack is to focus on something other than the darkness surrounding me. The blood tastes metallic on my tongue as I try to focus on steadying my breathing.

The thoughts racing through my mind grow quiet. I remember the bar we were drinking at, and I went to the bathroom.

It all comes back to me at once. The bathroom and the man who tried to break down the door. I thought I'd escaped when I jumped through the window, only for another man to catch me. He injected me with drugs, and now I'm in a basement.

Why the hell would anyone want to kidnap me?

A sense of dread floods me as I wonder if these people took the wrong girl. Aida or Gia make more sensible captives than me if these people are trying to get leverage over Milo or Fabio.

My body is weak as I try to free my arms from the ties around my wrists. They are so tight the rope is peeling the skin from my flesh. It's a painful sensation, yet I don't stop. The desperation to break free of the shackles forces me to keep trying.

I keep trying for God knows how long before realizing my skin is bleeding badly. I growl in frustration, letting out a frustrated cry. My life isn't supposed to end like this: caught by criminals and left to rot in a basement.

"Help," I shout at the top of my lungs, hoping that, if nothing else, my kidnappers will show themselves and explain why I'm here. Not knowing makes this ten times worse. "Help," I scream.

The deafening silence is all the reply I get. The drip of water nearby is the only thing that punctuates the air. Goosebumps rise on every inch of my skin as a sinking sensation ensues in my gut.

I tremble as the despair hits me hard. Tears flood my eyes, and I allow them to fall, knowing I'm powerless. The worst place for me to be tied up and subjected to is a basement in silence. I've woken up in one of my nightmares.

I'm utterly helpless as I stare into the darkness, wishing it would swallow me whole. It would be kinder to disappear than face the people who kidnapped me. I shut my eyes, wishing it would happen. I've seen enough movies to know that kidnapping never ends well.

I COULDN'T SAY how long I drifted in and out of consciousness. My mind plays tricks on me in the dark. More than once, I hallucinated I was on the beach in Palmero. Tricked by the trickle of the drain pipes running down the wall behind me.

My eyes snap open at the unmistakable sound of footsteps. I could be hallucinating again, or my captors may intend to reveal themselves, but I'm not sure which I want it to be.

The approaching footsteps are slow and deliberate,

making my heart pitter-patter in my chest erratically. I hold my breath, waiting for my captor to appear. The footsteps stop outside the rotten wooden door before someone turns the handle.

When the door opens, the breath from my lungs escapes. I stare at the monster of a man filling the entire door frame. His dark, almost black eyes seem to glisten from the dim light outside.

I swallow hard, trying not to let my fear get the better of me, even though inside, I'm more scared than I've ever been in my nineteen years.

He steps into the room and flicks a switch, illuminating the basement with a blinding light. The slam of the door shutting behind him instills an uneasiness I can't shake.

I squint through the pain, blinking as I try to get my eyes to adjust. "What do you want?" I ask, trying to sound confident. As my eyes adjust, it's impossible not to be in awe of the huge, muscle-bound man standing before me. He is wearing a tailored suit that hugs his muscles, and the tattoo up his neck is visible above the white shirt. He clenches his fists, drawing my attention to the ink covering the back of his hands, too.

He doesn't speak, walking toward me slowly, step by step.

I feel my confidence waning as I stare at the giant of a man approaching me. "Who are you?" I ask, feeling foolish for asking a second question when he didn't answer the first. Unfortunately, I'm not very good at keeping my mouth shut, a trait that used to irritate Gia when we were roommates.

The man stops a foot in front of me, glaring at me with enough intensity to stop my heart. "Does it look like you are the one asking the questions here?" He asks, his voice deep and unmistakably foreign. "Kukolka." He murmurs the word, but I do not know what it means.

I shake my head. "No."

He moves a hand to my throat and wraps it around it, making terror squeeze around my heart. My breathing comes fast and erratic, and I'm sure I'm about to die. This man is a dangerous criminal, and this has to involve Milo. "I currently hold you captive as my prisoner, Siena."

My stomach churns at him using my name.

How the hell does he know my name?

"Why?" I ask, swallowing hard under the squeeze of his hand.

He tightens his grip, making my eyes widen. "I said you are not the one asking the questions."

A shudder races down my spine at the coldness in his tone.

"Milo Mazzeo is about to agree to a merger with Bionantechnic Group. A merger I wish to stop dead in its tracks. You will return to him alive if he submits to my demands."

The blood drains from my face as I stare at this man, wondering if he's insane. I don't know Milo well, but I know he won't submit to threats, especially not over the life of his wife's friend. I mean nothing to him. "Milo won't care what you do with me," I murmur.

The man shakes his head. "Perhaps not, but his wife will care since she is your best friend."

I want to ask how this stranger knows so much about me, but I know better than to ask another question.

"Until he submits, I will do with you as I wish."

I raise a brow, wondering what on earth that is supposed to mean.

"You will be mine, Siena." He moves his hand from my neck lower, gently caressing my breasts through the thin fabric of the skimpy evening gown I'd worn to the bar as I left the black winter coat I had on at my table. "I'll do what I want with you when I want."

I swallow hard, realizing the grave danger I'm truly in. This man is talking about raping me. "I'll fight you every step of the way," I spit.

He growls and places a knee on the side of my leg, looming over me menacingly. The man digs his fingertips into my chin and angles it upward. "Reconsider. I like women who fight."

"That's sick," I mutter, knowing that this man scares me more than I'd ever admit.

He chuckles. "I'm sick, Siena." He moves his lips to within inches of mine, breathing heavily on my face. "My name is Mikhail Gurin, Pakhan to the Gurin Bratva." He bites my bottom lip between his teeth, making me shudder. "You will learn that I take what I want." He grabs a knife tucked into the band of his pants. Acute fear slams into me as I wonder what he will do with it.

I relax when he slices through one restraint, freeing my arm.

I want to thrash out at him, but he has me trapped.

He grabs my wrist and forces my hand against his crotch. My stomach churns at the hot, hard press of his cock under my palm. "See what you do to me, my little Italian kukolka."

I try to pull my hand away, but he's too powerful. Hopelessness sweeps over me as I stare into the eyes of the devil himself, knowing that there is no escape.

Mikhail finally releases my hand, and I pull it away from him fast. A sickness pulls at my gut I feel like I'm going to throw up. The entire situation I find myself in is overwhelming.

"Polina will bring you some food shortly." He pauses, glaring at me. "I want you to do as she says. Do you understand?"

I search the painfully handsome man's eyes, knowing that he's nothing but rotten on the inside. "I understand."

He grabs my throat again. "You will address me as master."

My eyes widen at the request, which seems so archaic. "Yes, master," I murmur.

He releases my throat. "Good girl," he purrs.

I can't understand the slight twinge I feel in my stomach when he calls me that. The validation from him is almost arousing. A sick but oddly true notion.

He turns his back on me, walking out of the basement. Once the door shuts and I'm alone, my emotions overwhelm me. Every muscle in my body trembles as the fear spreads through my flesh. Tears well in my eyes and spill down my cheeks.

I can hardly believe this is happening. Maybe I was naïve to think spending Christmas here with a mobster was safe. All my life, I've known about Aida's father's dealings. The threat of danger was always distant and didn't seem real. The situation in Boston is on another level to Sicily.

The question is, why did he kidnap me?

The door opens again, and a small lady with dark hair enters. She doesn't say a word, bringing in a tray of food.

I watch her, wondering if looking after her boss's captives is her job.

She looks like a housekeeper. She's wearing a black uniform with a white apron. "I'm Polina. You will eat," she says, freeing one of my hands and placing the tray on my lap. "Then, I will wash you."

My stomach dips. "Wash me?" I ask.

Polina looks at me with an indifference that chills me to the bone. "Yes, boss's orders." She returns to the door and brings in a large tub and a sponge. "Eat," she barks. Her accent is very similar to Mikhail's, and she is undoubtedly Russian.

I pick up the dry toast and nibble, feeling sick. I'm not hungry despite my empty stomach.

How can I eat after learning I'm being held captive by one of Milo's enemies?

Polina makes a tutting sound. "What are you, a mouse?" She walks over to me and grabs the toast. "Open."

I swallow hard, opening my mouth.

She shoves more of the toast into my mouth. "Eat," she orders.

I chew the bread, wishing that this was a terrible nightmare, but it feels too real to be a nightmare. They have dragged me to the gates of hell, and Mikhail is the devil in charge.

6

MIKHAIL

I pace the floor in front of my men, struggling to contain my rage. These three are the reason that Siena is in my basement, driving me fucking crazy.

"I want the three of you to explain to me how you took the wrong girl." I glare at Lev first and then move my attention to Yuri and Artyom, who stare down at the floor like the cowards they are. "Now," I growl.

Artyom steps forward, holding his hands out. "We are sorry, sir. None of us knew what Aida looked like, and the girl fit the description."

I shake my head. "Bullshit. Aida's hair is so dark brown it borders on black, and the girl you kidnapped has golden-brown hair." I run a hand across the back of my neck. "How am I supposed to blackmail Milo with a friend of his wife?" I glare at the three of them. "Now, talk me through what happened step by step."

Lev's Adam's apple bobs. "Yuri went after her in the bathroom to snatch the girl while I kept watch of the bar."

He pauses, taking a deep breath. "Artyom remained in the car so we could get away fast." Lev shakes his head. "The girl was smart and locked the bathroom door, escaping out of the window, but Artyom saw her and grabbed her outside."

Artyom nods. "Yeah, that sums it up."

"Right. Artyom, leave." He had no part in the selecting of the girl to kidnap.

Artyom glances between Yuri, Lev, and me. "Sir?"

I don't look at him, irritated by him questioning me. "I said you are free to leave."

He bows his head. "Of course, sir."

I watch him as he leaves. "As you two are aware, when a royal fuck-up like this happens, someone has to pay in blood."

Yuri trembles as Lev keeps his gaze steady and true. "Of course, sir." The only good thing Lev has going for him is that he's got balls of fucking steel.

"From what I heard, Yuri was the one to make a move on the wrong girl." I grab hold of Yuri's collar and lift him off the floor. "Is that right?"

Yuri stutters, unable to say anything coherent.

"That's what I thought." I grab my gun and shoot him through the head. Blood splatters my face and Lev's, who doesn't appear fazed by the sudden violence. My men are used to my ways by now. I can't tolerate mistakes, and although Lev was in charge, Yuri was the one to make a move on the wrong girl.

"Next time, it will be you on the floor with your brains

blown out." I glare at Lev. "Clean this up, and then get out of my sight."

"Right away." He heads toward the supply closet in the hallway in search of a mop and bucket.

I walk away from him and sit behind my desk, leaving him to clean up his mess. My heart is pounding hard and fast in my chest. I reach for a handkerchief tucked into the top pocket of my suit jacket and wipe away the blood from my face and hands. I feel irritated when I see it has gotten onto my tailored suit.

If Alexsandr had still been here, this never would have happened. I would have Aida strung up in my basement instead of the stunning little Italian gem they brought me instead.

I check my computer, pulling up my emails.

Nothing.

Milo hasn't replied to our threat against Siena. Maybe she is right; he doesn't care about her wellbeing. I sent him a photo of her via email and her dress stained in blood to his door. It wasn't her blood, but he does not know that.

It is three days until Christmas Day, and I don't expect him to respond by then. Despite being the pakhan of the Gurin Bratva, I appreciate that Siena is innocent in all of this. She was in the wrong place at the wrong time.

I will allow her the room adjoining mine. She has spent two-and-a-half days locked in a basement. It's time for me to allow her some freedom, and I fear that holding myself back will be an impossibility once I do.

Siena tempts me like nothing ever has. I fear my

threats to her will become a reality sooner rather than later with her.

I LOOSEN my tie as I walk up the steps to my home. The day's frustrations weigh heavily on me, and the most frustrating thing is that I can't get Siena out of my mind.

Lev should have been the one dead on the floor today, but I gave him a second chance. A chance to prove that he is worthy of standing by my side as my sovietnik.

Polina opens the door to me. "Good evening, sir," she says, stepping to one side to allow me in. "How was your day?"

I shrug off my coat and pass it to her. "Not great." I run a hand through my hair and walk toward the stairs, then pause. "Polina, can you ask the staff to prepare the room adjoining mine right away?"

Polina looks surprised. "Of course, sir. Are you expecting company?"

I run a hand across the back of my neck, knowing that staying away from Siena today has been hard enough. "The prisoner, Siena, will stay in that room instead of the basement."

Polina nods in understanding. "Okay. I will prepare the room myself." She is not a stranger to my perversions, and none of my requests ever shock her.

"Thank you." I walk up the stairs to my room to get changed. Most days, I enjoy wearing my suit, but today it is too confining. My skin is crawling over my flesh, and I can't explain why. Halfway up the stairs, I stop. "Polina," I call.

Polina rushes back to the hallway. "Yes, sir?"

"Can you also have dinner set up in the dining room tonight?" I ask.

"Of course. I'll instruct the kitchen."

I smile, but it is forced. "Thank you." I continue my ascent and walk to the door to my room, then open it.

The murder I committed today was nothing. Ten years as pakhan to the Gurin Bratva has left me indifferent to violence. Every murder I commit is nothing more than a daily chore, a part of the job description. It's a sick truth.

I shrug my jacket off and toss it into the laundry bin along with my shirt and pants. All of which are stained with the blood of a man who served as a soldier in my bratva for eight years. It's a fact that should move me, but it does nothing. I'm dead inside. Perhaps that's why I'm so drawn to the way Siena makes me feel. She's a beautiful, innocent creature that never should have landed in my hands.

I turn on the faucet to the shower and step under the water before it turns warm. The cold water helps cool the bubbling rage inside of me, and it shocks it out of my system. Lev and his men cocked up one of the most important jobs I've given him. It's about time I took Milan's opinion seriously. Now that Alexsandr has retired, Milan is the only person I trust in the Gurin Bratva, other than my sister, of course.

I wash the blood from my skin, watching as it turns the water a shade of crimson. Even the sight of blood washing away doesn't move me. This is my life, and it always has been and always will be.

When my father was alive, I worked by his side. Violence has been a part of my life ever since I can remember, and it's a fundamental part of who I am.

As the blood drains away, my mind drifts to more beautiful things, like Siena. My cock hardens at the mere thought of her name.

I wrap my hand around my shaft and lean my other arm against the shower wall, clasping my eyes shut. The hunger for Siena overwhelms me as I jerk my cock up and down roughly, envisaging her soft body writhing beneath me in ecstasy as I fuck her the way no man has ever fucked her before.

All the dirty things I want to do to her flood my mind at once as I tighten my grasp, thinking about her tight Italian pussy wrapped around my thick cock. It's all I want. Ever since I set eyes on her, tied up and unconscious in my basement, the sick side of me wanted to fuck her. I wanted to wake her up by my cock ramming into her so fucking hard she almost breaks.

I groan, imagining fucking her while she's unconscious. My balls tighten as I fist my cock even harder. My desire for her is violent, and I've never been so utterly consumed by thoughts of another person before.

"Siena." I groan her name as I picture her on all fours, her ass ready for the taking. The mere vision of her bent over with my cock lodged in such an intimate place tips me over the edge.

I groan as I unleash my cum, fisting myself even

harder as I drain every drop from my balls. The water washes it away. My breathing is uneven for minutes after I've orgasmed as I continue to rest against the wall for support. I've never experienced desire quite like this.

I press my head against the cold tiles, wondering what the hell has gotten into me. Siena has infected my blood, and she's under my skin even though I hardly know her.

It's pathetic.

I can't explain why I'm in the shower, jerking off over her when I could be inside of her. All of that will change tonight when I make good on my promise. I intend to take my little kukolka and mold her into the perfect slave and submissive.

By the time I'm through with her, she won't want to live without me.

7

SIENA

As I sit in the basement, I feel like days pass by, seeing no one other than Polina.

She forces me to eat, barking orders at me as if I'm nothing more than a dog.

Mikhail hasn't returned since our first meeting, which I count as a blessing. The man is wicked and scary as hell. I hear footsteps coming my way, but they are too slow and deliberate to be Polina's. Not to mention, she's always wearing high heels, which clack violently against the concrete floor.

I swallow hard, wondering if Mikhail is finally returning to threaten me again.

The door handle turns, and he appears, filling the void with his colossal form. I've never seen a man as tall and wide as him. He's built from pure fucking muscle. He's beautiful, even if he is pure evil inside. This time he's not wearing a suit but a casual shirt, only buttoned up three-quarters of the way. He wears a pair of tight-fitting jeans with it.

He says nothing, walking closer to me. "Kukolka."

I glare at him, wondering what that word means. "When the fuck are you going to let me go?"

He runs a hand across the back of his neck and circles me like an animal circling its prey. "Milo has yet to reply to my threats."

I shake my head. "I told you, Milo doesn't care about me."

Mikhail's strong hand wraps around the back of my neck, forcing me to look at him. "You better hope that's not true for your sake."

I swallow hard, remembering the threats he issued the last time he came down here.

"Since he hasn't responded, I am going to have some fun with you, Siena."

The tone of his voice is sinister. "What kind of fun?"

He doesn't answer my question, walking back around to stand in front of me. The dark onyx of his eyes mimics the darkness lurking under his beautiful exterior. A dangerous predator that is what he is.

"Can you at least tell me how long you have held me?" I ask, wondering if Christmas has already been and passed. The night at the bar was five days before Christmas day.

His brow furrows. "You've been here two-and-a-half days in total."

Cazzo.

It's true what they say. Time slows when you are held

against your will, especially when it brings up childhood experiences that I've struggled to bury for years. "It felt like days."

Mikhail grabs a knife from his belt and slices it through both restraints. "Do you remember what I told you the other day?"

My stomach churns as I remember it all too well. "Yes."

He grabs my chin between his finger and thumb. "Master," he growls.

I swallow hard. "Yes, master."

He moves his thumb over my bottom lip and caresses it gently. "I can't stop thinking about all the things I want to do to you."

I narrow my eyes at him. "That's because you are a sick bastard."

He smirks as if pleased by my outburst. "I love a feisty woman."

I bite my inner cheek, holding back my retort. Responding to him only spurs him on.

Mikhail grabs hold of my throat and squeezes hard, sending a flood of panic through my veins. "I'm going to remove you from this basement and put you in a room in the house."

His declaration surprises me. I can't understand why he'd allow me a room, considering I'm his prisoner. "Why?"

A vein at the side of his head appears as he clenches his jaw. "Or you can stay down here if you prefer sleeping in a chair."

I search his dark eyes, wondering what sinister plan he has for me. "A room sounds good as long as it has no strings attached."

He tightens his stranglehold on my throat. "There are no strings attached because I take whatever the fuck I want. If I want to fuck you, kukolka, then I'll fuck you while you scream for me to stop." He moves his lips to within an inch of mine. "The sickest part about it will be that you will love every thrust of my cock as I fill you better than any man has ever filled you before."

I whimper in both fear and an odd sense of arousal. Mikhail is a monster. An unapologetic rapist who has no care for my well-being. That alone should be a turnoff, but a twisted part of me I've buried longs for his rough treatment.

"That's right, my little Italian doll." Mikhail's accent thickens as lust overcomes his tone. "I'm going to fuck you so hard you won't know what has hit you. You will make noises you never knew were possible while I take what I want from you." He releases my throat, and I gasp for air, placing my hands around my neck where they were.

"What happened to you to make you so wicked?" I ask, searching his dark eyes.

Mikhail doesn't react to my question, clenching his tattooed hands by his side. "You have a lot to learn about this world, Siena, and I'm going to teach you."

The tone of his voice scares me. It's a threat if ever I heard one. "I don't want to learn. I want to go home," I say.

Mikhail's eyes flash as he turns his back on me. "That's not an option since Milo hasn't replied to my demands."

I sigh heavily. "I'm not a part of this world, and this has nothing to do with me." I shake my head. "If you wanted to get Milo to do something, why didn't you kidnap Aida?"

He growls. "That was the intention until my men fucked up and snatched the wrong woman." He paces toward me, clenching his jaw and stopping a foot in front of me. "Don't remind me of my men's incompetence, or you will experience the brunt of my rage."

It makes sense that the intended target was always Aida. Milo doesn't give a shit about me, so I can't see why Mikhail expects him to do as he says. "Then why don't you let me go? I'm not who you wanted."

Mikhail's eyes narrow. "Because Milo loves his wife and his wife loves you." He grabs hold of my chin and angles my face up to meet his gaze. "You are better than no leverage, Siena."

Despair claws at my insides, attempting to drag me down into a pit of darkness. I don't allow it to. I stare at the wicked man who insists on holding me captive, determined not to let him see how scared I am right now. Mikhail strikes me as a man who thrives off of people's fear. "Keeping me here is a waste of time, and we both know it."

Mikhail smirks. "Oh, I wouldn't be so sure about that." He tightens his grip on my chin and leans close, his lips mere inches from mine. "At least I can have some fun with you in the meantime."

I want so badly to hide my fear of this man, but it's impossible. A tremor pulses through me as I stare into the eyes of the devil. The solitude and silence I've endured in this basement are nothing compared to the hell this man intends to put me through.

Mikhail left me with the promise that someone would be by soon to take me to my room. I wish I were staying down here, as I fear his plans for me are far worse than sitting in a dank, dark basement alone.

The distinctive clack of high heels on the concrete echos through the basement, warning me that Polina is on her way. She appears in the doorway and walks over to me. "Follow me." She turns without another word and walks away, expecting me to get up.

When I don't move, she glances back at me. "Hurry. I don't have all day."

Every muscle in my body aches as I force myself out of the chair. I groan, struggling to balance on my feet. It feels like I've been in that chair for too damn long. It's hard to believe it's only been two and a half days.

Every step I take is an effort as I follow her out of the room and up a steep set of steps into a lavish home. A similarly large Christmas tree to the one Milo has sat pride of place in a large hallway. It's such a beautiful home for such a rotten, wicked man.

I've known that Fabio's world was dark and dangerous since I was a kid, but I never really comprehended the world he belongs to until the moment Mikhail Gurin stepped into that basement. Aida has lived with this kind of shit since she was born, so I guess it's less shocking to her.

"Up here," Polina calls, walking up the sweeping staircase to an equally lavish hallway. "This will be your room." She stops outside of a door and opens it, showing me inside.

When I don't walk forward, she clicks her tongue. "Inside."

I walk inside, frustrated by this woman's impatience. "Why such a nice room?"

Polina narrows her eyes at me. "No questions. You will not leave this room unless someone comes to get you. Do you understand?"

I draw in a deep breath. "Perfectly."

"Bathroom is behind that door." She points at a door on the left before walking directly opposite and opening it to reveal a large closet. "Wash and dress in this dress." She pulls out a dress. "In half an hour, I will return."

My brow furrows as I stare at the third door on the right-hand side of the bed. "What about that door?"

Polina shakes her head. "I told you. No questions." She walks away, slamming the door behind her with a thud.

I stroll around the room, taking in every detail. This home is a real estate agent's dream. They don't make many homes like this in Sicily. I'm fed up with selling homes, though. The job I accepted in Rome is a junior position in an interior design firm.

I stop in front of the third door and try the handle, finding it is locked. "Cazzo." I hate not knowing what is behind it, as it gives me the creeps.

I shake my head, trying to forget about it, and head toward the bathroom. Mikhail spared no expense in any aspect of this home. I take in the gold-plated bathtub sitting pride of place in the center of the room. I unzip my dress and step out of it, walking toward the huge shower cubicle and turn on the faucet. The showerhead is huge and lights up, surprising me.

I guess things could be worse. I could be in that basement tied to a chair. A part of me doesn't believe that. Mikhail's threat was very real, and just because he's keeping me in a gilded cage, that doesn't mean I'm no longer in danger.

Perhaps that's his intention, to get me to bring my guard down. I still can't understand why they snatched me to make Milo call off a merger. Surely, Aida would have been a better target than me.

I step under the rain-effect shower head, sighing as the water engulfs my skin in its warm embrace. For a moment, I forget that I'm trapped by a Russian mob boss, allowing the water to wash away all my worries.

The past two and a half days have been a childhood nightmare relived. I can't explain the relief I feel at no longer being in that basement. Although, I fear my relief will be short-lived. Mikhail has no morals. He will use me however he wants, which is a terror-inspiring prospect.

8

MIKHAIL

Polina is getting Siena ready, ensuring she dresses in the clothes I picked out.

Siena fears me. I saw it in her eyes when I threatened her. The things I want to do to her are unspeakable.

The knock at the door echoes through the vast room, warning me that my dinner guest has arrived. When I turn around, she's standing there in the stunning white dress I picked out, which accentuates her olive skin and golden hair that falls in waves down either side of her face.

Her eyes narrow as she notices me and then the food. "What the hell is this?"

She is feisty when she's not chained down to a chair. "Come and have a seat," I say.

She glares at me with those beautiful hazel eyes for a few moments before walking forward.

I clench my jaw, trying to ignore how tantalizingly beautiful she looks in that dress. The dipping neckline exposes her full breasts, and the tight fit of the fabric emphasizes her hips, making it impossible to contain my urges. Once she reaches the table, I pull out a chair for her.

She hesitates, unsure about getting too close to me after the threats I issued down in the basement. "Why are you doing this?"

I raise a brow. "It looks like you've forgotten my first rule. I ask the questions, not you."

Siena huffs out a breath before sitting in the chair.

The temptation to touch her is too great, so I place my hands on her shoulders, making her flinch. "Sit back and enjoy the food, kukolka."

Siena shudders at my touch. The effect I have on her is exactly how I like it. I fight my urges and remain in control, stepping away from her. I take my seat at the head of the table to her left.

"Eat," I order.

She stares at me with a confidence that surprises me, considering her position. "I'm not hungry."

I clench my jaw and shake my head. "It's a demand."

She crosses her arms over her chest, which only draws my eyes to her tempting cleavage. "I said, I'm not hungry."

I slam my hand down on the table, holding her defiant gaze. "Bullshit. You haven't eaten in over twenty-four hours. Eat."

She leans further back in her chair, proving she's going to continue to defy me.

I stand and move behind her, grabbing a fistful of her beautiful, golden hair. With a yank, I pull her head back and force her to look at me towering over her. "Listen carefully, Siena. You have no choice here, and you have no free will."

Her nostrils flare as she stares up at me, rage flooding her irises.

I can't understand what happened to the woman begging me to let her go half an hour ago. Now that she's dressed in a pretty dress, she's suddenly grown a backbone. "I own you until Milo submits to my demands. If I tell you to eat, you damn well eat. Do you understand?"

Her eyes narrow, and she keeps her mouth shut, driving me crazy. Siena angers me in ways few people do.

My patience is wearing thin. "I'll give you one last chance to comply."

When she doesn't say a word, I snap. I pull her from her chair by her hair and force her to bend over the table, pressing my straining crotch against her ass. "You have pushed me too far. All you had to do was eat and be civil."

She laughs at that. "Why would I be civil to a man who has threatened to rape me?"

"Because it's not sensible to provoke a monster," I answer, despite insisting I wouldn't answer her questions. It's the truth. The wickedness that rules me runs so deep it is a part of who I am. A gem like her could never understand the effect that pure darkness has on someone's soul.

I hold her over the table, ready to punish her for being such a brat about something so simple as dinner. It's natural for a captive to rebel against her captor, but she will learn that it's a terrible idea.

"You don't know the devil you are dealing with," I murmur, keeping my cock pressed hard against her ass.

She trembles viciously in my grasp, giving me a sick satisfaction. Fear is intoxicating, particularly when it radiates from the object of my desires, and Siena's fear fuels the lust clawing at my insides. "Let me go," she says, her voice quieter than before.

"Will you eat as you are told?" I ask, knowing it's best to give her a second chance to eat before things get out of hand too quickly.

There are a few moments of silence until she nods. "Yes."

I grab hold of the back of her neck and yank her upright, pushing her back down into her chair. "Yes, master," I growl as the need to dominate her outweighs all other needs.

Her slender throat bobs as she swallows. "Yes, master," she mumbles, her voice quiet and reluctant.

I accept it, for now, taking my seat to the left of her again.

She doesn't hesitate this time, spooning salad onto her plate, followed by a good helping of pelmeni.

"Have you eaten Russian food before?" I ask, helping myself to the pelmeni too.

She shakes her head. "No."

I watch her as she brings one of the pelmeni to her mouth, nibbling on it. The surprise in her eyes as she takes a larger bite satisfies me. Few people are aware of how delicious Russian food is, whereas people eat Italian food worldwide. "How do you find it?"

She meets my gaze, confusion in her stunning hazel eyes. "It's nice. Why the hell are you acting like this is a dinner date suddenly?" she asks, taking me aback with her direct question, considering I almost lost control and fucked her over the table a few minutes ago.

"Did you forget my rule, kukolka?"

She shakes her head. "No questions. But I need to know what the fuck is going on here."

"You need to know nothing. You are my captive." I turn my attention back to my food, irritated by her questioning. The women I spend time with are normally puppets I can force to do what I want. If I tell them to shut their mouth and stop questioning me, they normally comply. Siena may look like a flawless little doll, but she's anything but in reality.

"What does kukolka mean?" Sienna asks, getting the pronunciation right on the first attempt.

Another question. It's as though she's trying to anger me, trying to force me to lose control. I stand and step behind her, grabbing her throat hard enough to block her airways. "Enough pushing me, malishka. You are my captive and have no right to ask questions."

Her eyes widen as I force her to look up at me, leaning over her.

"You need to understand what defying me entails." I force her out of her chair and push her over the table for the second time. This time, she will not get another chance.

I force the hem of the beautiful white dress up her thighs, exposing her full ass cheeks. Siena is wearing a thong, which gives me a perfect view. "Beautiful," I muse, running my hand gently over her soft, unblemished skin.

"You are sick," Siena spits, fueling my irritation over her lack of understanding about what is happening here. She's my slave, my captive, and I will not stand by while she tests me at every turn.

I flatten my palm and bring it down against her taut, perfect skin with force.

Siena yelps, trying to move away from me despite there being no escape. I do the same on her other cheek, watching as the skin turns from lightly tanned to pink.

I clench my jaw and put her through as harsh a punishment as possible with my bare hands. Normally, I like to use an implement but didn't bring one on this occasion.

After accepting seven harsh spanks on each cheek, she's panting. "Stop," she shouts, trying to escape me again as she fights me every step of the way.

I admire the red welts my hand creates across her ass cheeks, stroking the tender skin with a foreign gentleness. "Are you screaming for me to stop because it's too painful or too pleasurable?"

Siena turns rigid as I slide a finger into the string of her thong and pull it away from her center.

I groan at the sight of her glistening pussy nestled between her thighs. It's a sight so erotic it's hard to stop myself from taking her over the table like an animal. "So wet, malishka." I run a finger through her dripping entrance before bringing my finger to my mouth and licking her sweet nectar off of them. "It looks like you enjoy being punished a little too much."

"Please." Siena's voice is quiet and broken as she begs me, but I don't know what she is begging for.

"Please, what?" I ask, wondering if she is enjoying this as much as I am.

A few moments of silence follow. "Please stop, master," she says, her voice bordering on breaking with emotion.

I swallow hard and clench my fist, struggling to stop myself from taking this further. As the pakhan of the Gurin Bratva, I take what I want no matter the consequences. Siena is disposable. A woman to fuck and use as I want and then discard once I get what I want. As I try to remind myself of that, Siena sobs.

My little kukolka is so vulnerable, and it ignites something inside me I can't comprehend. A need to protect Siena and keep her safe. Ever since I set eyes on her tied to that chair in the basement, I sensed she was different.

"Why would you want me to stop when you are enjoying this so much?" I ask, running my finger through the wetness pooling between her thighs again. "You are so wet."

Siena struggles against me again, but I hold her firm. "My body may react, but I hate you," she growls.

I can't understand why her outburst stings. Crouching down behind her and parting her thighs, I thrust my tongue into her cunt.

Siena gasps at the sudden sensation, trembling in my grasp. "Mikhail." The sound of my name on her lips is sensuous.

I move my tongue to circle her clit, longing to coax her climax from her. No matter what this little brat says, she enjoys the pain. She can beg me to stop all she likes, but I can't.

"You taste like sin, malishka," I murmur, moving my tongue to her ass and probing at her tight ring of muscles.

She gasps at the sudden sensation, tensing and trying to escape me. There is no escape. "Stop fighting." I spank her already welted ass, making her moan louder.

The need to master her body drives me as I slide three fingers inside of her soaking wet pussy. Siena moans deeply, her head lulling forward as I work her into a frenzy.

My tongue continues to probe at her tight little asshole as I finger fuck her toward orgasm. It takes all my self-control not to pull my cock out of my pants and replace my fingers with it. Siena isn't ready yet, because I want her to crave it. I want her to beg me for my cock, even though she fights the desire she has for me. In time, she will learn to yearn for me.

"Oh fuck," Siena moans, her thighs quivering as her orgasm hits her. Her muscles contract and then release.

"That's it. Come for me," I growl before fingering her through it. My tongue returns to her tight little asshole, a hole I would love to stretch open with my cock.

"Yes, fuck, yes," Siena cries as I prolong her orgasm with my fingers, making sure this one is the best she's ever received.

When she finally stops panting and quivering, I pull

my fingers from her and lick them clean, groaning at how good she tastes.

My cock is throbbing in my pants, desperate to be freed. However, I can't give her that yet. Not until she's desperate for it. I straighten and step back, pulling the hem of her dress down.

"Eat your food. Polina will show you back to your room when you are done." I don't wait for Siena to move, turning away and walking out of the dining room.

The woman affects me in ways I don't appreciate. If anyone else had been pleading with me to stop, I'd have increased the intensity of my punishment until she shut her mouth. Instead, I made her come and gave her pleasure when she needed pain. It's a miracle that I'm walking away without fucking her over that table.

I'm walking away from the danger she poses. Desire is a perilous feeling that I've always kept at arm's length. It is easy to be drawn in by the temptation, but I must fight it with her.

9

SIENA

I sit with my legs crossed, staring mindlessly at the gilt-effect wallpaper as the moon shines through the window, illuminating it. My tears are all spent, and now my eyes are dry, leaving me drowning in despair, unable to move from the crushing fear weighing me down.

Insomnia is a problem I've had to wrestle with since I was a child, but this is different. Fear keeps me awake as I try to ignore the terrible pain coursing through my brutalized butt cheeks.

Mikhail is a wicked man.

A sense of shame and shock mingle together as I recall the way he made me come afterward. It was the best orgasm I've ever had. He ripped my guard down by putting me in a pretty dress and having me to dinner, only to treat me like nothing more than a pet. I pushed him too far, which is a mistake I will try not to repeat.

Fear isn't the only thing keeping me awake, though.

It's the sickening shame I feel over his beating. I enjoyed his beating too much, and the pain wasn't a punishment but a reward, which freaks me out a little.

Mikhail knows it too after he saw how wet I was. It gives that sick bastard something over me, a kind of control. And I don't like it. At least, that's what I keep telling myself.

Mikhail broke me. I stare at the wallpaper, wishing I wasn't so helpless.

Milo won't help me. That's one thing I'm damn sure of. If it had been Aida in this position, he'd submit to Mikhail's demands in a heartbeat, but Milo doesn't care about me. I glance at the clock on the nightstand, noticing it's one o'clock in the morning.

The thud of approaching footsteps outside of the room makes me tense. They stop just short of my room, and I hear someone enter next door. I can't understand why I'm certain it is Mikhail.

The door that is locked no doubt adjoins my room to his. The fact both terrifies and intrigues me. I shudder as I hear his footsteps on the other side of the wall. As I expected, they come to a stop outside of the locked door. I keep my eyes on it, wondering if he will enter at this time of night.

The lock's turning sinks my stomach like a lead weight. I swallow hard, knowing that the handsome, brutal Russian who beat my ass so hard with his hand, I'm left bruised and sore, is about to enter.

Mikhail is probably expecting me to be asleep, but I remain sitting, keeping my eyes on the door like a hawk.

The door swings open, and he appears. His vast body takes up the entire frame as he steps through it. I notice that he's no longer wearing a tie, and his shirt is unbuttoned halfway, giving me a teasing view of the dark, brutal ink that scrolls over his body. Deep down, I want to see every inch of the masterpiece that scrolls over his hard, muscled body.

His eyes widen when he notices me sitting upright in nothing but my panties. I don't even move to cover myself, forgetting I'm practically naked. "Why aren't you asleep?"

I shake my head. "How can I sleep when I've been kidnapped and beaten?"

I see a muscle in his jaw flex before he speaks. "You got off pretty lightly if you ask me, Siena." He steps further into the room. "I may have spanked you, but I also made you feel better than any man ever has in your life."

He says that with the cockiest certainty. I wish it weren't true, but it is. A wicked smirk twists onto his lips. "Since you don't deny it, I guess it is true."

"I've not had much experience to compare it to," I mutter.

His brow furrows. "You can't be a virgin."

I shake my head. "No, but I've only ever been with one man."

"Hard to believe." He tilts his head to the side. "How do I know you aren't lying?"

I narrow my eyes. "Are you suggesting I'm a whore who sleeps with loads of men?"

The smirk remains as he stands there in silence,

watching me. He has no intention of answering my question.

"Please leave me alone," I say.

He clenches his fists by his side. "Why would I do that when you are sitting here awake and ready for round two?"

A shiver travels down my spine as he moves closer to me. "No, I'm not."

He takes four more steps, stopping at the edge of the bed. "You need to understand that I'm in charge here, Siena." He lowers himself down onto the edge of the bed, mere feet from me. "If I want you, then I will have you."

I shuffle further away on the bed, glancing at the bathroom door to my left. Perhaps I can make it in there and lock the door before he can stop me.

"Don't even consider it. I'll break the fucking door down if I have to."

My heart sinks. *Was I that obvious?*

I don't ask as I know I won't receive a response, anyway.

"I'm not sure what you mean," I mumble.

Mikhail laughs a wicked laugh that makes goosebumps rise across my exposed skin. "You are a terrible liar, malishka." Mikhail moves fast, grabbing hold of my throat. "I'm going to show you what it means to be owned," he whispers into my ear, biting my earlobe hard.

I yelp in shock at the sting of pain that goes through me. "Please don't." It's a pathetic and weak plea.

"You may not want to admit it to yourself, but you want this." He moves his lips to mine and kisses me. "You want me to claim you because you know it will feel so fucking good, malishka."

I shake my head, knowing that I can't admit to enjoying anything he inflicts on me. The man is a sadist. A hot and wickedly handsome one, but he's dangerous. Mikhail doesn't care about consent or what I want. He cares only about himself and getting what he wants from Milo. "How does this help you get Milo to comply?"

Mikhail frees my throat, but he moves his body even closer to mine. "It doesn't. I take what I want, and right now, I want you."

I swallow hard, resigned to the fact that Mikhail will take what he wants from me, no matter what I say or do.

"Do you understand?" he asks.

I search his dark brown eyes, looking for an ounce of humanity. He doesn't show any sign of remorse as I nod my head, glancing down at my hands. "I understand, master," I mumble, not wanting to have my ass beaten again.

Mikhail gets up off the bed, putting distance between us. "Stand," he orders.

I do as he says, watching him intently.

His gaze dips from my eyes to my breasts, which are entirely exposed. The lust that ignites in them is hot and all-consuming. I notice the way a muscle in his forehead tenses. The tension in the air heightens as we both stare at each other.

I can't understand why I'm so wet between my thighs. Mikhail stalks toward me, and it entices both fear and excitement. This man is a criminal and evil to the core, and he proved that the moment he bent me over the table and spanked me before licking my pussy like it was his right.

I can't understand why desire twists at my gut when he's near, considering he intends to use me. He grabs hold of my hips tightly and spins me around, forcing my back to mold against his rock-hard chest.

The throb of his heavy cock pulses against my skimpily clad ass. "It is going to be far easier for you if you comply with my demands." His tattooed hand snakes up my chest, and he squeezes my left breast forcefully. "I'm going to use you however I want," he growls. "I will ruin you for all other men." He reaches for me and grabs hold of my thigh, clutching it firmly. "Once you return to your life, you will think of me always because no man will make you climax the way I do." His hands move lower, dipping into my panties. He rubs my clit with his fingers, making my knees shake. "Then, I will let you go back to your life, and you will think of me all the fucking time."

His voice is so stoic that it sends a chill deep into my bones. I can't understand how him talking about releasing me sounds like a threat, which makes no sense. That's all that I want; to return to my life.

"Do you understand, malishka?"

I swallow hard, trying to find my voice. "Yes, master," I murmur, knowing that it doesn't matter if I understand or not. Mikhail is going to do what he wants to me, no matter what I say. He's a mob boss, and all bosses are dark, twisted, and dangerous. Tears prickle my eyes as the whole situation overwhelms me.

Why the hell didn't I go to Hong Kong?

It's a choice I'm regretting. Mikhail's fingers dig deeper into my hips as he spins me around. He pulls me tight against him, wiping away a stray tear from my cheek. It's a gentle move that doesn't match what is going on here. The warmth of his skin penetrates my chilled flesh. The scent of vodka on his breath, coupled with his masculine musk, is inviting.

Mikhail yanks me even closer, our lips a mere inch away. "It's time for me to show you how good I can make you feel." Before I can say anything, his lips cover mine. Mikhail kisses me so passionately it shocks me. No one has ever kissed me like this. It's frantic as though he wants to devour me from the inside out.

Mikhail groans into my mouth, his hands roaming over my body as he touches every inch of me as if his life depends on it.

I hate that the moment he plays with my nipples, I moan. It's hard not to when a man so utterly beautiful touches me the way he does. His possessive grip on my hips tightens as he forces me toward the bed before pushing me onto my back.

He stands, staring at me in all his intimidating grandeur. After a few seconds, he crawls over me on the bed. The position gives him control and power over me, which makes it impossible to escape. His weight pins me down to the soft mattress below as his lips move down my neck toward my breasts.

Mikhail's tongue draws a path around my sensitive, hard nipple. Then he sucks on it, turning me into molten lava beneath him. He does the same to my other nipple, making me moan. Mikhail knows how to drive me crazy with need.

It's been too damn long since I had sex. Three years to be exact, with my first boyfriend in high school. It wasn't great, and we broke up not long after. Sicily doesn't have many prospects.

Mikhail moves past my breasts and kisses my stomach, sending goosebumps rising over every inch of my flesh. "I'm going to make sure no other man ever compares to me, malishka," he says, reminding me of his intent to "ruin me for all other men." It's such a cocky, self-assured thing to say, but something tells me after the way he made me come over that dining table, it may be true.

Mikhail pulls my panties down my thighs, exposing my soaking wet pussy to his hungry gaze.

"You are so wet for me." The desire in his voice deepens his alluring accent.

Everything about this situation is arousing, except that the man touching me is also the man who kidnapped me. I try to forget that as his tongue connects with the sensitive nerves. It's as if Mikhail has struck a match and set me on fire as desire blazes through me.

"Fuck," I say, biting my lip as I try not to moan too loud. I don't want to give him the satisfaction.

"Sweeter than sin, malishka."

I raise a brow, glancing down at him. "What does malishka mean?"

He looks up at me from between my thighs. "It means

baby girl." He says nothing else, sliding his tongue through my pussy and driving me wild.

I clench the comforter beneath me, feeling confused by the undeniable pleasure he's giving me for the second time tonight.

Mikhail slides a finger inside of me, finding the spot that lights me up almost instantly.

"Oh my God," I cry, clenching my muscles as his tongue connects with my clit again.

He's masterful as he plays my body like a goddamn instrument, turning me into a wanton, panting slut.

I always wondered how people could develop Stockholm Syndrome. Well, it seems it's quite easy when the man who has you is beautiful and a god at eating pussy.

I push my fears over being here to the back of my mind. All I can focus on is the man between my legs, driving me higher with each touch. My hips buck as he sucks my clit harder, bringing me to the edge of no return.

Mikhail places his large hand on my stomach, holding me down with it. "That's it, malishka. I want you to come for me."

I moan softly, letting my head rest against the pillow again as his teeth graze against the sensitive bundle of nerves at the apex of my thighs. That's all it takes to tip me over the edge.

My muscles contract around his finger, which is still lodged inside of me. Every part of my body tingles with unsurmountable pleasure as I come for him as he demands.

He pulls out his finger and buries his tongue inside of me instead, tasting me deeply. Once he comes up for air, he's panting. "You taste perfect, kukolka."

I bite my bottom lip as Mikhail moves to lie beside me. My breathing steadies as we remain in silence.

As the effect of the orgasm wears off, the shame returns.

Mikhail wraps an arm around me and pulls me close, kissing my lips. I reach out for him, touching his hard, muscled body. My heart pounds in my chest as I let my hands dip lower, finding the waistband of his pants. I let my hand move down to the hard, enormous bulge at his crotch. The moment I touch his cock, it stokes the need inside of me back to life. I want it from him. I want everything.

I grab hold of his belt, intending to undo it, but he grabs my hand and stops me. "Not tonight," he murmurs, surprising me. "Goodnight, kukolka." He turns away and gets off the bed, leaving me watching after him.

It takes a few moments for the deep shame to kick in. I wanted Mikhail to fuck me, even though he kidnapped me. The man is more confusing than anyone I've ever met.

The past few days have been a rollercoaster ride that I'll never forget…if I make it out of here alive.

10

MIKHAIL

I step out of the house, feeling unfocused. I can't get the little brat locked in the room next to mine out of my mind.

She knows how to push my buttons. I'm used to being with submissive women who wouldn't dare stand up to me. Siena is a challenge that I long to conquer.

Like a drug addict, I couldn't stay away from her mere hours after our dinner together. I treated her more gently than I should have last night, and my actions involving her make no sense.

I try to forget about her as the car comes into view down the driveway. Lev picked up my sister yesterday morning in Maine from the Syndicate Academy. He parks in front of me, exiting the driver's side. I allow him to walk to her door and open it for her.

Natalya smiles as she gets out of the car, dashing toward me. "Brother." She launches herself at me, forcing me to take her weight.

"Welcome home, sister." I squeeze her. "How was the trip?"

Natalya releases me, and I set her down on the floor. "It was long and boring. When is Yana arriving?"

I know Natalya misses her eldest sister the most, even more than our mother. Natalya has always harbored anger at my mother for abandoning her when she had a choice to stay.

"She will arrive the day after next. Mother will be here tomorrow."

Natalya rolls her eyes. "Great. Who the hell invited her, anyway?"

I set a hand on her shoulder. "She's our mother, Natalya, no matter what she did in the past."

She gives me a skeptical look. "So it was you."

I shrug. "It's been three years since we last saw her, and I felt it was time, especially since you are graduating from the academy soon."

She huffs and glances back at the car, where Lev is wrestling with three enormous suitcases. "Should I help him?"

I shake my head and guide her toward the house. "No, he has pissed me off. Let him deal with it."

Natalya glances at me. "I wondered why your sovietnik had turned into a cab driver for the day. What did he do?"

I clench my jaw as the reminder of his mistake brings Siena to the forefront of my mind. The girl I locked in the adjoining room to mine is waiting for my next move.

If Lev had gotten it right, Aida would be in the basement waiting for her husband to comply. Instead, our threats have gone unanswered. He doesn't care what happens to Siena and will keep the truth from his wife. It's what I'd do if I were in his position.

"He fucked up a very important plan, but it's nothing for you to worry about." I smile at her. "When you take charge of this family, you better find a better sovietnik."

She laughs. "I wondered why you chose Lev, as he's not the smartest of your men."

I clench my jaw as she's now the second person who has questioned that decision. "Who would you have picked?"

She raises a brow, reflecting for a moment. "There is only one option: Timur, for sure."

I growl as she is not the first to say Timur would have been a perfect choice. Lev has been with the bratva longer. He's a safe choice. Perhaps that's why I picked him. "Milan said the same." I rub a hand across the back of my neck. "Perhaps it's time for a reshuffle of the leaders."

Natalya rests a hand on my back. "It's Christmas, brother. Let's forget about the bratva and not worry about it for now." The remark is so innocent, reminding me she's a long way off becoming the leader of the bratva.

I force a smile, knowing my sister means well. In time, she will learn that there is no forgetting the bratva when you are pakhan. Work is on my mind all the time, as one mistake could lead to our downfall. "Of course. Come inside." I gesture for her to enter the house.

Natalya walks up the steps and stops still, staring up at Siena, who somehow escaped her room. All she is wearing is my shirt buttoned up, and the outline of her nipples are visible. "Who is she?"

"Natalya, go into the kitchen. I will be there in a minute."

Natalya looks uncertain, but she walks toward the kitchen without questioning me.

I shake my head. "Who let you out?" I head up the stairs to join her, irritated that she's walking around my home half-naked as though she has the right to.

Siena's throat bobs. "A woman came in and said she needed to clean the room." She shrugs. "I wasn't sure where to go."

I grit my teeth, realizing I forgot to tell Olga not to clean my adjoining room for now. "Come with me." I yank her back toward her room, opening the door.

"Olga, I apologize. I was supposed to tell you not to clean this room for now."

Olga looks startled by my appearance, but she bows her head. "Of course, sir." She grabs the vacuum and cleaning caddy, then heads back out of the room.

Siena shuffles from one foot to the other, anxious as I turn all my attention to her.

"Under no circumstances are you to leave this room unless I say so." I pull her toward the walk-in closet and open the door. "All the clothes you need are in here. Get dressed and join my sister and me in the kitchen for breakfast."

Siena nods. "Yes, master."

I shake my head. "No, call me sir from now on. Do you understand?"

Siena meets my gaze with those tempting hazel eyes that drive me crazy. "Yes, sir."

The word sounds more natural when she says it. My cock stirs to life, and the need to take her overwhelms me, but I don't have time. I step toward her and wrap my hand around her slender throat, forcing her to look at me. "Never leave this room looking like that again. Only I get to see you like this," I murmur, moving my lips over hers and claiming them.

Siena moans as my tongue tangles with hers. It's a sound that is almost impossible to resist, but I force my lips away. "Now, get dressed, as I want you downstairs in five minutes."

I walk away from her and out of the room, heading toward the kitchen. Natalya won't let me hear the end of this until she meets Siena. It's easier if Natalya believes that Siena is a girl I'm sleeping with rather than my captive.

Although Natalya knows the wicked role I must play as pakhan, I don't like my sister seeing me like that.

Natalya gives me a questioning glance when I enter the kitchen. "Who is she?"

I shake my head. "No one important. Her name is Siena, and you will meet her."

Natalya sighs. "You ought to find a girl to settle down with, brother."

I glare at her, as she knows I hate being told what to do. "It is not in the cards for me."

She looks disappointed. "If you would find a nice girl and have a kid, I wouldn't have to take over the business."

My brow furrows. "I thought you wanted to be pakhan?"

There's a conflicted expression in her eyes. "I'm not so sure anymore. You are asking me to reform a centuries' old construct that relies on men alone."

I always knew it would be difficult, but I have hope that it will work out in the end. My men are loyal to the Gurin family and have been for many years. It's hard to believe that they would turn against my sister because of her sex.

However, it is naïve to believe there wouldn't be some resistance. It's something I hoped I wouldn't have to worry about for quite a while, but life is never certain. If the bratva is about to go to war with the Italians, anything could happen.

"Okay, well, as you said, let's not talk of work for now. We can discuss it after Christmas."

Natalya smiles and lifts a ponchiki to her mouth, and pops it in. Our cook makes all our favorite Russian food since she's from Moscow. "I missed Katya's cooking."

I chuckle and pick one up myself, tasting it. "I thought the food was amazing at the academy?"

"It is, but nothing beats Russian food."

I have to agree with her there. I think it's only natural to love the food your parents brought you up with.

Siena appears at the doorway, hugging her arms around herself.

"Siena, come and meet my sister." I approach her and wrap an arm around her back, leading her toward Natalya.

Natalya smiles and jumps to her feet. "It's nice to meet you. How did you two meet?"

Siena's brow furrows, and she's about to open her mouth when I cut in first.

"A bar the other night." I tighten my grip on Siena's shoulder. "We just hit it off, isn't that right?"

Siena nods. "Yeah."

Natalya, as always, is welcoming. "It's great to meet you, Siena. Why don't you come and have some delicious ponchiki?"

Siena follows her. "What is ponchiki?"

"They are like donut holes but different." She grabs one and passes it to Siena. "Here, try it."

Siena smiles and takes the small pastry, placing it in her mouth. I notice the surprise when she tastes it, nodding. "Wow, not bad." Siena takes a seat at the island in the middle of the kitchen. I can't deny that seeing her there gives me an odd sensation I can't quite explain. She looks like she belongs.

"Where are you from?" Natalya asks, brow furrowing. "Your accent is strong."

Siena glances at me before answering. "Sicily."

Natalya claps her hand. "My best friend was born in Sicily. What part?"

"Palermo," she says, not so enthusiastic.

"Ah, Giorgia was born in Messina." Natalya glances at me. "I've meant to mention that she invited me to visit with her extended family during Easter break next year. I miss her so much."

I frown. "No chance."

Her shoulders dip in disappointment. "Mikhail, please."

I hold my hand up to silence her. "No, I won't hear any more about it." There's no chance in hell I'm sending my sister into the territory of Fabio Alteri, Milo's greatest ally when we are on the brink of war.

Natalya pouts and gives up, for now. I know she will not give in so easily.

I take a seat next to Siena, resting my hand on the small of her back.

She tenses at my touch.

I reach for the pot of coffee and two cups. "Coffee?" I ask her.

She meets my gaze, and there's surprise in her stunning hazel eyes. Surprise because I'm treating her gently, considering my beating of her over dinner last night, but I can't let my sister see me mistreating her.

"Sure," she says.

I pour her a cup and pass it to her, watching as she sips it. "That's pretty good too."

Natalya and I laugh. "That's because it's Italian," Natalya reveals.

"Yes, we like Russian food, but we're not known for our coffee," I add.

A calm silence falls upon the room as we eat our breakfast. The atmosphere is too normal, considering Siena is my captive. I'll indulge my sister for now, but I'll have to clarify to Siena that this changes nothing.

She is my slave and plaything. A means to end, as she

has no rights while she is my captive. Until Milo gives me what I want, I own her.

11

SIENA

Today has been weird, and that's the only word I can use to describe it.

I spent the day with Mikhail and his sister, acting as if I was here by choice. A few times, I even forgot that I'm being held for ransom by the man who dotes on his little sister.

Mikhail approaches me as I sit in front of the raging fire and sinks onto the couch close to me. "It's time for bed, malishka," he murmurs into my ear, sending shivers down my spine.

I swallow hard and meet his gaze. "Why are you treating me like this?"

His eyes harden at my question. "Like what?"

I shake my head, trying to describe it. "As if me being held captive by you is normal?"

He glances behind him at his sister, who is busy watching a movie. "I don't wish for my sister to know that side of me."

I nod and glance down at my hands, a sinking sensation in my gut. The moment he gets me back in that room, I sense everything will change, like the flick of a switch. His wicked ways will return the moment he has me alone.

"Bed, now," he orders.

We both stand, and he sets a hand on the small of my back gently. He guides me toward his sister.

"We are going to bed, Natalya. See you in the morning."

Natalya smiles and waves. "Of course. Will Siena be joining us for the holidays?"

Mikhail's jaw clenches. "We haven't decided yet. Possibly."

"Great. I look forward to getting to know you better," Natalya says, unaware that I'm not here by choice.

I force a smile despite feeling nothing but turmoil battling inside of me. "Yeah, see you tomorrow," I say.

Mikhail leads me out of the room and up the stairs, never once saying a word. His domineering silence foreshadows the darkness I will encounter once we're alone. He could not show his true colors, hating any of the times I spoke out of turn.

He doesn't lead me into the bedroom I was in earlier. Instead, he leads me to the one adjoining it: his room.

"What are you—"

He tuts, cutting me off mid-sentence. "Remember the rules. No questions."

Mikhail is more confusing than anyone I've ever met.

"Bullshit. I questioned you plenty of times today."

Mikhail growls and yanks me into his room, slamming the door behind us. I watch as he turns the key in the door before stowing it in his inside jacket pocket. “Yes, you have. That’s why I have to punish you.” The intensity in his voice scares me, but I’m fed up with bowing to him like a pathetic, scared woman.

“Whatever. You can do what you want with me, but I’m done with being your pet,” I spit, crossing my arms over my chest.

Mikhail turns around slowly and glares at me with wicked violence brewing in his eyes. It’s such a dark, dangerous expression that I wonder if I’ve made a grave mistake.

I swallow hard, taking a step back. Mikhail’s gaze is enough to make me retreat. The silence only heightens the tension as he continues to watch me. The back of my thighs hit the bed, meaning I’ve got nowhere to go. There’s no escape from the dangerous man staring at me like he’s ready for blood.

I notice the door to my room and make a split-second decision. Rushing for it, I open it and slip the key out of this side of the lock.

Mikhail growls and chases after me, but I’m too fast. I slip into the other room and slam it behind me, sliding the lock-in and turning it before he can get to the door.

I’m not stupid. I know Mikhail can come through the main door to my room, so I rush for the bathroom instead. I lock it from the inside, sliding onto my backside and hugging my legs into my chest.

Mikhail’s thudding footsteps echo on the wood floors

outside of the bathroom. He growls like an animal and slams his fists against the door. "Open the door, Siena."

If he thinks I'm going to open the door to him, then he is out of his mind. I'd rather die of starvation than face a man who has far too much rage inside of him. "No," I call back.

"You've seen the size of me, Siena. I can break this door down with little effort." There are a few moments of silence. "Don't make me throw you back in the basement where you belong."

I stare at the door, wondering if my running is making things worse for me. A sadness pulls at my chest as I should be with my two best friends, and instead, I'm stuck in a fancy prison with a monster.

"All you are doing is making this worse for yourself, malishka." His voice sounds calmer.

I know he's right, and I know that I'm fighting the inevitable.

Today made me see the man outside this door in a different light. I hate that I see him as a person now, not just a dangerous mobster with no morals, as it means I'm at more risk than ever of allowing him to get under my skin.

Even if he kidnapped me, our chemistry since the moment our eyes met has been palpable, and I've felt nothing like it before.

"I'll give you three seconds to open this door, or I'll break it down," he calls.

I stand from my position on the floor and step toward the door, unlocking it.

The door handle twists, and Mikhail opens it, standing in the doorway with a frantic look in his eyes. He looks manic.

I shut my eyes as he walks toward me, waiting for the inevitable.

Mikhail wraps a hand around my throat and squeezes hard. "I don't understand why you continue to defy me." He sounds confused as I open my eyes, meeting his gaze.

"Because I'm not a puppet that you can order around, Mikhail. I'm a woman with rights, even if I am your captive," I declare, stilling the fear inside of me.

I expect him to snap and hurt me, but he forces his lips over mine. The kiss steals the air from my lungs as he yanks me closer, forcing me to cling onto his powerful frame for support. "I'm going to fuck you," he murmurs.

The declaration sends my heart rate spiking. If I'm honest, I'm shocked that Mikhail hasn't taken what he wanted before now. The sick thing is that I want him as well. "What if I don't want you to?" I ask.

A wickedly handsome smirk twists onto his lips. "Then you would be a liar, malishka."

I shudder as he lifts me like I'm a doll, carrying me back to his room.

He sets me down in his room. "Lie on your back for me."

I hesitate, glancing between the huge four-poster bed and the man ordering me around. "Mikhail, I'm not sure about this."

He growls. "Have I ever given you a reason to believe you have a choice?"

I shake my head. "No, but have I ever given you any reason to believe I wouldn't fight you?"

Mikhail rushes for me, grabbing my hips hard and flinging me onto my back on the bed. His rough treatment only seems to turn me on. "This is not a game, kukolka."

I narrow my eyes at him. "You still haven't told me what that word means."

He moves over me, unbuttoning my dress in the front. "It means little doll in my language." The front clasp in the bra makes it easy for him to undo, and he frees me of that as well. He roughly tears the fabric away from me, chucking it off the bed.

Mikhail captures my lips, kissing me passionately. He grabs my right wrist, clapping a restraint around it, before doing the same to my left wrist.

"What are you doing?"

He glares at me. "Why do you always insist on asking so many questions?"

I narrow my eyes at him. "Why do you always insist on not answering them?"

Mikhail moves over me on the bed, kissing my neck softly. I groan when he bites my collarbone so hard, it will bruise. Until I'd met Mikhail, I hadn't realized how much of a masochist I am. The pain is almost addictive.

"I like you like this," he muses, staring at me with profound admiration. None of this makes sense, as I should hate this man for kidnapping me and holding me for ransom.

I glare at him. "What, restrained?"

"Yes, and entirely at my mercy." He bites my lip hard enough to hurt before kissing a path down my neck.

Mikhail kisses my breasts, making goosebumps prickle on every inch of my body. I moan as he sucks on my hard nipples, melting me into a puddle of desire for him.

I can hardly draw enough air into my lungs as he moves lower, parting my thighs wide. Mikhail presses his nose to my panties and inhales. It's oddly arousing as he groans, "I love the way you smell, malishka."

I watch him as he tears my panties apart with his bare hands. The act is so aggressive as if he can't hold himself back from ravishing me.

Mikhail devours me the moment he has them off, thrusting his tongue deep inside of me. I can't understand why I love being touched by this man. Maybe this is what Aida and Gia meant about being with a criminal. They are a different breed of man. Alpha in every way imaginable and so fucking demanding.

I've never desired a man the way I desire Mikhail. No matter how wicked he can be to me, he's everything my life has been missing. He rules me with an iron fist. He's a man that doesn't take any shit, and I love it more than I should.

"Oh fuck," I cry as he thrusts two thick fingers inside of me.

This man knows how to turn me into a molten puddle with his tongue and fingers. I don't think I'll ever tire of him touching me. His tongue pushes me higher and higher as he circles my clit with the tip.

When his teeth graze the sensitive flesh, all rhyme and reason shatter into a million pieces. The pleasure is unlike anything I've experienced before, as it hits me like a freight train. Every muscle in my body spasms as the most intense orgasm washes through me. "Mikhail," I cry his name, knowing that no one could ever make me feel the way he does.

Mikhail smirks up at me with that wicked smirk that is both handsome and cocky. "That's right, malishka. Scream my name." He spanks my thigh, heightening the pleasure. "Now, it's time for you to make me feel good."

He pushes off of the bed and stands, moving his hands to the button of his shirt. I've not seen him even half-naked yet. It's ridiculous that excitement builds inside of me as he opens his shirt, tossing it to one side.

My heart rate spikes as I drag my eyes down from his face to his neck, admiring the colorful tattoos that cover his muscled chest and arms. He's the most gorgeous man I've ever seen.

He moves his hands to the belt of his pants, pulling it off and setting it down on the edge of the bed.

I watch in anticipation, waiting for him to lose his pants. He teases me, dragging them down slowly until he's only wearing a pair of tight boxer briefs, which leave nothing to the imagination. He's huge.

I feel my stomach twist as he hooks a finger into the waistband and drags them down, releasing himself. The length of his vast cock jutting out between his powerful thighs is enough to turn me into jelly.

"Like what you see?" Mikhail asks, his accent thicker

than I've heard it before, and it only adds to his sex appeal.

I swallow hard, torn about giving him the satisfaction. "I guess."

His eyes narrow, and he fists his cock in his hand, drawing my attention back to it. The idea of Mikhail driving that inside of me makes me anxious. "Open your mouth, Malishka."

The order scares me. If he's going to shove that thing in my mouth, I need some control. My restrained wrists mean he'll have unrestricted access to my mouth. Mikhail isn't gentle, and he will take what he wants without mercy. "No."

Mikhail growls softly. "It was an order."

I glare at him. "I need my hands if you want to put that thing in my mouth."

The anger on his face is clear as he reaches over to the nightstand, grabbing something out of it. "If you won't comply, I'll force you to."

My heart sinks when I see some contraption with a hole in the center. It appears to be a gag. "No, please. I will comply," I say.

Mikhail clenches the gag in his hand before placing it down on the bed. "One wrong move and I'm putting the gag on you."

I open my mouth, shutting my eyes and waiting for his assault.

"Look at me, kukolka."

It takes all my courage to open my eyes.

"I will not hurt you. Trust me and enjoy it."

I search his dark eyes, wondering why he would ever expect me to trust him. A man who has kidnapped me spanked me over a table and told me he has no problem raping me if I don't want to give him what he wants. It's ludicrous that a part of me trusts him not to hurt me.

He straddles my chest and then pushes his cock through my open lips.

I moan at the taste of him as precum drips from his cock, coating my tongue.

Mikhail grabs hold of my hair and thrusts his cock deep into my throat, making me gag. "Relax and breathe through your nose," he murmurs, coaching me through it.

I do as he says, conflicted over the deep desire to please him. It makes no sense, as Stockholm Syndrome is all too fucking real right now. I'm becoming addicted to the man who holds me captive.

He's like no man I've met before. Dominant, self-assured, and wicked as sin. I want him despite myself. It's ingrained so deep inside me: the desire to submit to a man who longs to dominate me.

I get the rhythm of it as I breathe through my nose, accepting every thrust down my throat. It's electrifying being at Mikhai's mercy, trusting him not to choke the life out of me with his vast cock. I shouldn't trust the man thrusting into my throat, and yet, for some twisted reason, I do.

"Fuck, malishka. Your throat is like fucking heaven," he growls, pulling his cock out and allowing me a moment to breathe. "It's time to find out if your pretty little cunt feels as good."

My stomach churns at the thought of his huge dick stretching me open. Mikhail is going to fuck me, no matter what I say. I can see it in his eyes. I want him to take me while I beg him not to. Maybe I'm messed up as him for desiring such terrible treatment from a man who holds so much power over me.

12

MIKHAIL

Carnal hunger overwhelms my senses as I line my cock up with her entrance, holding her uncertain gaze as she watches the space between us.

"I'm going to fuck you so hard they'll hear you scream in Sicily, malishka," I murmur, grabbing her throat. "You will be mine after tonight, held captive by thoughts of me long after I release you."

Siena shudders, eyes dilating. "Mikhail, please."

I press my mouth over hers, drowning out her pleas. She may be pleading with me to stop, or she may be pleading with me to fuck her. It doesn't matter which, as I'm not stopping.

Thrusting my hips forward, I slide every inch into her hard. Siena cries out, pulling her mouth away from mine at the sudden invasion. "Fuck," she pants, eyes wide as she stares at me.

"That's right, malishka. You are going to take everything I give you and enjoy it." I pull out, only to slam back inside of her with force.

Siena cries as I take her roughly, entirely lost to the sensations as our bodies combine for the first time.

When I saw her tied up in my basement, I knew we would end up here. My desire for my little kukolka was too much to resist. Siena fell into the hands of a man who doesn't take no for an answer.

"It's too much," she pants, fighting against the restraints on her wrists. "I can't take it—"

I silence her with my mouth, kissing away the pain. Her cunt is so damn tight. "You can take it, malishka. Relax."

Siena moves her lips to mine, kissing me this time. I allow it, loving the way her tongue tangles so desperately with my own. She wants me as badly as I want her.

The call to claim her is so strong. I sense the threads of control slipping through my fingers. I groan as my body takes over. I thrust my hips toward her hard, fucking her with all my strength.

Her small, lithe body is so gentle, and I'm so brutal. We're so polar opposite to each other in every way that it makes no fucking sense that I long for her with every fiber of my being.

Siena moans as I increase the pace, fucking her like the animal that I am. Her eyes roll back in her head as I give her everything, and she takes it. Our bodies collide in a clash of skin against skin as I lose all control.

"It's too big," she whimpers as I dig my fingertips into her hips.

I kiss her neck and nibble on her ear. "A perfect fit. Take it for me like a good girl," I groan, continuing to fuck her viciously.

Siena cries out as she races toward her climax. The beautiful little Italian doll writhes beneath me frantically, trying to find some control over the situation. There is no way for her to gain control, as I control everything, including her orgasm.

I still inside of her, stopping her on the precipice of pleasure. "Not yet, malishka."

"Please, Daddy," she murmurs, shocking me at her choice of word.

Siena tenses beneath me when she realizes what she said. "Sorry, I don't—"

I kiss her, silencing her words. Right now, she can call me whatever the fuck she wants. All I need is to claim her. "You will come only when I say so. Do you understand?"

Siena searches my eyes before nodding. "Yes, sir."

I clench my jaw, wondering why she didn't call me Daddy again. It's clear she has an affinity for that nickname, and it sounded more natural than when she called me sir or master. I ignore my desire for her to call me what she wants. All that matters right now is making sure I'm etched into her brain so damn deep that she will never stop thinking about me long after she returns home.

I want to be the only man she craves for the rest of her life. Since I won't keep her, it may be wicked, but that is the man I am. The darkness inside of me knows no bounds.

"Harder," Siena moans, shocking me as I slam back into her.

I grab her throat. "Look at me, malishka."

Her hazel eyes are dilated as she gazes at me with lust like none I've ever seen before.

"You like it harder, do you?" I ask, tightening my grip on her throat.

She nods. "Yes, sir."

I shake my head. "Be careful what you wish for, my kukolka. You might break." I bite her collarbone hard, making her whimper.

"Please, Mikhail, fuck me harder," she moans again, breaking the reins on my control.

I growl like an animal and release the restraints around her wrists and ankles. "If that's what you want, then that's what you will get." I force her onto all fours and grab hold of her hips with all my strength.

Siena arches her back as I drive my hips forward ferociously. She moans as if she enjoys it, taking the brutal assault as I lose my mind. All I want at that moment is to satisfy her. To break her so that when she leaves here and sleeps with other men, all she will think of is me.

The mere thought enrages me, and I increase the power of my thrusts. Our bodies entwine in a violent clash of skin against skin as sweat beads on my forehead. I've never worked this hard for any fucking woman, but then, Siena isn't just any woman. She's a rare breed of woman. Special in ways I can't explain.

"Take my cock," I growl, digging my fingertips so hard into her hips I know they'll be bruised in the morning. I reach down and grab my belt on the edge of the bed, struggling to control the desperate urge to inflict pain. The sadistic side of me is rearing its ugly head. I bring the belt down over her ass, making her scream in both pleasure and pain.

My cock throbs as her pussy clamps down hard, coming undone from one lash of the belt. "Fuck, you love the pain, malishka." I lean over her back and grab her throat, biting down hard on her shoulder. "You love it as much as I enjoy giving it."

"Give me more, Daddy," she moans, letting herself go. This time she doesn't correct herself or get embarrassed. Siena is too far gone to the pleasure, and it drives me wild.

I bring the belt down on her other cheek, groaning at the sight of welts forming across her golden skin. I continue to pump in and out of her hard, our bodies writhing together in a storm of passion so intense I'm not sure either of us will survive it.

I give her two more lashes on each cheek before setting down the belt and continuing to impale her relentlessly. "That's it, malishka. Take my cock," I growl, feeling very close to the edge. If I have to hold out much longer, I'll explode.

Clenching my jaw, I force myself through it, giving her what she wanted. Siena wanted it harder, meaning she's a masochist at heart, even if she didn't know it before we met. "I want that tight little pussy to come for me, baby girl."

Siena moans, arching her back, so my cock plunges even deeper inside of her.

I grit my teeth and crouch behind her, so my cock sinks even deeper at a different angle. I force her back downward, pressing her into the mattress.

"Fuck, yes, Daddy!" she screams after three thrusts. Her tight as fuck cunt is squeezing my cock so hard it almost breaks me.

I roar as I come too. The explosive sensation beats any I've ever felt in my life. No woman has turned me on the way Siena just did. My balls draw up as every drop drains into her tight little pussy. Our cum mingles together as it drips out of pussy and down her thighs. We're both panting for air, struggling to draw it into our lungs.

When I come down from the earth-shattering sensation, I pull out of her. My cock is still rock hard and ready for more. I lie down on the bed and wrap an arm around her.

Siena allows me to pull her against my chest, resting her head on me.

We remain in silence as we lay together. The tension hangs heavy in the air, but I try to ignore it. I try to forget that this woman is my captive, and I intend to release her in the end. The idea of living the rest of my life without being inside of her every fucking day almost breaks me.

It is Christmas Eve, at least in America. Despite our Russian heritage, we conform to the western dates for Christmas. I've given up hope of hearing from Milo. Despite the threats we sent, the Italians haven't responded.

Four days she has been in my capture and two days in the room next to mine.

I shut down my computer and sigh, loosening my tie. My mother appears at the door, leaning against the door-frame. "Just like your father, never switching off," she mutters.

I don't respond as I stand and walk toward her. "I have finished work until after Christmas. Are you, Yana, and Natalya still going shopping today?" I ask.

My mother nods. "Yes. When they can get themselves ready and out of the door." She rolls her eyes. "I don't know why they take so long."

I smile and lead my mother out of my office, shutting the door.

My mood changes the moment I see Lev heading toward me. "Excuse me, mother. I must speak with Lev alone."

She gives me a frustrated look before walking away.

"What is it?" I ask.

Lev is pale as he runs a hand across the back of his neck. "The auction last night got hit." He shakes his head. "It is the Italian retaliation for Siena's kidnapping."

I raise a brow. "What do you mean, hit?"

"Milo has lost it. His men killed five of the virgins and three of the men in attendance." Lev shakes his head. "Many more were injured."

“Raspizdyay kolhoznii,” I growl.

Lev nods. "He is acting like a maniac. The police are involved now, and we won't be able to run another auction until the heat dies down."

"I should have known he wouldn't comply with my demands over his wife's friend. I will take some photos of Siena roughed up a bit to send to him." The moment I say it, I feel a tight sensation in my chest at the thought of hurting her. We're in this mess because Lev couldn't get it right.

Milo's reaction would have been very different if it was Aida in my capture rather than Siena.

I grab hold of Lev's shirt and yank him close. "This is your fault for fucking up the kidnapping. Find me a way to sort it, or you'll be the next casualty."

Lev shudders like the coward he is. "Of course, sir."

I release him and watch as he scurries away from me. Natalya and Milan are right. It's time I put my faith in a man more worthy than Lev. Timur is an intelligent and worthy man. I guess a part of me preferred the idea of surrounding myself with weak idiots who would not try to cross me.

This response isn't what I'd hoped for, as it means that Siena will be with us for Christmas. My mother is not as gullible as Natalya, and she will see through my story of how we met in seconds.

I'm not too fond of the idea of having Siena with the family for Christmas, as it feels a little too personal. My questionable desire for my captive is the main reason I don't want her around. I was relieved when Lev told me that Milo had reacted with retaliation, as I never want to let Siena go, which is a dangerous complication.

"Mikhail, where is Siena?" Natalya asks, making my stomach churn.

I turn to face my sister. "She is sleeping."

Her brow furrows. "That girl sure sleeps a lot."

I clench my jaw and shrug, walking on down the hallway. "Remember, I've booked out the club tonight for a party for the bratva. Be there at seven o'clock."

Natalya calls back, "Is Siena coming?"

I don't answer the question as I can't decide whether to take her. It would be a little questionable if the woman I'm using to blackmail my enemy attends a bratva party, but a part of me wants to have her on my arm. My captive on display as mine in every sense of the word.

I finally took what I wanted from her last night, but I've been more out of control, thinking about Siena nonstop. The mouthy Italian girl has wormed her way under my skin like no other woman has ever done.

My cell phone rings, and I pick it up. "Andrei, what can I do for you?" I'm still waiting for Milan to find out why this bastard is in talks with Spartak Volkov.

"It's merely a courtesy call, as I wanted to wish you a great Christmas." There are a few moments of silence, as I'm not stupid. That isn't why he has called. "Also, I've moved my meeting up to the fifth of January. Does that work for you?"

I grit my teeth together. Certain Milan can get me an answer by then. "Sure, that should be fine."

"Perfect," Andrei says.

I'm impatient to get off the phone. Until I know that I can trust Andrei, I prefer to limit our interactions. "If that is all, I am currently preparing for the festivities."

"Yes, that's all. See you soon, Mikhail."

I cancel the call, feeling frustrated that he dares to call me on Christmas Eve. It could have waited until the New Year, but Andrei is up to something. I sense it deep in my soul, and I trust Milan will bring me an answer soon. Milo's merger might be the least of my worries if Milan's theory is correct. Spartak has had it out for my family for years.

13

SIENA

My stomach twists with nerves as I slide into the car next to Mikhail.

He doesn't even glance my way, focusing his attention on his phone. This is the first time I've been out of the house since he captured me. A part of me wonders if Milo has accepted Mikhail's demands.

When the car moves and Mikhail hasn't so much as glanced at me, my irritation grows. "Are you going to tell me where we are going?"

Mikhail sighs before glancing at me. "A party," he says.

His intense gaze turns me to jelly as I break eye contact. I can hardly think of anything other than him since he fucked me last night.

"Have you heard from Milo yet?" I ask.

Mikhail growls this time, turning angry. He puts down his phone and moves closer to me, grabbing hold of my throat in that possessive way he always does. "Why do you think you get to know the answer to that question?"

I hold his gaze, no longer as afraid of the bratva boss. "Because it affects me whether he responds."

"He attacked me instead of complying, which doesn't bode well for you." Mikhail's brow furrows. "Unless you enjoy me using you for the rest of your life."

I hate that my stomach flutters at the word "life." The idea of leaving Mikhail makes me sad, and yet a few days ago, it was all I could think about. He made good on his promise and has ruined me for all other men. "You will get bored with me if he doesn't do as you say."

A flash of irritation enters Mikhail's eyes. "Don't be too hopeful, kukolka." He moves his attention away from me, staring out of the window.

A tense silence fills the air as we both stare out of opposite windows. I can't understand why Mikhail would dress me up and drag me along to a party. "What is the party for?" I ask after five minutes of silence. I've never been good at sitting in silence.

Mikhail groans. "Do you want me to punish you before we get there?"

The tone of his voice makes my stomach tighten. I can't help but wonder if there is something wrong with me for craving his rough treatment. "No."

"Then keep your mouth shut, malishka."

I swallow hard and glance down at my fingers, wondering why I insist on pushing him all the time. "I'm not good at staying quiet," I say.

Mikhail huffs, shaking his head. "You don't need to tell me that."

I laugh at that, and a small smirk twists onto the

wicked bratva boss's lips. "My roommate always got pissed off with me because I hate the silence." I worry my bottom lip between my teeth.

Mikhail straightens. "Why do you hate the silence?"

It's a question I don't like to reflect on. It all stems back to my early childhood living in Rome. My parents would often get my grandparents to take care of me while they worked, and they were both archaic in their punishments. They had a deep basement under their old townhouse, and they would lock me in there for hours on end.

It traumatized me. Silence always reminds me of those endless hours in the dark. It's why I loved Sicily so much; I escaped that torment. It's also why I've put off moving back to Rome, despite the lack of prospects for me in Sicily.

"Siena?" Mikhail pushes.

I shake my head and hug my arms around myself. "I don't know."

Mikhail growls. "Don't lie to me. You went somewhere then. Why do you hate the silence?"

I meet his dark, brooding gaze. The treatment I endured from my grandparents was nothing in the grand scheme of things. Many children suffer far more than I did, but it affected me. "My grandparents used to punish me by locking me in a dark, silent basement." I shrug. "It always takes me back if it's too quiet."

Mikhail nods as if he understands. "My father did the same to me when I was young, but I guess I enjoyed it. The silence helped me reflect on my actions."

We fall silent for a short while. Both caught up in

thoughts of our past. This time, it isn't me who breaks the silence, but Mikhail. "Do you have a good relationship with your parents?"

The question surprises me. Until now, Mikhail has shown no interest in learning anything about me on a personal level. I smile. "Yes, my mother and I got on well when I lived at home. My father traveled a lot, so he wasn't around much of the time." My brow furrows. "How about you?"

Mikhail's expression turns sad. "My mother can be difficult, but I love her, of course. My father died ten years ago, and our relationship was strong despite his questionable disciplinary techniques."

I set a hand on Mikhail's arm, wishing to comfort him. "I'm sorry about your father."

He shakes his head. "Don't be. Death is a part of life, and the sooner everyone comes to terms with it, the better." He turns cold and glances out of the window, pulling away from me the moment it gets too real.

It shocked me how civil our conversation was. Normally, Mikhail shuts me down the moment I ask a question. The car comes to a stop outside of a building in downtown Boston. "Where are we?" I ask.

Mikhail glances at me. "One of my clubs."

My brow furrows, as the place doesn't look like a club. There is no sign of a bouncer outside, and it looks like a nondescript warehouse building. "Weird looking club," I murmur to myself.

Mikhail doesn't comment on my observation, getting

out and walking around to my door. He opens it and holds a hand out to me.

I stare at his hand, wondering why he's acting like a gentleman. Despite my reservations, I take it and allow him to help me onto the sidewalk. Once we're on the sidewalk, he grabs my hips and pulls me close. "Now, I want you to be a good girl tonight, Siena. Do you understand?"

His deep voice makes me tremble as I nod. "Yes, sir."

"Good girl," he replies, placing a hand on the small of my back. Mikhail leads the way into the nondescript-looking building. The entryway is bare, but once we step through the doors, everything changes.

It's a lavish and fancy nightclub, with a dancefloor at the front that appears more like a stage. A mezzanine at the top wraps around three sides of the place. Several tables surround the dancefloor. "Wow, this isn't what I expected from the outside."

Mikhail leans toward me. "Haven't you heard the saying, never judge a book by its cover?" he murmurs, his voice alluring.

I meet his gaze, and my heart skips a beat. If it weren't for the circumstance we met, I would be glad to be attending a party with such a gorgeous man. "True." If I didn't know who Mikhail was, I wouldn't know the true darkness within him.

He's wearing a tailored suit, and only a glimpse of his tattoo is visible on the side of his neck. Mikhail could be mistaken for a wealthy businessman rather than the leader of the bratva. "Let me get you a drink," he says, squeezing my hip.

The wetness pools between my thighs despite the touch being so innocent. Mikhail has broken me, and I can't keep my mind out of the gutter. He was true to his promise that he would ruin me for all other men, as I'm already ruined. "Sure."

He leads me over to the bar, keeping his hand on my hip in a possessive way.

I can't explain why it makes me feel so special and wanted.

"What will you have to drink?" he asks, looking at me.

I shrug. "Surprise me."

Mikhail turns to the woman behind the bar. "Two kvasya, please."

I raise a brow, wondering what he just ordered. Whatever it is, it sounds Russian.

The bartender makes our drinks quickly, despite other people waiting. I guess it's because Mikhail owns the place. He takes one drink and passes it to me. "This is a famous Russian cocktail."

He takes his and clinks the glass against mine. "Za zdarovje."

I assume it means cheers in Russian. "Cin cin." I bring the glass to my mouth and sip it, surprised by the flavor. "Cinnamon?" I ask.

Mikhail nods. "Yes, it's a cocktail with kvass, vodka, and cinnamon syrup. A good winter drink."

I nod, taking a large gulp of it. "It is delicious."

Mikhail leads me away from the bar, holding a chair for me at a table next to the dancefloor. I notice that most people are speaking Russian around us. "Is this a party for your bratva?" I ask.

Mikhail nods. "Yes. Think of it as an annual Christmas party like you might have at work."

The music isn't too loud as people dance nearby.

Mikhail notices me watching the dancefloor. "Do you want to dance, malishka?"

I love dancing, but it feels wrong to dance with a man who is holding me captive. "I'm not so sure."

He stands and holds a hand out to me. "Okay, I demand you dance with me then."

I roll my eyes but take his hand.

He pulls me onto the dancefloor, whisking me into a twirl as he does. The faster song ends, and a slow song starts, making my stomach flutter. Mikhail pulls me close, wrapping his powerful arms around me as he leads.

I let him guide me, enjoying the warmth of his body against mine. Mikhail should be the furthest thing from safe, sp I can't understand why his embrace feels so protective.

"You dance well, malishka," Mikhail whispers in my ear, his breath teasing the shell.

I crane my neck to glance up at him. "You're not too bad yourself."

He chuckles. "I should hope I'm not bad. My father forced me to take dance lessons when I was young, as he believed it built character for a man to do things others deem as feminine."

"That's a strange thing for the leader of a criminal

organization to get his son to do." I raise a brow. "I thought it was all about being manly and scary."

The smile that twists onto Mikhail's lips is the most genuine I've seen from him. "It is, but having an open mind about the world is the most important aspect, as it helps you see things more clearly from all angles." He bites the inside of his cheek. "Not to mention, my sister is next in line to take the throne."

"Natalya?" I ask, wondering if she has it in her to be the leader of an organized crime gang. She seems so nice and normal.

"Yes. She has a long way to go, but it is my hope she can succeed me." Mikhail twirls me around again before pulling me back against his hard, warm body.

It makes little sense, but I enjoy our dance. I may be Mikhail's captive, but he looks at me in a way most women dream about. He has gotten under my skin already. I love everything about this moment; the way he smells, the way he feels, everything about the dangerous Russian criminal is alluring.

Fear is what I should experience in the presence of this man. Instead, I am falling prey to his charm, and it's a dangerous notion that may get me hurt.

14

MIKAHIL

"Sir, can I have a word?" Milan asks.

I let go of Siena's wrist, glaring at my spy. He wouldn't disturb us if it weren't important. "What is it?"

He glances at Siena and then back at me. "I think it would be best if we speak alone."

I lean toward Siena. "Stay here and out of trouble, malishka. Or your punishment will be severe," I murmur into her ear.

Siena nods. "Yes, sir."

I give her one last lingering glance before following Milan to a room at the back of the club. An unease sweeps over me at leaving Siena out there with the wolves. The men in the bratva aren't exactly saints, and Siena is stunning.

"Talk fast," I say once we're alone.

Milan looks torn. "Sir, I found out that Andrei intends to join forces with Spartak." He runs a hand across the back of his neck. "I'm concerned they may intend to take you down."

I growl, shaking my head. "I should have known Andrei couldn't be trusted."

Milan shrugs. "At least we've learned his intention, which means we can stop him in his tracks."

I run a hand through my hair. "The two together will be unstoppable. We need an ally if we're going to hold off their threat on our territory."

Milan bites the inside of his cheek as if unsure about speaking. "I have an idea, but you will not like it."

"Spit it out then."

He draws in a deep breath. "Perhaps we need to form alliances with our enemies in Boston?"

I pace the floor as anger builds inside of me. "You're right. I don't like it," I say. The Petrov Bratva may have given us no choice but to create an alliance within the city. It's unspeakable. No city in the states has an alliance with all nationalities, yet I believe Milan is right. We have little choice if we want to turn Boston into a stronghold that Andrei can't touch. "I hate to say it, but I think you are right."

Milan crosses his arms over his chest. "How can we unite everyone, though?"

I shake my head. "It's something we will need to think about over Christmas." My brow furrows. "It won't help that I just blackmailed Milo to stop him from signing the merger with Bionantechnic Group."

"No, Milo isn't known for being forgiving. Perhaps you

can use the girl to get a meeting with him at least to discuss an alliance?"

It's insane to think about joining forces with the people we've called enemies for years. "The difficulty is proving to Milo that Andrei and Spartak pose a threat to his business, too. Can you get me some evidence?"

Milan nods. "Yes, sir. I'll get on to it right away."

I shake my head. "No, take tonight and tomorrow off, Milan. It's Christmas, and you need to be with your family." Milan has two young children and a wife who must get frustrated with him working. "Is your wife here tonight?"

"Yes, sir," he replies.

I pat him on the shoulder. "Then enjoy the party with your wife."

He nods and walks away, leaving me to process my thoughts. An alliance with Milo and Malachy would stop their stupid war, but it would also be volatile. If I know anything about the Irish and the Italians, they hate keeping the peace, and it's almost as if they want war when they get bored.

I return to the party, searching the room for Siena. When I don't find her, I feel panic clutch around my heart. Milan is standing nearby with his wife. "Have you seen Siena?" I ask.

Milan shakes his head, but his wife nods. "Yes, I saw her heading toward the restroom about five minutes ago." She points over at the sign toward the restroom.

"Thank you," I murmur, heading toward it. I told Siena not to move. Milan and I were less than ten minutes, which means she could have waited until I returned. Siena always ignores my orders, which drives me crazy.

I open the ladies' restroom door to find Ivan leering over Siena with his hands on either side of her, boxing her in.

"No, please don't," she cries, tears streaming down her cheeks.

"Such a pretty little thing. I can't wait to see how you feel," Ivan says, making me sick to my stomach.

I clear my throat, and Ivan looks up into the mirror, seeing me behind him.

He pales and takes a step back from Siena. "Sorry, sir. Did you need something?"

Acute rage floods my veins as I step closer to him. "Yes, my date. Who you seem to be harassing."

Fear floods his irises as he moves to the side, holding his hands up. "I didn't know she was yours, boss, I promise."

I can't understand the surge of possessiveness and rage mingling as I stare at the man who put his hands on my malishka. "You should have listened to her when she told you no, then." I don't have time for men like him. Cowards who don't own up to the fact that they are rotten on the inside. "Siena, leave us."

Siena meets my gaze, her brow furrowing. "Why?"

I clench my jaw, wishing she wouldn't question me, especially not right now. "I said leave."

Siena steps forward and places a hand on my chest. "Please don't do something you will regret, Mikhail."

I don't look at her, keeping my attention on the man in front of me. "Leave. I won't ask again."

Siena walks out of the bathroom, leaving us alone.

"Please, sir. I did not know she was yours." He keeps his hands held up in front of him.

"What did you intend to do to her, Ivan?" I ask.

His Adam's apple bobs as he swallows hard. "I was having some fun. I wouldn't have raped her, I swear."

Coward. Liar.

The two often are the same, but I don't have space on my team for men like him. He was going to rape her, so he should be a fucking man and own it. Perhaps then I would have allowed him to live after a bit of a beating. Instead, this man is obsolete. I don't need his kind in the bratva, and no one leaves the bratva alive unless permitted to retire by the pakhan.

I step closer to him and grab the collar of his shirt. "Do you know what I hate more than a coward?"

Ivan is shaking now. "No, sir."

"A liar. And you, Ivan, are both," I breathe, sensing my rage overwhelm me. The image of Siena, so helpless and vulnerable, backed against the sink with his hands all over her floods my mind. Red is all I see as I lose control. My clenched fist pummels his face. I don't even know how many times I hit him, as I'm no longer present.

Rage is a powerful emotion, and it can control and dominate you if you let it.

A shocked cry behind me brings me back to my senses as I glance at the pulp of a man still in my hands. Blood covers everything around me, including my white shirt and fists.

When I glance into the mirror, my heart skips a beat. Siena has returned.

I growl, "I told you to leave."

Fear floods Siena's eyes as she shakes her head before running out of the restroom.

Ivan is on the brink of death, barely breathing.

I pull my gun out of my holster and shoot him through the heart, putting him out of his misery. The gunshot draws the attention of several men, who flood into the bathroom. I turn to them. "He messed with what is mine. Clean it up," I say, walking out of the bathroom and toward the back office of the club to clean up.

Siena shouldn't have seen the carnage I inflicted on that man. I hate the way she looked at me.

I charge through the door into the office and walk into the adjoining bathroom, turning on the faucet of the tap. When I glance into the mirror, I see why she was so shocked.

The image would frighten most people, but I'm used to it by now. Ivan's blood covers my face in splatters, barely leaving an inch of skin clean. I look like a psychopath.

Ivan was unrecognizable when I came back to my senses, but I don't regret what I did. The man would have raped what is mine, and it's an offense punishable by death, especially when he didn't have the balls to admit it.

I shove my blood-stained hands under the water, watching the crimson gore wash down the plug-hole. This party is a celebration of the bratva thriving for another year. I've never spilled blood at one of these events, and the difference this year is Siena.

Ivan no doubt saw me already with Siena. He just believed that I wouldn't care who touched the woman on my arm—and normally, I don't.

I splash the lukewarm water onto my face, washing off the rest of the blood. Once my skin is free from Ivan's blood, I turn my attention to my clothes. The shirt is burnable, as are the pants.

I unbutton the shirt, tossing it into a metal trashcan, before unbuckling my belt and throwing it along with pants into the trashcan too. I search the desk in the office for a lighter and some lighter fluid, and I find it and then return to the bathroom and place the trashcan in the washbasin, setting light to the fabric.

As I watch the flames ravage my clothes, it feels a little insane that this is just everyday life for me. I go through the motions, knowing how to cover my tracks like it is second nature.

The creak of the door alerts me to an intruder. I go to the bathroom door and find Siena standing with her arms wrapped around herself. "What are you doing in here?" I boom.

She jumps, unaware that I was in here. "Shit. I thought it was a place I could be alone." She turns to walk away.

I rush after her, grabbing her hips to stop her from leaving. "What is the hurry, malishka?"

She shudders and tries to writhe out of my grip. "Don't touch me."

I move my hands to her shoulders, working the tension. "I'm sorry you saw what you saw, malishka."

She shakes her head. "So you're sorry I witnessed that you're a murderous psychopath, but not that you killed a guy?"

I laugh, wondering why she is shocked. "I'm a mob boss, kukolka. I kill people; it's what I do. Not to mention, we met because I kidnapped you." I force her to turn around and face me. "Did you think I was a good guy?" I search her eyes, which are brimming with tears.

"I thought you had enough decency not to kill a man just because he made a pass at me." She shakes her head. "I don't understand why you killed him."

I grab her throat, squeezing. "I killed him because you belong to me, malishka. I'll kill any fucking man who so much as looks at you the wrong way because I can. Do you understand?"

Her nostrils flare, and she glares at me with a mix of both lust and hatred. "Perfectly."

I release her throat. "Good. Now, wait for me by the bar before I fuck you right here so everyone can hear you scream."

Her eyes flash with anger as she turns away without a word, walking out of the office. I let her go, knowing that the longer she is in my grasp, the more likely I will snap and fuck her here. It's not right for the boss of the bratva not to be present at his party.

I walk to the closet in the back office and select an old suit. It's not great, but it will do. I need to present myself as the pakhan that everyone fears. I need to retain control and not lose my mind over a woman who is nothing more than leverage.

15

SIENA

I'm falling for a psychopath.

What I witnessed in the ladies' bathroom was horrific. I can't get the image of Mikhail's face coated in blood out of my mind.

The scariest part of it is that it was his reaction to a man making a pass at me. He wasn't just making a pass at me. There is no doubt in my mind that he would have raped me if Mikhail hadn't come in when he did. I find it too difficult to accept that Mikhail's reaction is to beat a man to death with his bare hands.

This world that I've stumbled into is maniacal.

Mikhail returns to the party wearing a different suit. If I hadn't witnessed the bloody scene, I wouldn't have known he just pummeled a man to death. I duck down and sit at a table where I can still see him as he searches the room, no doubt looking for me.

The thought of his hands on me right now makes my

skin crawl. I don't want him to find me, as all I want is to disappear off the face of this earth so he can never find me again.

Gia and Aida accept their husbands' brutal nature, but I highly doubt they've seen the men they love in action. I search the room, looking for somewhere to escape to. My heart skips a beat when I notice the bouncer is no longer at the club's main exit.

This is my chance to escape Mikhail's capture. I can grab a cab back to Milo's home and get Aida or someone at the house to pay the fare. Although my hopes of actually getting out of here and into a cab before Mikhail finds me are slim, it's worth a shot.

I make the split-second decision as Mikhail turns his back on the door. I dash for it. My heart is pounding in my chest so hard and fast it feels like I might puke. A sense of relief hits me when I step out of the club and begin rushing up the stairs toward my freedom.

Mikhail will realize I'm no longer in the club sooner rather than later. I need to move fast. I walk into the deserted alleyway where the club is located. The sound of traffic isn't too far away, and I follow it, knowing that there must be a cab nearby since we're in central Boston.

I've got a good chance of getting caught before then. I take one glance back at the club before heading past the car park toward the bustle of the city.

The sound of the door bursting open once I'm two hundred yards away spikes my anxiety. I glance back to see Mikhail has followed me out of the club. He can't see me as I remain close to the wall, hidden in the shadows, but I can see him lit by the streetlights outside the club.

I swallow hard and continue to creep away, only one hundred yards from the main street.

Mikhail is a monster.

I'm not sure what he will do to me if he catches me out here.

"Siena, there's no escape from me," he calls, glaring right at me as if he can see through the dark. "I know you're there, as I can smell your perfume, malishka."

My stomach churns. This man is like a fucking wolf, sniffing me out. I break into a run, panic consuming me as I try desperately to make it to the main street. Mikhail can't catch me.

I am a step away from getting out of the alleyway when a powerful arm wraps around my waist, lifting me off the sidewalk. "Let me go!" I cry, hoping someone might hear my plea and come to my rescue.

I'm wrong. People walk down the streets, oblivious to my cries of help. In Sicily, there is no way someone wouldn't stop to help me. I long to be back at home, enjoying the mild Sicilian winter.

"You can't run from me, Siena." Mikhail's voice is rough and laced with anger. "I own you."

I shudder, feeling repulsed by the man behind me. "You're a sick fucking murderer."

Mikhail chuckles. "Again, I do want to know what you thought being a mob boss meant when we first met. I find it hard to believe you thought I didn't kill people."

My stomach sinks. I never gave it much thought. Of

course, I knew he might rough people up and order hits, but Mikhail is a wickedly vicious man. He killed a guy with his bare hands, and the way the blood covered his face was like something out of a horror movie. "I didn't know you were capable of such violence."

Mikhail drags me deeper down the alleyway, away from the main street. "I'm capable of anything for you, Siena."

The way he says it is full of emotion that makes no sense. Mikhail captured me, and I'm his slave, and he has made that abundantly clear from the moment I met him.

Maybe I'm just a fool for thinking that Mikhail had some decency. I underestimated how dark that bratva boss who holds me captive is.

"You should be ashamed of yourself. It wasn't for me; it's for your fucking ego. You are just annoyed that another man touched me."

Mikhail growls and spins me around, grabbing my throat and forcing me to crane my neck to look up at him. "Would you have preferred that I let him rape you?" He moves his face to within an inch of mine. "Is that what you want? Maybe you'd like me to strip you naked and offer you up to all my single bratva men." There's rage in his expression, a rage so dark it scares me.

"No, but I–"

"But nothing," he roars, nostrils flaring. "I protected you because, believe it or not, I care what happens to you."

The admission hits me hard as I stare into his dark, onyx eyes. It makes no sense, as Mikhail shouldn't care about me because he's using me for his gain. "That makes no sense."

There's a flash of disappointment in his eyes. "It makes no sense, but I don't want any other man touching you." He loosens his grip on my throat and places his hands on my hips, pulling me against his hard body. "I own you until I have to release you. Do you understand me?"

He's saying that he will act like a psychopath and kill anyone who touches me until he is bored and tosses me aside. "I understand perfectly. You don't care about me. You care about your ego. If you cared about me, you'd let me go."

Mikhail groans and lets go of my hips, grabbing my legs and hoisting me over his shoulder.

"What the fuck? Let me down right now," I shout, banging on his hard, muscled back.

"No." He walks toward the car park. "We're going home so I can teach you a lesson."

I shudder, longingly staring at the main street that I almost reached. Freedom was so close and yet so damn far. Mikhail won't let me go. He's a beast with no soul. A man who doesn't care about anyone but himself, despite what he says.

Mikhail puts me down, keeping a tight grip on my wrist. "Get in," he orders.

I stare at the black town car, feeling a sinking sensation in my gut.

"Now," he growls, making me jump.

I swallow hard and open the door, sliding inside.

Mikhail follows me in, sitting closer to me than I'm comfortable with. He sets a hand on my thigh and squeezes. "You will get over what you saw and come to realize what I did was for you."

"Bullshit," I say, moving further away from him in the spacious town car.

Mikhail growls and launches himself toward me, wrapping his fingers around my throat. "Don't make me punish you in here, malishka."

I shudder, fear overtaking my body. The man with his hand wrapped around my throat is dangerous in ways I hadn't comprehended before tonight. "Please let me go," I say, hating how pathetic I sound.

Mikhail moves his lips to within an inch of mine, making my stomach churn. "In time, you will be thankful that I killed a man who had no regard for your wishes." His grip loosens on my throat. "He would have raped you while you screamed, and yet you expect me to let him live."

I shake my head. "That's rich, considering you did the same thing to me."

My comment makes him snap as he moves over me on the seat of the car, boxing me in. His bodyweight holds me down to the seat, immobilizing me. "You wanted me to fuck you; it's entirely different." He wraps his tattooed hand around my throat again. "Are you telling me you didn't enjoy it when you came on my cock three fucking times?"

I stare into his dark, manic eyes, feeling heat flood my

cheeks. "Even if I hadn't enjoyed it, you would have raped me just like that man would have today."

He shakes his head. "There was no way you wouldn't have enjoyed it with me because I cared about making you feel good. Ivan only wanted to get his dick wet, and he would have fucked you while you cried and screamed in pain rather than pleasure."

My stomach sinks, as I know that it's probably true. But I still can't match up the crime to the punishment. A death sentence for attempted rape. I'm certainly not condoning his actions, as rapists are the scum of this earth, but he should be in prison, not beaten to death. "You could have got him arrested for the crime rather than murdered him."

Mikhail releases me and sits back down, loosening his tie. He pinches the bridge of his nose. "With you, malishka, I struggle to think straight." He meets my gaze. "Although I don't regret killing him for trying to rape you, I snapped when I saw his hands on you." He sighs heavily. "I try every day to control my rage, but sometimes it controls me."

Rage that I have witnessed on more than one occasion. I turn away from him and focus my attention on the wintery scenes passing by the window. It reminds me of how blissfully happy I felt when I arrived in the city, excited to explore the snow-filled parks. Mikhail has taken all of that away from me and replaced it with darkness and blood.

Now I can't get the image of Mikhail's bloody face out of my mind. Or the ridiculous amount of blood on the floor. Thankfully, since Mikhail's back was to me, I didn't see the man's face, as something tells me that would have been horrific.

The most horrific thing is that I'm at the mercy of this wicked man. Milo will never submit to Mikhail's demands, which means I'm destined to be enslaved by this man forever.

16

MIKHAIL

I don't regret murdering Ivan. Hell, I'd do it to any man who tried to rape what is mine.

Siena believes I'm selfish and that my defense of her honor was born from a need to prove my status as pakhan of the bratva. She is wrong, and I intend to prove that to her.

Siena opens the door the moment the car pulls up to the house, trying to go ahead without me. I let her go, knowing that she can't escape me.

"Sir, shall I park the car in the garage for the night?" Popov, my driver, asks.

I meet his gaze. "Yes, we won't be going anywhere else. Thank you, Popov." I reach for the door handle, get out of the car, and then pause and stare up at my home.

Siena can't accept the monster that I am, as she shouldn't have witnessed that dark side of me. The only thing I regret is not dragging that piece of shit far away from her before murdering him.

I walk toward the house, knowing that I need to make her understand why I act the way I do. I'm the Pakhan of the Gurin Bratva, and I have to do things that she wouldn't agree with every day.

Siena is nowhere to be seen when I walk into the entry hall. I hear voices coming from the library, as my mother and Yana decided not to attend the bratva party. Natalya is still there, but she took her car.

I head up the stairs and walk to her bedroom, listening for any sign that she's in there. It's quiet, and when I try the door, it's locked. Siena is becoming a headache I don't need, yet I want her in my life.

I walk into my bedroom and unlock the door that separates our rooms. Siena isn't in the bedroom, but she has shut the door to the adjoining bathroom. The rush of water sounds behind the door.

Dirty thoughts flood my mind at the idea of her naked behind the door. I know my naughty little Italian brat will have locked the door, and I try it, frustrated when I find she has locked it as I expected.

"Siena, open this door now," I growl.

There's no response as the flood of water drowns out all other sounds.

I notice a hairpin on the dresser to my left and grab it, sliding it into the bathroom door lock. After a minute or two of messing with the lock, it clicks open. I push the door open slowly and step into the room.

Siena is in the shower with her back to me, washing her beautiful golden-brown hair. It makes no sense why she'd want to shower since she showered before we left.

The desire to join her rules me, so I pull off my tie and unbutton my shirt, chucking them onto the floor.

Siena is blissfully unaware of my presence. I free my belt quietly and take off my pants and boxers, placing them on the floor gently. She thinks she's safe from me in here, unaware that I have the skills to break into any room she tries to keep me out of.

I approach the shower and clear my throat. "You should know by now that there is no escape from me, malishka."

Siena jumps, turning around in shock to face me. "How the fuck did you get in here?" She moves her arms across her breasts to hide them from me.

I step into the shower, making it impossible for her to escape. "Don't hide from me." I grab her arm and pull it down, groaning at the sight of her nipples, hard and erect. "I want to see every inch of you." I move closer to her, forcing her against the shower wall with my body.

"I don't want you, Mikhail. If you want to protect me, then protect me from you." She glares at me with a rage that makes me want her more.

I chuckle and bring a finger to her face, gently caressing it. "Siena, that's the worst lie I've heard yet." I move my fingers between her thighs and part them, teasing a finger through her entrance. "You are so wet you are practically dripping."

Siena huffs. "That's because I'm in a shower."

I thrust my finger inside of her. "No, your pussy is soaking wet."

She bites her lip most deliciously as if trying desperately to stop herself from moaning. "You're a monster, Mikhail," she murmurs, but there's lust in her voice.

"A monster who intends to devour you, malishka." I move my lips to her neck and kiss her there, finally breaking her resolve.

Siena laces her fingers in my hair and moans. I've always hated being touched during sex, but I don't mind when Siena touches me. On the contrary, I want her to touch me. Her hand moves from my hair down over my chest as she touches me for the first time. "Why do you have so many tattoos?"

"It's tradition when part of the bratva." I raise a brow. "Don't you like them?" I ask.

Siena doesn't answer the question, staring at me with a mix of hate and lust in her eyes. "I don't like you for what you did to that man."

I grab her hips and pull her against me, enjoying the softness of her skin against mine. "No, you're just scared to admit that you love the way I make you feel, despite what I did tonight."

Siena searches my eyes before finally caving. "Whatever. Either fuck me or get out."

"That's not a very nice way to talk to the man in charge of your orgasms, is it?" I wrap a hand around her throat. "Do you want me to fuck you, Siena?"

Her lip quivers as she looks at me with a torn expression. Siena fights with her issues over my lack of morality and her desire. "I don't know what I want anymore," she says, her voice uncertain.

I move my hands lower and grab her hips, pulling her

against me. "I want you, malishka." My cock is hard against her abdomen.

She sets her hands on my chest as I move my lips to her neck, nibbling on her sensitive skin. "Mikhail." She murmurs my name in her sexy accent.

I move my lips to her breasts and suck on her hard nipples, making her shudder. "You may have seen the monster I truly am tonight, malishka, but your body still craves my touch."

Siena makes a frustrated noise. "You are so frustrating," she says, her voice exasperated.

"Because you know I'm right." I look into her eyes. "I'm going to tie you up tonight, Siena. Would you like that?"

Her brow furrows. "You've tied me up before."

I chuckle. "No, I haven't. I'm going to tie you up with rope."

She raises a brow, looking uncertain. "What's the difference?"

My innocent Sicilian gem makes me so damn crazy. "Rope is more restrictive but can feel so much better if done right."

Her throat bobs as she swallows, drawing my attention to her slender neck. A neck I love to wrap my hands around while I'm inside of her. "I don't know why you are asking me, as what I want has never mattered before."

I shake my head. "That's not true, malishka. You've always wanted everything I've given you."

Her brow furrows as she glares at me. "That's a lie."

I tighten my grip on her hips and lean toward her.

"Then why is your pussy always dripping every single time I touch you?"

Her nostrils flare, giving me an odd sense of satisfaction. Siena doesn't have an answer as she glares at me.

"Since you don't have an answer, I'm going to assume you want me to tie you up." I bend down and hoist Siena over my shoulder, still dripping wet.

"What the fuck? I haven't finished showering."

I chuckle. "After what I intend to do to you, you'll be dirty as fuck, anyway." I spank her pert ass. "No point showering before."

Siena grunts in response, turning limp over my shoulder.

My cock is painfully hard in my boxer briefs at the mere thought of fucking her senseless. Siena is becoming a compulsion I can no longer resist. No matter how hard I try to think of other things, it is impossible. She enslaves me with thoughts of her day and night. Even in my dreams, I can't escape her.

I may have kidnapped her physically, but she has arrested me in ways I can hardly contemplate. I place her down on her back, not caring that she's making the sheets wet. "Wait here and don't move," I order.

The rope I intend to tie her up with is in my closet. For a long time, I've had an affinity with Shibari rope bondage techniques. It's an art form that I enjoy inflicting on my subject, but I can't be sure whether Siena will like it or not. I collect some ropes and return to the bedroom.

Siena lies in the center of my bed with her arms crossed over her chest, waiting for me.

"Before we start, do you have any part of your body you aren't comfortable being accentuated?"

Siena stares at me blankly. "I don't know what you mean."

I rub a hand across the back of my neck. "Is there a part of your body you don't want me to put too much pressure on with the rope?"

Siena shakes her head. "No, I don't think so."

I nod. "Okay. If you want me to stop, you say a safe word." I tilt my head. "What would you like the safe word to be?"

She smiles. "Palermo?"

"That should work." I kneel on the bed between her legs. "I am going to tie you up now, malishka. If you feel anything wrong, numbness or tingling, you let me know."

Her brow furrows as if she hasn't quite comprehended what I mean by tying her up. I want her immobile and stimulated beyond compare. "Okay," she says simply.

"Good girl," I say, grabbing her hips. "Stand up for me, as it's easier that way."

Siena does as I say, standing in front of me.

I take a moment to admire every dip and curve of her body. I start with a basic chest harness with the rope in my hand, wrapping the rope under her breasts and tying the knot at the back. I let the rope go down her spine before wrapping it above her breasts next, using her body as a canvas.

The mere sight of the rope against her tanned skin drives me wild.

Siena whimpers softly.

"Are you okay? It's not too tight, is it?"

Siena shakes her head. "No, it just feels strange."

Once I finish tying the harness, I grab another rope. "Next, I'm going to tie your waist and hips, as well as your arms."

She licks her lips before nodding. "Okay, sir."

I shake my head, lifting her chin, so she looks me in the eye. "I know you don't want to call me that, Siena. Call me what feels right."

Siena looks torn as she searches my eyes. "I don't know what–"

I spank her beautiful, round ass. "Don't lie to me, malishka."

"Sorry. Yes, Daddy," she says, her voice soft and innocent. It's so delicate I'm sure I will break her with the things I'm going to do to her.

I start to tie the shibari rope around her hips and thighs, linking it into the chest harness to give me better leverage on her body.

Siena remains still, submitting to me as I have my way with her. Once I'm finished, I step back and admire my work, groaning. My hard cock leaks precum onto the floor beneath me as I fist it in my hand. "You look amazing. How does it feel?"

Siena's brow furrows. "I'm not sure how to describe it."

I grab hold of the rope at her hips and push her onto the bed. "I want to show you how amazing it can feel when you are at my mercy, tied like this."

I position the head of my cock at the entrance of her

dripping wet pussy.

"Wait," Siena says, stopping me as I'm about to thrust into her. "We're not using any birth control."

The statement surprises me as I stare into her stunning hazel eyes. "Don't worry, malishka. I can't have children."

Her brow furrows. "How do you know?"

"I had a vasectomy three years ago."

Siena looks like she wants to ask why I'd do that. It was a choice I made after a woman I'd slept with tried to claim I'd gotten her pregnant. It turned out that I wasn't the father of her child, and she was trying to exploit me, but it highlighted a weakness. Someone could trick me into getting them pregnant and hold it over me as leverage, so I opted for the treatment.

"Oh," she says simply.

I wonder why I detect disappointment in her eyes. Children will never be a part of my future, as I never wanted them, and nothing will ever change that.

An odd tension passes between us as she stares at me. I can't understand why the mention of my inability to have children has made things so awkward. I move my lips to hers and kiss her, diffusing the tense atmosphere as she moans into my mouth.

I slide every inch of my cock into her, and she cries out louder than ever before.

"Oh fuck, Mikhail." Siena's face is a picture of perfection as her pleasure is painted all over it. "That feels so fucking good."

I smirk at her. "That's the art of shibari, malishka." I kiss her lips, silencing her again. A part of me longs to force a gag into her mouth, removing more of her senses, but I know that is a step too far for a beginner.

I reach down and rub her clit, making her arch her back. "I want you to come so many times on my cock you won't know your name once I've finished."

Siena whimpers as I slam my cock as deep as possible inside of her. The violence of my desire for her is difficult to describe. After three more thrusts, my Italian gem comes undone, her body trembling viciously as the first intense orgasm tears through her body.

"That's it. I want to feel you come for me," I murmur, licking a path down her neck.

Siena's eyes roll back in her head as I continue my wicked assault on her body. The intimacy of sharing these moments with her is so polar opposite to how our relationship should be. She is a slave and a means to an end, nothing more.

The more I think that the less I believe it is true. Siena is more precious to me than stopping any stupid merger Milo might be planning. She's becoming my world. A dangerous notion, considering the instability that surrounds me right now.

"Oh God," Siena moans as I continue to thrust into her without mercy. The violence of my desire translates into a rough assault as our bodies collide. I feel her getting close, knowing it deep in my soul.

"Not God, baby," I murmur, sucking on her hard, puckered nipple.

"Fuck, Daddy!" she cries as she tips over the edge for the second time.

It's hard to believe how natural she is at this. Everything I've thrown at her, she's excelled in. Siena loves pain, and she loves being tied up. God knows what else she loves. I need to find out and explore every fucking avenue with her.

I grab hold of the rope and force her onto her knees. "Stay like that for me like a good girl," I purr.

Siena arches her back as much as the rope will allow, panting frantically. "Fuck me harder."

I grind my teeth together at the utterly ludicrous request. Any harder, and this girl might tear in two. I grab the rope at her spine and pull her onto my cock with all my strength. Her tight little asshole draws my attention to it. The idea of fucking it makes me crazy, but I know I have to take this one step at a time.

Shibari bondage as a beginner is a lot to take in, and adding anal to it would be overwhelming. I don't know why I even care, since normally I take whatever the fuck I want. With Siena, I know I can't, as it would break this weird, twisted thing we have together.

Siena screams in what could be pleasure or pain. I don't know. Right now, I'm not entirely with it enough to know what is happening. All rational thought eludes me as I drive my cock in and out of her harder, deeper, faster. The clash of skin against skin is so loud it fills the room along with her screams.

"Yes, Daddy, yes," she repeatedly cries like a broken record.

I keep the tempo, pushing her over the edge for the third time. Her body spasms out of control. It's the hottest thing I've ever seen as her muscles spasm and contract around my cock. "Fuck, baby, that's right. Come on my cock like a good girl," I roar, slamming into her once more and unloading my cum deep in her pussy.

Our rasping breaths fill the air as I pull my cock out of her, watching as my cum drips from her. It's a sight so fucking erotic, I feel a twinge in my balls as my desire reignites.

I loosen the knots on the rope, knowing that I have tied her up long enough. The knots will leave bruises on her skin by the morning. I'm starting to wonder if I'll ever be able to let my little kulkoka go. She's becoming too precious to me.

17

SIENA

I wake to find Mikhail's side of the bed empty. My heart sinks as I realize it's Christmas morning.

Today would have been filled with so much joy if I had been with my two best friends. Instead, loneliness will fill my Christmas day. Mikhail keeps me locked in this room, and I know today will be the same.

A bang in the bathroom startles me, and I sit upright brow furrowing. Then the door opens, and Mikhail walks into the room with nothing other than a towel wrapped loosely around his hips.

It's frustrating that despite what I saw him do and everything I know about him, I feel a hungry need ignite deep inside me.

"Happy Christmas, malishka," he says as if we're a normal couple waking up on Christmas morning.

I glare at him. "It would have been happy if you hadn't kidnapped me."

He walks toward the bed and sits down. "I understand you are angry with me for what you saw last night. If we are going to enjoy today, then I need you to put that aside and play a part for me in front of my family."

I narrow my eyes at him, wondering what he's talking about. "Your family?"

He nods. "I will not leave you locked in here alone on Christmas Day, but I need you to be on your best behavior." He moves a hand over my exposed thigh. "Can you promise to do that for me?"

I search his eyes. The man sitting in front of me is different from the man I saw last night with blood coating his face. His touch is gentle, and his request is the most civility he's given me since I arrived here. "I promise," I say, despite my reservations.

I don't want to be locked in here for the entire day, even if that means spending the day with Mikhail and his family, as at least I won't be alone with him.

He moves the covers off me and grabs my hand, forcing me to my feet. "I have something for you." He reaches under the bed and pulls out a parcel wrapped in gold.

My stomach flutters with nerves as he places it into my hand. As I stare at the neatly wrapped gift, I don't know what to do with it. A part of me doesn't want to accept anything from a man like him. "Why would you get me something?" I ask, glancing up and searching his dark eyes.

Mikhail's jaw clenches, and he folds his arms over his chest. "Open it. You know I don't like questions."

I turn the long, thin box over in my hands. I don't like the idea of accepting anything from a man holding me captive. "Why should I accept anything from you?"

Mikhail runs a hand across the back of his neck, pacing away from me. "Don't open it then." He marches into the bathroom and slams the door, making me jump.

I sit back on the bed and throw the gift down next to me, glancing at it.

Why would Mikhail buy me a gift?

I'm his damn prisoner, but he's treating me more like his damn mistress. It makes no sense. All of this is making it more difficult to comprehend my feelings for him. Before I saw him kill that man, I was falling for his wicked ways hard.

The question is, have I witnessed his true colors too late?

Deep down, I'm sure that I have already lost my heart to him. I don't know when it happened, but Stockholm Syndrome is more real than I ever could have imagined.

I turn my attention back to the gift and sigh, pulling open the red ribbon. The gift wrap is well fixed, and I take a while to free it. Once I do, I reveal a long black velvet box, and I instantly know it's jewelry.

Mikhail remains in the bathroom as I force open the box, gasping when I see what is inside. It's a stunning diamond collar necklace that has to be worth more than anything I own in this world. My stomach flutters as this is a necklace that a man would buy for his girlfriend. I have to wonder whether Mikhail has feelings for me in return. The man who promised to ruin me for all other men.

I sigh and shut the box, placing it down next to me.

Mikhail returns.

"I can't accept the gift," I say simply.

Mikhail notices the black velvet box strewn on the bed. "You can accept it, and you will, malishka." He moves toward me with such self-confidence. "Stand for me."

I stand up despite being naked.

Mikhail grabs the box and pulls out the disgustingly expensive necklace. He slides it around my neck and does up the clasp at the back. "This is a sign of my ownership over you," he murmurs into my ear.

"Great. So this is just a pretty collar?" I ask as he circles back around to stand in front of me. "What next? Will you get me a leash to go with it?"

Mikhail's lips twist into a wicked smile that makes my stomach churn. "Not a bad idea. Don't tempt me."

I shake my head. "I was joking." I glance down at the beautiful diamonds adorning my neck. "You better remove it so I can shower."

Mikhail shakes his head. "Shower with it on. It won't harm it." His eyes dip down my body slowly. "You look fucking perfect like this."

I turn away from him and walk toward the bathroom without a word. His footsteps trail behind me, following me into the bathroom.

My nipples tighten, and I feel the wetness pooling between my thighs. No matter what I think of the man stalking behind me, he affects my body like no other man ever has, and I long for him on an intuitive level.

"Wait," Mikhail orders.

I stop still, trembling as I feel him approach me.

"I want you to take a bath." Mikhail walks in front of me, eyes full of lust as they travel down the length of my body again.

"Why?" I ask.

He growls softly, shaking his head. "Don't question me."

I make my way over to the bath, bending over to put the stopper in.

Mikhail groans behind me. "I'm so fucking hard I want to take you right now," he growls.

I glance over my shoulder at him, feeling need spread through me at the sight of his huge, hard cock in his hand. He fists it up and down viciously, eyes manic with lust. "Then fuck me," I say simply, feeling my knees shake.

He growls. "Bathtub, now."

I swallow hard and walk toward the huge jacuzzi bathtub in the center of the bathroom. I reach for the faucet, but Mikhail places a hand over mine, stopping me.

"No, get in. Let me handle that."

I glance at the commanding Russian mob boss behind me before doing as he says. It feels strange as I lie down in the empty tub and place the stopper in, waiting for Mikhail to fill it. He turns the faucet on, and the water runs cold at first, making me shiver. "How does that feel?"

I meet his hot and heavy gaze. "Warm, but I like it hotter."

He smirks and mutters something in his language.

I watch as he turns the faucet more to the right and the water heats. "Yes, that's perfect," I murmur, feeling my muscles relax as the balmy water rises around my body.

"Not as perfect as you, kukolka," Mikhail says gruffly, moving his hands to my shoulders and gently kneading them.

His gentle touch is a little scary, considering he's always so rough. Last night was no exception, and I forgot all about his sick and perverse ways the moment his hands were on me. Maybe I'm the one that needs to see a shrink.

"Let me take care of you today," he murmurs, working out the knots in my shoulders.

I sigh as his hands feel like heaven as they work my muscles. "You are good at this."

"I'm good at everything I do, malishka. Haven't you figured that out yet?"

I roll my eyes at his unapologetically cocky attitude. "I guess not."

He makes a tutting sound in response, grabbing a bottle of soap off the side. "Time for me to get you clean."

Mikhail lathers the soap in his hands before rubbing his hands over my arms and chest. His dark eyes are intense as they follow his hands over my body. He doesn't say a word, paying attention to every part of me as he washes me. It's both a tender and erotic moment.

I feel my need increase as he finishes washing me between my thighs, rubbing my clit hard. "Mikhail, that feels so good," I moan.

That wicked smile I've grown to love twists onto his lips. "I think it's time you give me my present, isn't it?"

I feel my cheeks heat, wondering what he means. "What is that?" I ask.

Mikhail climbs into the vast tub next to me. He wraps an arm around me and forces me to straddle his lap. "I want your ass, malishka," he whispers into my ear.

I tense. "Ass?"

He groans. "Yes, I want to fuck your tight little asshole."

I swallow hard at the thought of his immense size invading such a tight space. "I'm not sure you will fit."

He chuckles. "Oh, believe me, I will." I feel his finger probe at the ring of muscles gently. "Have you ever had your ass fucked, kukolka?"

I shake my head. "No, sir."

Mikhail tightens his grip on my hips. "What did I tell you?" He looks into my eyes. "I know that sir doesn't come naturally to you."

He's right. I can't understand why I want to call this wicked, brutal man "Daddy." It's ingrained in me for reasons I don't understand. "No, I've never had my ass fucked."

His onyx eyes fill with a feral lust that scares me. "Good, because I'm going to be the first and last man to fuck your ass. Do you hear me?"

I don't question the logic. Yes, Mikhail will be the first, but he can't guarantee he will be the last. I've always wondered what it would feel like, fantasized about it.

"Have you ever fingered your ass?" Mikhail asks.

I swallow hard, feeling embarrassed by the answer to the question. "A few times."

He groans. "Dirty girl. I like to think of you with your fingers up your ass, moaning." He kisses my lips, restricting my arms with one hand behind my back. "So fucking sexy. Wait until my cock is stretching that tight little hole instead."

I shudder. "It's too big."

He smirks. "Don't worry. I'll get you suitably stretched before entering." He sucks on my left nipple. "Trust me." He then moves to my right.

Mikhail asking me to trust him is insane. He kidnapped me, for fuck's sake. And yet, I do trust him. "Turn around for me."

My brow furrows, but I do as he says, straddling his legs with my back to him.

Mikhail groans as he forces my ass cheeks open. "Such a tight little hole."

I feel his finger tease the sensitive ring of muscles. "Mikhail."

He grabs my hips and lifts me enough to free his cock, lining it up with my lips. I moan as he drags the head of his cock through them before thrusting his hips upward.

"Fuck," I murmur, enjoying the way he fills me so completely.

"Ride it, malishka." He spanks my ass cheek firmly, making me moan.

I rise and fall on his cock, impaling myself harder and faster with each movement.

The click of a bottle cap opening makes my heart skip a beat. I slow down the pace, waiting for Mikhail's next more. It unnerves me he has unrestricted access to my asshole. I have no control here, even though I'm the one in the driver's seat.

I feel the cold liquid as he squirts it onto my ass. My clit throbs with need as I move my hand between my thighs, rubbing myself as I ride his dick. Anytime I played with my ass before, it was fucking amazing. I just don't trust that a huge cock in my ass will feel so good.

Mikhail thrusts a lubed finger into my ass. It feels even better than when I did it to myself, and perhaps it's because his thick cock is stretching my pussy still.

I grind against his cock, forcing his finger deeper into my ass.

Mikhail spanks my ass cheek with his free hand. "You love having your ass played with, don't you?"

"It feels amazing," I murmur, rising and falling faster on his cock. "Give me more."

Mikhail laughs and squirts more lube onto my eager hole before sliding two fingers inside of me this time. "Such a good girl, begging me for more." He spanks my ass cheek again with his free hand. "Keep riding my dick," he orders.

I move my hips up and down, driving his fingers in harder with each movement.

Mikhail doesn't warn me as he adds another finger, stretching my ass, making it ready for his thick cock.

It shocks me how good it feels, along with his cock still in my pussy. It's a sensation I'd never believe I'd enjoy. The idea of being stuffed in both holes is both arousing and scary.

Mikhail adds his fourth finger, groaning. "Fuck, you take my fingers so well in that tight little ass."

His dirty talk is enough to tip me over the edge. My body trembles as I come on his cock, panting for air. I feel my muscles relax further as Mikhail stretches my ass more.

"You are ready," he murmurs, squirting more lube into my asshole.

My stomach clenches at the thought of his cock filling such a tight space. He may have gotten four fingers in, but Mikhail is so long and thick. "Are you sure it will fit?"

Mikhail doesn't answer my question. Instead, he forces me off his cock and moves the enormous length to my asshole. I feel the tip of him pressing against the tight ring of muscles, and I tense instinctively at the mere thought of such a huge thing entering a confined space.

I feel the pressure as he pushes his cock into the confined space, wincing as it stings a little. My clit throbs, and I reach down, rubbing it as he continues to inch his way deeper into my virgin hole.

I bite my lip, trying to ignore the stinging pain.

"Relax, malishka."

I breathe deeply, shaking my head. "It's too damn big."

Mikhail groans. "No, it's almost inside, malishka." He spanks my ass cheek. "You look so good with my cock deep in your ass."

I swallow hard, struggling to believe that he's almost all the way inside. "Really?"

He laughs that deep, rasping sound. "If you didn't realize, then you are ready for me to fuck you." His fingertips dig into the skin at my hips as he forces me to rise higher, so I can feel the thick length of him pulling at my tight hole.

I groan as he forces his hips upward while yanking me down, impaling himself inside of me. "Oh, fuck," I cry.

Mikhail grunts as he fucks me harder with each thrust, taking my anal virginity roughly. I expected nothing less, but I didn't expect to love it this much. The sensation is unlike anything I've ever felt.

I move my fingers to my clit, rubbing it as I meet Mikhail's thrusts. "It feels so good."

Mikhail groans. "It looks so fucking good too, malishka. I love the way your hole clings to my cock." He stills inside of me, sinking his teeth into my back. "I want you to turn around for me."

I rise off his cock, groaning at the sudden empty sensation. Mikhail practically lifts me and turns me mid-air, forcing me to straddle his legs facing him. He kisses me deeply, his tongue caressing mine.

Without any warning, he slides every inch back into my ass. "Fuck," I pant. It feels even better in this position as Mikhail thrusts his hips up to meet my movements.

"Good girl, malishka. Ride my cock," he groans, wrapping his tattooed hand around my throat. "I want you to come while my cock is deep in your tight little asshole." He squeezes my throat hard enough to block my airways partially, heightening the unparalleled pleasure of him fucking my ass.

"Fuck, Daddy!" I cry, resting my hands on his hard, chiseled chest as I increase the tempo. "I'm going to come."

"Good girl. Come for me," he murmurs, thrusting into me hard. "Then I'll fill that tight little asshole with my cum."

My eyes roll back in my head as an intense wave of pleasure crests through me. I moan incoherent words, knowing that this man has made me lose my mind. As my muscles spasm, I feel my ass tighten around his cock as he continues to thrust.

Mikhail roars as he comes undone. Our bodies continue to gyrate together as we both struggle to stop, overwhelmed by our orgasms. When he finally stops thrusting into me, it feels like my entire body is made of jelly.

Mikhail lifts me off his cock and turns me around, forcing me to sit between his legs. His powerful arms wrap around me as he holds me against his chest in the warm water.

"This was the best gift I've ever gotten, malishka," he whispers into my ear.

I smile. "I think it was the best one I've ever gotten to."

Mikhail tenses beneath me. "Not the two million dollar necklace I gave you?"

My heart skips a beat. I knew it was expensive, but that is ridiculous. "Two million dollars?"

He chuckles. "Yes. If I'd known all I needed to please you was some rough anal sex in the bath, I wouldn't have splashed out on it."

I shake my head. "No, I love that too."

He presses his lips to my shoulder, kissing me softly. Christmas day as a prisoner should be a nightmare, but it feels like a dream right now.

18

MIKHAIL

Siena laughs at something Natalya says, drawing my attention to her.

The Italian goddess fits into this family better than I ever imagined. Even my mother seems to like her, which is rare indeed.

The necklace I bought her sits proudly around her neck, serving as a mark of my ownership on her, ownership that I never want to end.

"Mikhail?" My mother says my name, and when I look at her, she shakes her head. "Did you listen to a word I said?"

"Sorry, mother, I wasn't—"

She clips me on the ear as if I'm a damn child. Only she would dare lay a hand on me. "You were too busy ogling your pretty woman."

I narrow my eyes at her. "Siena is just a friend. I told you."

"Don't treat me like a fool. I see the way you look at

her." She glances between her and me. "I've never seen you look at a woman the way you look at her, Mikhail."

My stomach dips as I know she's right. Siena is different. Ever since I set eyes on her in my basement, I've wanted her in a primal way. Relationships are messy, and it's the reason I never got serious with anyone, as it's easier to remain alone.

Siena fell into my arms, and now I can't imagine my life without her in it. It's a ridiculous notion, considering I met her five days ago.

Is it even possible to know that you want to spend the rest of your life with someone that fast?

"I don't know what you mean, mother."

She makes a disapproving sound and shakes her head, turning to speak with Yana's husband instead.

I grab my vodka glass and bring it to my lips, knocking the contents backs.

Siena glances over at me, and our eyes meet, sparking that deep, hungry tension in an instance.

My mother's archaic seating plan means I'm sitting too damn far away from her. I want to touch her under the table and feel how wet she is just thinking about me.

She smiles at me, and it is enough to make my heartache. Her cheeks flush as she finally breaks our eye contact, saying something to Natalya. Those two get on well, but I hate that I'm thinking about our future together when it is impossible.

My staff prepared the meal this morning before heading home to spend Christmas with their families. For one day a year, our family isn't waited on hand and foot.

"I shall see if the food is ready." I stand, struggling to keep my attention off of Siena.

Siena stands too. "I'll help."

I raise a brow at her eagerness to be alone with me before nodding and leading the way out of the dining room.

Siena follows close behind me, her presence ever felt from her scent and the soft sound of her footsteps. "Your family is nice."

I swallow hard and glance at her. "They like you, it seems." I turn left into the kitchen, a room I rarely spend any time in. "The goose should be ready."

Siena laughs. "I don't know why hearing you say that is so funny."

I grab the oven mitts off the counter and open the door to the oven. "Perhaps it is because I'm not exactly the cooking type?"

Siena moves closer to me. "Why don't you let me handle it, then? I love cooking." She tries to reach for the mitt, but I hold it out of her reach.

"Do you? I didn't know that about you, malishka."

Siena purses her lips, glancing at the open oven door. "You are letting all the heat out of the oven, Mikhail."

I smirk at how adorable she is. "The goose is done, so it doesn't matter."

She grunts and walks away from me. "You are so frustrating."

I get the goose out of the oven and place it on the center island to rest. Most of the other food to accompany it is cold, and the potatoes are ready. "You are so adorable when you get angry."

Siena glares at me. "I'm going to go back to the dining room."

I walk toward her, each of my steps equaling two of hers. "You aren't going anywhere unless I say so." I grab her wrist and yank her against me. I press my lips to hers, overwhelmed by the pressing desire coursing through my veins.

Once we break apart, I notice that her cheeks are flushed a rosy pink. "I've wanted to do that all damn morning," I murmur.

Siena's breathing deepens. "I've wanted you to do it all morning, and that's why I offered to help."

I groan and lift her onto the edge of the counter. "I shouldn't need to have you already. I fucked your perfect little asshole before we left the room. But with you, I'm insatiable." I kiss her neck, moving my lips toward her ear and nibbling there. "I thought it would stave off my hunger for you at least until tonight, but if anything, it has made me more ravenous."

Siena digs her fingertips into my shoulders, moaning. "What about the food?"

"Fuck the food," I growl, tightening my grip on her hips. "All I'm hungry for is your sweet little pussy." I bite her earlobe, making her yelp.

She quickly covers her mouth. "I don't know how to stay quiet with you."

I move down her body, lifting the hem of her pretty gold dress to reveal her skimpy white thong. "Then don't."

I pull the fabric aside and press my mouth to her dripping wet cunt.

All rhyme and reason evaporate when I'm like this. Siena controls me as no woman has ever been able to. I'm like an animal for her—a beast that can't control my cravings. It's as if the more I have of Siena, the deeper the craving roots itself in my blood.

I lick her throbbing clit before burying my tongue in her pussy, tasting her sweet nectar.

Siena laces her fingers in my hair as I devour her, sucking and licking at her as if my life depends on it. It feels that way. The last few days with her have been a whirlwind I will never forget.

"Oh fuck," she moans, head lulling back as I thrust my fingers into her dripping cunt.

I'm so wound up by the woman I'm feasting on, addicted to her in ways I never knew possible. If Milo rang me tomorrow and agreed to stop the merger in exchange for Siena, I don't think I'd be able to let her go.

I thrust three fingers in and out of her greedy pussy, groaning at how wet she is. "You are so fucking wet," I murmur before plowing my face against her lips again and tasting her deeply.

Someone clearing their throat startles both of us apart as I stand quickly.

Siena's cheeks turn a deep red as she notices Natalya standing in the doorway, hands on her hips. "Friends, hey?" She shakes her head. "I thought I'd see if you guys needed a hand bringing the food, but it looks like my brother was more interested in feasting on you, Siena."

I growl, feeling irritated that I don't have the chance to finish what I started.

Siena jumps off the counter. "I'm so sorry you had to see that." She shakes her head. "We best get the food into the dining room."

I give my sister a warning look as I follow her, grabbing the carving knife out of the block on the side. "I'll bring the goose after I've carved it. You two go ahead with the rest of the food on those trolleys." I nod at the trolleys in the corner.

Natalya helps Siena load them up as I carve the goose. They both wheel one out each, leaving me alone with my thoughts. I shouldn't have lost control like that in here. This day is supposed to be about spending time with a family I rarely see. Instead, I can't stop thinking about a woman I met five fucking days ago.

I take my frustrations out on the goose in front of me, carving it rather roughly. It all tastes the same, no matter how it looks. Once I'm finished, I carry the enormous platter to the dining room.

My family helps themselves to the delicious food as I make a place on the table for the large meat platter. Siena keeps her eyes off of me with purposeful intent. Her cheeks redden as I get closer to her, brushing her hand as I move something out of the way. Her bashfulness is adorable.

I sit on the opposite side of the table, grinding my teeth as I long to be next to Siena. My cock is still hard in my pants after our moment in the kitchen. It's highly inappropriate, considering I'm sitting down to dinner with my family, but my desire for Siena is uncontrollable.

"How is work, Alex?" my mother asks, drawing my attention.

Yana sets a hand on his arm as he smiles. "It's good, and I'm up for a promotion next month."

My mother smiles widely, always taken in by Alex's act. "Oh, how wonderful." I believe I'm the only one in this family, except for Yana, who knows the truth about Alex. He's a glorified criminal for a cartel in Mexico, nothing more. It may appear that he has a legitimate job on the outside, but it's all a front.

Yana clears her throat. "We have some rather exciting news."

I tilt my head, observing my eldest sister. She's pregnant, as I noticed the slight bump on her stomach and the glow of her skin the moment she arrived.

"We are expecting a baby in six months." She squeezes Alex's hand.

My mother claps her hands. "A baby. I'm going to be a grandmother." Tears well in her eyes, which is a show of unexpected emotion from a woman who always seems so cold. "I do wish you'd both consider moving to Russia."

Yana shakes her head. "No chance of that. I love the warmth, and Russia is far too cold."

My mother looks disappointed as she picks at her food before glancing at me. "You, my son, need to get a move on and have a child of your own. If you want stability for the family business, a child is imperative."

Natalya meets my gaze, as we've never told my mother our intention.

"I have no intention of having children. Natalya will be next in line once I'm gone."

My mother's eyes widen. "Like hell, she will."

Natalya sighs. "Why do you think I'm attending the Syndicate Academy, mother?"

I sigh heavily, realizing I forgot to tell Natalya not to mention the Academy. My mother hates that place, as she thinks it's barbaric to have a school set up to teach pupils how to be criminals.

"Mikhail." The tone of my mother's voice sends shivers down my spine. Even to this day, she has this power over me, I can't quite explain. "You told me that you enrolled Natalya in a normal school," she booms, glaring at me with an expression that could turn most people to stone.

"I knew you would not approve." I glare back at her. "Perhaps if you hadn't abandoned us and left me as her sole guardian, you would have had more say."

My mother stands, the chair scratching on the wooden floor. "I will not stand for this insolence from you, Mikhail." She glowers at me intensely. "Natalya is my daughter, and you knew I didn't want her going to that joke of a school."

Natalya stands. "Mikhail is right. You aren't my mother, and Mikhail has raised me for the last ten years."

I glance at Siena, who has gone pale as she glances between the three of us. Yana and Alex remain silent but unsurprised. Anytime all three of us are in the same room, tensions arise at some point.

I clap my hands. "It is Christmas Day, and this isn't the time to discuss it." I gesture at the food on the table. "Eat before the food gets cold."

Natalya does as I say while my mother continues to glare for a few moments. Finally, she sinks back down into her chair, muttering to herself in Russian about how terrible I am.

I take my seat last as a tense silence floods the air. My mother doesn't know the truth about the procedure I had three years ago. A family wouldn't be an option for me because of it, even if I wanted children. She will have to accept that Natalya is the only option for the future of the Gurin Bratva.

19

SIENA

"I've eaten way too much food," I groan, holding my stomach.

Natalya laughs. "Tell me about it."

Mikhail remains sitting by my side, silent. He has said little all day, and all he does is sit there and observe. It's unnerving being watched by a man as intense as he is.

"What time is it?" I ask.

Mikhail checks his watch. "It's almost midnight."

Natalya yawns. "I think I'm going to get some sleep."

I swallow hard at the thought of being left alone with Mikhail and his mother. "Goodnight," I say.

Natalya smiles. "Goodnight. See you tomorrow." She walks away, and I notice Mikhail's mother stand too. She's a very serious woman, but nice enough.

"Goodnight, son," she says, walking over to Mikhail and kissing him on the cheek. She glances at me. "Goodnight, Siena. It was lovely to meet you."

I smile. "Goodnight, Mrs. Gurin." Once she is gone, it

will just be the two of us. I've felt his gaze on me throughout the day. The heavy tension that clouds the air every time I meet it makes my stomach flutter with nerves.

Despite feeling Mikhail's gaze on me, I focus on the door as his mother leaves. He is the most intense man I've ever met.

Once she's gone, Mikhail breaks the silence. "Look at me."

I move my gaze to him, expecting him to speak.

Instead, he stands and approaches me, placing a finger under my chin and lifting it. "You were a very good girl today," he murmurs. "Do you want a reward?"

I tilt my head to the side. "It depends what the reward is."

He smiles, and it is the most genuine smile I've seen all day. "You will enjoy it, I promise."

I swallow hard as the last thing I should do is trust a word this man says. It's ridiculous that I do trust him. "Okay."

He takes my hand in his and leads me out of the grand reception room we'd spent the evening lounging around in. I feel my heart pounding hard and fast in my chest as I allow this criminal to lead me God knows where.

Mikhail leads me into the hallway and then out toward the front door.

"Where are we going?" I ask.

He squeezes my hand in warning. "It's a surprise."

I sigh and resign myself to the fact that Mikhail won't

tell me where he's taking me. Mikhail opens the door, and the cold evening air hits my bare skin, making me shudder. He glances at me and notices I'm only wearing a maxi dress, which isn't suited to these conditions. I'm surprised when he shrugs off his jacket and wraps it around my shoulders.

"It's so warm in the house I almost forgot it is winter," he says, keeping an arm around my back.

His touch is gentle as he steers me toward a small building on the grounds.

"Are you going to tell me where we are going?" I ask.

He chuckles. "I don't think I've ever met anyone who asks as many questions as you." Mikhail doesn't answer the question as he leads me to the building entrance, sliding a key into the lock and turning it.

Mikhail guides me inside a large room with a mezzanine above. My heart skips a beat as I look up, noticing a vast glass dome above us and the stars twinkling overhead. "Is this your very own observatory?" I ask.

He smiles and nods. "Yes, and I like to come here to clear my mind." Tightening his grip on my hip, he guides me toward the steel circular staircase, rising to the mezzanine. "The view is better up here."

At the top of the staircase is a huge telescope. "Wow, does that work?" I walk over to it and run my hand over the smooth metal case.

Mikhail smiles, watching me from a distance. "Why don't you look and find out?"

I hate the way my stomach flutters every single time he looks at me like that. Despite being very aware this man is sick in the head, I long for him with every bone in my body. I crouch down and glance through the eyepiece of the telescope. The image knocks the air from my lungs: a crystal clear view of thousands of twinkling stars millions of miles away. "That's stunning."

Mikhail's hand lands on my shoulder, shocking me. "Not half as stunning as the star in front of me."

I swallow hard as I meet his gaze. That intense longing ignites inside of me. "Don't be silly." I shake my head. "Nothing beats the beauty of the solar system." I have always had an obsession with space, ever since I was little. My parents were sure I would become an astrologist, but I was never good enough at school.

Mikhail growls, grabbing my hips. "That's not true, malishka." He pulls me against him, forcing me to crane my neck to look into his onyx eyes. "For me, there is nothing on this planet that is as beautiful as you."

It's an oddly tender expression that makes me wonder if he feels this deeper connection between us. A connection that shouldn't exist between a captive and his captor.

"The solar system isn't on this planet," I point out.

Mikhail cups my face in his hand and shakes his head. "You don't know how to take a compliment, do you?"

I smile at the man who has inexplicably captured my heart. It's ridiculous but true. Five days he has had me as his prisoner. In those five days, I've fallen prey to his charms. He told me he would make sure I'd never forget him. "It doesn't seem like it."

Mikhail kisses me softly. The passion in his kiss makes my heart swell. I can't love a man who has held me against my will. It is illogical, and yet love knows no logic. It's a fundamental truth that I have learned to be true in a short space of time.

I thread my fingers through his dark hair, pulling him closer.

Mikhail plunges his tongue into my mouth frantically. Our bodies writhe together as the desperation between us increases. He pulls his lips from mine, panting. "Shall we lie down and look at the stars?" he asks.

We both know exactly where this will go the moment we lie down. There will be no star gazing tonight. The tension between us is too high. We both need each other, want each other. Ever since Natalya interrupted us in the kitchen, I've been desperate to be alone with him.

"Yes," I murmur, allowing him to pull me down onto the soft cushions scattered over the mezzanine floor.

Mikhail pulls me against his chest and looks up at the glass ceiling. "When it's a really clear night, you can often see Mars."

I smile at him. "Do you know the constellations?"

He shakes his head. "I never have time to learn, but I like looking at them, as it puts everything in perspective."

I gaze up at the twinkling stars. "I always wanted to learn. Maybe we can learn together." I hadn't thought about what I was saying until after I said it. It makes no sense. Once Mikhail gets what he wants from Milo, he will return me, which will be the end of this twisted relationship.

My chest aches at the thought of this ever ending.

"Maybe," Mikhail murmurs, pressing his lips to my

forehead. "Right now, all I want to do is learn the location of every blemish on your body."

I shudder as he moves over me, covering me with his heavyweight. The hard press of his cock is evident between us. "I need you," I murmur.

"I will not lie. When we first met, I never thought I'd hear you say those words."

Neither did I.

He presses his lips to my collarbone and kisses me there softly, moving lower. There's a tenderness that has never existed between us, and the gentleness in his touch is a foreign sensation.

"Take this off," he murmurs, tugging at my shirt.

I unbutton it before shrugging it off onto the floor.

Mikhail groans before sliding his hand around the back and unhooking my bra. He yanks it away and slings it across the floor. "I will never tire of seeing you naked."

Before I can say anything in response, he captures one of my hard nipples in his mouth. My back arches as he sucks on it, making me needier than ever before. Our unfinished business in the kitchen before dinner has left me longing to feel him touch me ever since.

"Fuck me," I say, wanting nothing more than to feel him inside of me.

Mikhail chuckles. "Since when are you in charge?"

"I'm not, but you didn't finish what you started in the kitchen." I pout at him. "I've been going crazy ever since."

He grazes the tip of his teeth over my collarbone. "I intend to finish it now." He plants soft kisses over my chest and stomach, lifting my skirt. He grabs hold of the lace fabric of my panties and tears them apart.

He acts like such an animal, and that turns me on like nothing ever has. His all-consuming need to fuck me is addictive.

Mikhail makes me feel wanted, something I've never felt in my entire life.

His tongue switches between my throbbing clit and my pussy as he devours me.

"Yes, Daddy," I moan, uncertain why I love calling him that. He asked me to call him master, but it didn't feel natural.

Mikhail thrusts his fingers into my pussy, finding the perfect spot inside of me as if he knows my body better than I do. I scream as I feel my orgasm rushing toward me, which is long overdue.

Mikhail realizes and stops finger fucking me. "Not yet, kukolka."

I grunt in frustration, glaring down at him. "Why not?"

The wicked smirk I've come to know and love twists onto his lips. "You know I'm in charge." He caresses his lips against my abdomen teasingly, moving to my breasts next.

I whimper as he asserts his lips over mine dominantly. His tongue thrusts into my mouth forcefully as he takes what he wants, entangling our tongues in a dance of fiery passion.

He breaks away, breathing against my lips. "I don't want you to come until I'm inside of you, malishka."

I gasp, desperate to feel him inside of me. It feels like I'll explode any moment if he doesn't fuck me. "Then what are you waiting for?"

He searches my eyes before freeing his cock from his pants. "Nothing," he says simply before plowing every inch into me.

My eyes roll back in my head as he fills me so completely. I moan, wrapping my fingers around the back of his neck and pulling his lips to mine.

He obliges, kissing me deeply, our tongues entangling in a war of passion as we both struggle to get enough of each other.

I know at that moment that I will never have had enough of Mikhail Gurin. It's an absurd but true fact. A man who kidnapped, threatened, and unapologetically took whatever he wanted from me has become my obsession. I wake up thinking of him, think of him all day, and then fall asleep only to dream of the man who has enslaved me so completely, as he promised.

I know that if he ever releases me, he'll break me for the rest of my life. Doomed to long for the man I can never have. Destined to compare all others to him.

I will ruin you for all other men.

There has never been a truer statement than that.

20

MIKHAIL

I sit at the head of the boardroom table, waiting for Milan to deliver the news.

"I've found you the hard evidence to bring to Milo and Malachy. He's been buying up real estate in Boston already." He walks toward me, shuffling the papers in his hands. "It took some digging, but I found out he's created a company under an alias as a front for his operation here." Milan sets the papers down in front of me. "The cocky son of a bitch had already made a move in Boston before we knew it."

I pick up the papers, which are contracts for purchases his company has made in my territory. "This is an act of war, Milan," I say, feeling oddly calm considering I just found out the man I'm in business with intends to pull me down and replace me.

"I know, sir. What I'm concerned about is that Andrei isn't likely to be doing this alone, which means he must have someone on the inside."

The idea angers me. "A mole in our organization?" I ask.

He nods. "I don't know how he bought up all this real estate from under our noses without someone in our outfit being aware."

It makes sense. A rat in our ranks, however, is the least of our worries. "You're right. Make sure only you and I know of Andrei's treachery. We don't want him changing his plans once he realizes we know."

"Of course, sir." A few moments of silence pass between us. "How do you feel we should proceed with Andrei and Spartak?"

I stand and walk to the floor-to-ceiling glass window in the office block, staring out over the city I have ruled for ten years. I can't believe that it has come to this. "Set up a meeting with Milo and Malachy, and make sure neither knows that the other will be in attendance." I clench my jaw, knowing the vast challenge I have ahead of me to get them to talk, let alone work together. "If they found out, they wouldn't attend."

Milan nods, "Of course, sir. I'll set up the meeting." His brow furrows. "What do you want me to state as the reason for the meeting?"

I run a hand across the back of my neck. "Tell them that the meeting concerns a business opportunity and be vague."

"Okay, I will call you as soon as I have their answers." Milan turns his back to walk away.

"Milan, how was your Christmas?" I ask.

He turns around and smiles. "Lovely, sir. The children

are at that age where everything is so exciting." He rubs a hand across the back of his neck. "They were up at six o'clock Christmas morning."

I nod. "I'm glad to hear it. Try to take more time over the next week with them. You don't need to be working non-stop."

"Thank you. I will." He walks away.

I turn my attention back to my computer screen, flicking through the photos of Siena on social media. She has turned into my sick obsession. I stop at a picture of her kissing a guy, feeling envious rage flow through me, although this photo is from two years ago. Siena hasn't mentioned a boyfriend, so I can only assume she is single.

A knock at my door startles me as I thought Milan and I were the only ones to come in today. "Come in," I call.

Lev steps inside, walking toward my desk. "Morning, sir."

I raise a brow. "Why are you here?" I'm still angry at Lev for fucking up such a simple job as kidnapping the right girl. If it weren't for him, I wouldn't be sitting here like a stalker trawling through Siena's photos.

"Andrei Petrov is here in Boston." His brow furrows. "I saw him at the Four Seasons this morning as I went to meet my family for breakfast."

"We have a meeting set for the fifth. Do you know why he's here early?" I ask, wondering whether to trust Lev with the information Milan brought me.

Lev's brow furrows. "No, sir. Did you want me to find out?"

I straighten. "Did you not speak with Andrei when you noticed him at the Four Seasons?"

Lev and Andrei are acquaintances, so I find it hard to believe they didn't speak if they saw each other.

He shakes his head. "Andrei didn't see me, and I thought it best to bring you the news that he is in town first."

"I misunderstand your meaning, Lev. Andrei is an ally. Why would it matter if he is in town?"

His face pales. "I thought you ought to know if another pakhan is in the city. That is all."

I run a hand across the back of my neck, unease sweeping over me. Milan's theory that someone in our outfit is helping Andrei returns to the forefront of my mind.

I glance up at Lev, studying him.

Would he have the audacity to cross me?

I know the answer deep down. Lev isn't as stupid as he'd have me believe. He has been playing with me, feeding Andrei information, and I need proof before I act. I can't let him suspect I know the truth of Andrei's plans.

"Why don't you head back to the Four Seasons and greet him?" I ask, shuffling the papers on my desk. "That way, he knows we are aware of his presence in the city." I glance back at Lev. "Find out his reason for arriving early."

Lev's Adam's apple bobs as he swallows. "Of course. I'll head there now." He turns to leave. "Is there anything else you need from me today?"

I control the anger raging inside of me over his potential treachery. "No, that will be all. Enjoy the rest of Christmas with your family."

Lev glances back at me. "You too, sir." He walks away stiffly.

Once he's gone, I stand and make sure no one else is in the office. Then, I call Milan.

"Sir, is everything okay?" he asks.

"Lev just came to see me. Don't ask me why, but I feel he may be our mole." I clear my throat. "Andrei is in town, and somehow he knew before you did, which he blames on coincidence."

"Fuck. Does he suspect you know?" Milan asks.

"No," I say. "Can you find out if he's working with Andrei for me?"

"Of course. Do you know where Andrei is staying?" Milan asks.

"The Four Seasons hotel. Get me answers, Milan." I cancel the call. I'll kill him with my bare hands if Lev has been working for Andrei this entire time. The rage bubbling away under the surface is like a volcano ready to erupt. I can feel myself losing control, and all hell might break loose when I finally blow.

I RETURN BEFORE MIDDAY, opening the door to the sound of Siena laughing, and it's a sound I've become addicted to hearing.

"What time is Mikhail back?" Natalya asks.

I walk toward the small study they are sitting in and clear my throat. "Now," I answer.

My sister smiles and jumps to her feet, hugging me. "Where were you, brother? It's Christmas."

I sigh and loosen my tie. "I know. I'm sorry. There were pressing matters to attend to." My attention remains fixed on Siena, who hasn't looked at me. "What have you been up to?" I walk into the room, unable to pull my eyes away from Siena's dazzling beauty.

Natalya sits back down next to Siena, forcing me to take a seat further away from her. "I was showing Siena our childhood photos."

I groan when I see the baby photos of us spread out on the coffee table. "Great," I murmur.

Siena smiles, lifting a photo of me from when I was two years old. "You were so adorable." She shakes her head. "What happened?"

I narrow my eyes at her, irritated that she's delighting in this. "Don't push me, Siena."

Natalya rolls her eyes. "Don't listen to him. He's such a grump whenever I bring out the photos."

"Which is every fucking Christmas," I point out.

My mother appears behind me, tutting. "Language, Mikhail."

I roll my eyes. If she thinks the language I use is bad, she should see what I do on a day-to-day basis. She knows the darkness that surrounds my world as pakhan.

Natalya chuckle. "Wasn't Mikhail adorable as a baby, though?" she asks my mother.

"Yes. I'm not sure where I went wrong." She takes a seat next to Natalya. It has surprised me this Christmas how well they've got on. Maybe Natalya can finally put the past behind her.

"Siena, can you come with me?" I ask, hoping to steal a few moments alone with her.

Both my mother and Natalya raise their brows at my request, but Siena stands. "Sure. Excuse me," she says to Natalya and my mother.

I lead her out of the room and toward the library down the hall. A perfect, quiet spot.

"What's wrong?" she asks when I shut the door and lock it.

I turn around, shaking my head. "Nothing, I just need to touch you." I walk toward her. "I didn't think it would be very appropriate to do that in front of my sister and mother."

I set my hands on her hips and pull her against me. "Every time I see you I have this powerful need to fuck you."

Siena shudders. "We don't have time for that. It will be too obvious."

"Bullshit. I can make you come within minutes if I want, malishka. You won't know what hit you." I wrap my arms around her waist and lift her against the bookcase.

"Have you forgotten what happened yesterday?" she asks, hinting at my sister walking in on us.

"No. That's why I locked the door this time." I move my lips to her collarbone, kissing her there. "I need to be inside of you." Only Siena can take away the tension.

She's like a drug that I can't get enough of. The bane of my God damn existence ever since my men fucked up and kidnapped her instead.

"Mikhail, wait." Siena's voice sounds strained as she looks into my eyes.

"What is it?"

She shakes her head. "I just started my period."

I smirk, wondering if she thinks a bit of blood is going to stop me right now. "So what, malishka?"

Her eyes widen. "Won't it be messy?"

I groan and tighten my grip on her hips. "If you haven't learned by now, I love messy, malishka." I lift the skirt of her dress and grab hold of her panties. The intensity of my need for her forces me to tear them at the crotch, feeling overwhelmed by the need to be inside of her. Nothing is stopping me from entering this woman right now.

I run my finger through her lips and find the string of her tampon, then yank it out of her. A small waste bin with a bag at the side of the desk catches my attention. "Don't move." I grab it and place it beneath her, chucking the tampon in there.

Siena glances back at me questioningly. "Are you sure—"

I slide my cock inside of her, filling her up.

"Oh, fuck—"

I slam my hand over her mouth, silencing her. "I locked the door, but they can hear us through the walls." I remove my hand and slam into her hard from behind, forcing her to arch her back.

Siena moans loudly, forgetting that my mother and sister are only down the corridor. I can't find it in me to care. They both know that Siena and I aren't just friends.

I dig my fingertips into her hips hard, using my arms to pull her to meet my thrusts. The violence of my feelings for this woman makes it hard to control myself, and it consumes me. Every waking moment, all I think about is her beautiful body and addictive scent that calls to a primal side of me I never knew existed until I met her.

"You feel so damn good," I growl into her ear, pressing her harder against the bookcase. "I can't get enough of your pretty little cunt."

Siena shudders. Her body reacting to my words. "Give it to me harder," she moans, her back arching more.

I growl at the utter desperation in her voice. "I'll give it to you so hard you won't know where I start, and you begin." I grab hold of her throat from behind, choking her as I ram my cock into her as hard as physically possible.

Siena cries her moan a half-scream as I start my passionate assault on her.

In the short time I've known Siena, I've learned her body like a second language, and it's a language I've become fluent in.

I pound into her with all my strength, making sure I give it to her hard enough. The need to erase the memory of any other man is strong, as I want to be the owner of her thoughts, dreams, and world.

Every time she touches herself, I want my face to come into her mind. The possessiveness when it comes to Siena is insuppressible, and it drives my every action with her, turning me into an animal whenever she is close.

Siena's hoarse breaths fill the room as I feel her getting close, her muscles already spasming and contracting. "Fuck," she moans softly, her voice quieter now.

I spank her pert ass as I continue to drive into her, forcing her over the edge with all the power I possess.

Siena will be sore from this rough fucking. It's a certainty, and yet she will be ready for more before I know it. The woman is insatiable. A siren sent to me to destroy me in every sense of the word.

I grab her throat from behind as she tumbles over the edge. "That's it, malishka. Make that pretty little pussy come for me."

She cries out as the pleasure racks her body. Siena's legs tremble beneath her as I hold her steady, continuing to drive in and out of her with all my strength. I groan as my release hits me hard.

"I want you to take every drop of my cum in that eager little cunt," I growl.

Siena arches her back as I hold myself deep inside of her, unleashing every drop of my cum.

My labored breathing takes a while to subside before I slip out of her. I grab a box of tissues off the desk and wipe myself clean, tucking my cock back into my pants.

Siena stiffens as I turn my attention to her, cleaning her. Once done, I throw the tissues in the waste paper bing and pull her panties up. "I think we should move this to the bathroom, malishka," I murmur into her ear, sliding the fabric of her dress back down over her ass.

She shudders and glances at me over her shoulder, eyes full of lust. “Okay, Daddy,” she whispers.

I feel it right to my cock. My need for her knows no end. I feel like I’m free-falling, spiraling anytime I’m not close to my little Italian gem.

21

SIENA

I rush down the stairs only to be stopped midway by Mikhail.

He looks irritated.

"What's wrong?" I ask.

"Natalya told me you agreed to go shopping with her."

My brow furrows. "Let me guess. You are going to forbid me?"

Mikhail grabs my shoulders and shakes me. "You are my captive, Siena. I can't have you swanning off and meeting up with Aida."

It hurts more than I can explain. Mikhail believes my agreeing to go shopping with his sister is an attempt to escape. "That's bullshit. The likelihood of me running into Aida is slim."

"Go back to your room before I drag you there." He glares at me with a gaze that could turn most hearts to stone.

"No." I cross my arms over my chest. "I want to go shopping with Natalya."

He shakes his head. "Tough. I told her you weren't feeling well, and she already left with Yana twenty minutes ago."

I narrow my eyes at him. "Bastard." I turn to walk away, only to be stopped by his powerful hands on my hips.

"Don't turn your back on me, malishka," he whispers into my ear, letting his breath tease my ear lobe. "Or I'll fuck you right here on the stairs and make a mess for everyone to see."

A shiver races down my spine at the mere thought. His mother is still in the house, as far as I'm aware.

"Now, I have to go to work today. I want you to be a good girl for me and lock yourself in your room."

I tense at the request. "Can't I—"

He bites my shoulder hard, making me yelp. "No. My room now, before I fling you over my shoulder and lock you in there myself."

I don't doubt that he'd do exactly that. Instead of pushing him, I free his hands from my hips and nod. "Fine." I walk away, only for Mikhail to grab me again.

"Give me a kiss, malishka."

I bite the inside of my cheek. Mikhail is right that I shouldn't have the freedom to go shopping with his sister while he holds me as his prisoner. I'm angry that he got in my way. This house is a luxurious prison that I can't escape.

"Now," Mikhail growls.

I turn around and look into his dark eyes, wondering why I'm inclined to do anything he says. The Russian boss is a monster in disguise. A handsome, beautiful man that is nothing but evil. "Why would I kiss you?"

He grabs my hips and pulls me hard against him. "Don't push me, Siena. I'm going to be late."

"And, whose fault is that?" I ask, knowing that all I'm doing is winding him up.

Mikhail's nostrils flare. "Yours." He pulls me harder against him and melds his lips over mine, thrusting his tongue into my mouth possessively.

The grip on my hips tightens so much I'm sure he's trying to bruise me. Mikhail makes me feel owned. It's a sensation that should go against my feminist side that believes men and women are equal, yet it is tantalizing in the bedroom.

I lace my fingers in his dark hair, yanking on it as I try to claw him closer to me.

Mikhail groans and laces his fingers in my hair, yanking me away from him. "I can't go to a meeting hard. On your knees."

My eyes widen, and I glance around the hallway. "Not here. What about your—"

"I said on your knees."

The tone of his voice is demanding, and I don't have it in me to deny him. Instead, I drop to my knees on the step in front of him.

Mikhail unzips his pants and pulls out his erection,

pressing the tip of his cock to my lips. "Open wide, malishka."

I moan as I open my mouth, taking his thick shaft into my mouth. He tastes like heaven, pure masculinity on the tip of my tongue.

Mikhail's cock leaks onto my tongue as I close my lips around him, moving my head up and down.

"That's it, suck my cock like a good girl," he purrs.

I long to hear him call me that, and it turns me on so much. I circle my tongue around his thick head before taking his shaft deeper into my throat.

"Fuck," Mikhail says, grabbing a handful of my hair. "Be careful, malishka. Or you might tempt me to fuck that pretty little throat of yours."

I look up at him, batting my eyelashes. This time, I take him even deeper.

"That's it." He tightens his grip on my hair and rams the entire length of his cock down my throat.

Thankfully, I've always been devoid of a gag reflex.

Mikhail looks pleasantly surprised as he thrusts his hips in and out, fucking my face hard. The look on his face is one of unadulterated pleasure. It is difficult to breathe, though, as he blocks my airways, forcing me to breathe through my nose. Saliva spills down my chin and all over Mikhail's cock.

Mikhail groans as I feel his cock twitch against the back of my throat. "I'm going to shoot my cum down your throat, and I want you to swallow. Do you understand?"

I nod my head as best I can with his dick lodged deep.

"Good girl," he murmurs, picking up the pace as he fucks my mouth harder.

I gag this time as the force is too much, struggling to keep up with his strength.

Mikhail roars as his orgasm hits him, shooting his creamy cum into my throat.

I swallow, loving the taste as it spills onto my tongue. There's so much that it's impossible to swallow it all at once.

Mikhail pulls his cock from my mouth, holding it in front of my face. "Lick it clean for me, as I want you to swallow every damn drop."

I grab his shaft and eagerly lick off every drop of cum, feeling filthy but loving it.

Mikhail grabs my chin and moves his face to within an inch of mine. "You are such a good girl, Siena."

I swallow hard. "Only for you, daddy."

His eyes mist over with lust as he pulls me closer and slides his tongue into my mouth, tasting himself on me. We both moan as we kiss like this for God knows how long.

Mikhail's mother clears her throat at the bottom of the stairs, shocking both of us. He is fast to shove his cock back into his pants, and I jump to my feet.

"Good morning, Mrs. Gurin," I say, feeling ashamed that I just did that where anyone could have seen.

Her eyes narrow. "Good morning. Mikhail, you really should leave your fornicating to the bedroom." She turns around and walks away, leaving me burning with embarrassment.

"Oh my God, I can't believe she caught us." I meet Mikhail's gaze, which is unreadable. "How long do you think she was there?"

He shakes his head. "Not long. Otherwise, we wouldn't have heard the end of it." He steps around me. "I need to get to work. Remember, stay in your room." He turns away and walks out of the house without another word.

I don't go upstairs as I have no intention of sitting in the room all day. Instead, I head toward the library down the hall where no one ever spends time. It will be private and peaceful.

Mrs. Gurin is sitting in the living room as I pass the door. "Siena." She calls my name, making my stomach churn.

I walk cautiously toward the door, uncertain about facing her at all after she caught us in such a compromising position on the stairs. "Yes, Mrs. Gurin?"

She waves me into the room. "Please, call me Anya."

I enter the room and sit opposite her. "Of course, Anya," I say.

She smiles, but it is forced. "I have never seen my son look at another human being the way he looks at you."

I feel my stomach churn at her observation. His mother is entirely unaware of how we met, and if she knew, she might think differently about the two of us. "I see," I murmur.

"My son is under a lot of pressure because of work, but he needs to have a family of his own." She looks at me expectantly, as if she expects me to have Mikhail's children. For a start, he already told me it's an impossibility. His mother is unaware of his decision to have a vasectomy.

"Well, I haven't known him very long." I twist my fingers together in my lap, wishing the sofa would swallow me whole. Mikhail is my captor and nothing else. At least, he was supposed to be.

Her eyes narrow. "Do you love him?"

I avoid her gaze, trying to find the answer to that question. It should be no. I can't love a monster who kidnapped me, a man who has done nothing but threaten me and order me about ever since we met.

Even as I try to find the answer I know I should give, it's not true. I love Mikhail, and I've fallen for him so fiercely I hardly saw it coming. "Yes," I say.

His mother nods. "Then, it is never too soon. If you love someone, act." She sits forward. "Mikhail believes Natalya can run the family business when he's no longer around, but she can't."

My brow furrows, as that seems like an unfair statement. "Why not?" I ask.

"Let's just say the line of work Mikhail is in requires a male touch." She looks wistful. "Russians aren't used to taking orders from women. While the modern world is changing, Russian men do not change."

"That seems rather archaic, especially since Natalya wouldn't be in line to inherit control of the business for quite a long time." I know it's not my place to tell her about Mikhail being unable to have children, but it seems unfair that she hopes he will have a family.

"That is the Russian way." She tilts her head slightly. "Do you know what work Mikhail does?"

"Yes," I say. Mikhail is involved in dangers I can't even begin to comprehend.

"I thought as much." She glances at the clock on the wall. "I assume you didn't meet my son at a bar, then?"

I swallow hard, shaking my head. "No. How did you—"

She holds her hand up to silence me. "I was you once." The ghost of memories twinkle in her eyes. "Young, naïve, and utterly taken captive by the dominance of a pakhan." She pauses a moment. "Mikhail's father. He kidnapped me in a feud with my father in Russia."

My heart skitters in my chest, making me feel a little lightheaded. "You married the man that kidnapped you?"

She laughs. "It may sound crazy, but it happened. We fell in love." Her brow furrows. "It is why we moved to America: to escape my father." Tears brim in her eyes. "When Valery, Mikhail's father, died, I couldn't face staying in a country where we were so happy. Everything reminded me of him."

"I'm sorry about your husband," I say.

"If you have found a love like that with my son, you should not let it go." She meets my gaze. "I see the way he looks at you, and it reminds me so much of the way Valery used to look at me." She reaches for my hand across the void between us.

I give it to her, and she squeezes.

"Cherish the time you have with him, even if the way

you met wasn't traditional." She shrugs. "There are no rules in matters of the heart."

"I will," I murmur, knowing that she is right. What I feel for Mikhail is real, even if it's insane.

I have fallen in love with Mikhail, which means I have fallen in love with a wicked monster who could toss me aside as quickly as he claimed my heart.

22

MIKHAIL

Siena trails behind me as I lead her into my office block, wishing I didn't have to bring her to the meeting. It was one of Milo's demands to agree to this meeting. Aida is going to be in attendance and wants to see that her friend is unharmed.

We have given Malachy the same location for the meeting, but he should arrive ten minutes later, giving me enough time to diffuse tensions before he arrives.

"Keep up, malishka," I say, glancing at her. She doesn't know what this is about.

Siena hugs her arms around herself, picking up the pace.

I stop in front of the elevator, pressing the button.

Siena makes sure not to stand too close to me, which grates me.

I slide an arm around her and pull her against me. "Don't stand so far away."

She glances up at me, brows knitting together. "I don't want Milo seeing you fawning over me."

I tilt my head. "Why not? Until he gives me what I want, you are mine to do with as I want."

A flash of hurt enters her beautiful hazel eyes. I know why. This captive and kidnapper relationship has been turning into something deeper so damn fast that I'm not sure either of us saw it coming.

Eight days it has been since Lev kidnapped the wrong woman.

Siena glances away, not answering my question.

I don't let go of her, as I can't. We're both scared that this meeting could lead to me letting her go, which neither of us wants.

We get into the elevator and ride it to the top floor. When the chime sounds to alert us that we've arrived, I finally let go of Siena's hip and step away.

Siena glances up at me questioningly before returning her attention to the doors, which slide open.

Milo, Piero, and Aida are there waiting for us. The moment Aida sees Siena, her countenance changes, and she rushes at us. "Siena, thank God you are okay." She slams into the beauty by my side, wrapping her in a tight embrace. "I'm so sorry," she blubbers, tears running down her face.

I clear my throat. "Don't you two want to take this somewhere private while we talk?" I glance at one board-room with glass walls on every side, meaning I can monitor her. "That room would be suitable."

Aida gives me a disapproving look. "I can't believe you

stole my best friend." She shakes her head. "Come on, Siena. Let's go."

Siena exchanges a glance with me, looking a little shell-shocked that Aida is here at all. She looks disappointed that I didn't warn her. Perhaps it was a wicked thing to do since she wasn't mentally prepared to face her best friend.

"Gurin, let's get down to business. I don't want to be here any longer than necessary," Milo says, drawing my attention to him.

I narrow my eyes. "Indeed." I nod toward the opposite boardroom. "In there."

Milo goes ahead first, addressing his capo. "No need to come in, just keep watch outside."

"Sir," Piero says.

I walk past his capo and join him in the boardroom. "Take a seat," I say.

Milo glares at me. "Was this childish kidnapping necessary, Mikhail?" Milo asks, not sitting down. "I mean, I expect this kind of shit from Malachy, but from you?" He shakes his head. "I thought you were above all that."

I cross my arms over my chest. "I said, sit down."

Milo glares at me. "Do I look like I take orders from a fucking Russian?"

I hold my hands up, knowing that I need to end this pissing contest before it starts if we want to make progress. "Fine, we can do this standing if you prefer."

Milo holds my gaze for a few moments before dragging out a seat and sitting. "What is this about, Mikhail? I'm not breaking my merger with Bionantechnic Group."

I shake my head. "Things have changed rather drastically. It's not about that." I pull the folder out of my briefcase that Milan put together. The evidence of Andrei's purchases here in the city and evidence of what he has done to other cities across the United States in the past three years. "We have a new mutual enemy, I'm afraid."

Milo glances between me and the folder, and I push it over to him. He opens it and reads through a few of the pages, shaking his head. "Andrei Petrov? I thought he was your ally."

"As did I, until my spy brought me this evidence." I tap my fingers on the desk. "It seems his greed knows no bounds."

Milo meets my gaze. "What do you want me to do about it?"

"This concerns all of us in Boston City. Not just me. If Andrei intends to make a move on Boston, he won't leave anyone standing." I grab the folder and pull out the evidence of what he did in San Diego. "The only criminal operation running in San Diego now is Petrov Bratva."

Milo rubs a hand across the back of his neck. "What makes you think he has the power to destroy my organization?"

"He has teamed up with Spartak Volkov."

Milo's face pales at the mention of the dark and twisted Chicago bratva leader. The man takes the meaning of a psychopath to a whole new level. He should be in a mental asylum, not leading a criminal organization. "Fuck." His brow furrows. "Are you proposing what I think you are?"

"Probably," I say, wishing it hadn't come to this. While I don't want war any more than the next man, it is a big pill to swallow requesting an alliance with one enemy, let alone two. "We need to work together if we are going to keep this son of a bitch out of our city."

The elevator dings, signaling that Malachy has arrived.

Milo's attention moves to the elevator, and he jumps to his feet the moment he sees him. "What the fuck is he doing here, Mikhail?" His hand moves to the hilt of his gun at his waist.

"Considering the threat we are facing, three is better than two for facing the Petrov and Volkov bratva."

Milo shakes his head. "No chance. I may agree on an alliance with you, but not with that Irish scum."

I stand in front of him, breaking his attention from Malachy. "I heard tensions between the two of you are waning, and this is the perfect opportunity to agree to a truce." I pat Milo on the shoulder. "Wait here."

It's an order, but I know Milo doesn't take orders from anyone. He's much like me in that respect. "Malachy, thank you for—"

"Why the fuck is the Italian here?" He glares through the window at Milo, who looks just as angry.

"I know the two of you don't get on, but I have a pressing matter that involves both of you." I place a hand on his shoulder to steer him toward another office.

He wraps his fingers around my wrist and twists my hand hard, glaring at me. It hurts like a bitch, but I don't let him see my pain. "We aren't friends, lad." He shakes his head, tightening his grip on my wrist. "I may have attended your auctions, but that's because they were the only decent auctions in town."

I grab his fingers and pry them from my wrist, reclaiming my hand. Malachy is tall, but compared to my six feet nine inches, he's short. I cross my arms over my chest. "You are going to want to hear what I have to say."

He holds my gaze with surprising confidence. I'm aware of his title as a bare-knuckle fighter, but he has never faced me in a fight. "Fine." He crosses his arms over his chest. "Talk."

"We can take this to the office down the hall." I nod to an open door a few meters away.

Malachy's eyes narrow. "I'm good here."

These two men are as childish as ever. Milo's ego is too big even to consider the idea of agreeing on a truce when they are bordering on the war ending anyway, and Malachy has to have a pissing contest with everyone he meets.

"The file I need to show you is in that room." I hold his gaze. "Either come with me to the room, or we can stand here staring at each other all day."

Malachy glances at Niall, his second in command.

Niall approaches. "I'll check it out first."

I roll my eyes, wondering if Malachy thinks I'm stupid enough to invite him here to wipe him out. The Irish have never been my problem as it is the Italians that the Gurin Bratva have more history with.

Niall returns after a minute and nods. "All clear, sir."

Malachy nods. "After you then, lad."

I walk past the window of the office where Siena and

Aida are. A part of me longs to look at her, but I need to remain focused right now. Enemies surround me, and a distraction could prove fatal.

"Have a seat," I say, gesturing to the chair in front of the folder. "Look at the folder on the desk."

Malachy stares at me for a few beats before taking a seat and opening the folder. He skims through some of the information before glancing up at me. "Why don't we cut the crap? Tell me why I'm here, Mikhail."

"Andrei Petrov is making a move on Boston." I rub a hand across the back of my neck. "I don't need to spell out to you what that could mean for all of us if he is successful."

Malachy shakes his head. "No, but what do you propose we do about it?"

"Andrei has Spartak Volkov on his side. He's a powerful ally who I can only defeat if I make alliances with both you and Milo."

A sly smirk twists onto Malachy's lips. "Are you saying you need us, lad?"

"I'm saying we all need each other if we are going to survive." I grab the folder and pull out the in-depth details of San Diego, where Andrei took control. "This happens when he takes over cities, and he takes control of everything, obliterating all of his competition."

Malachy takes the paper, scanning over it. Once he's finished, he passes it to Niall.

"Shit," Niall says, shaking his head. "Why is it we never heard about this?"

"Andrei is clever. Inter-city alliances didn't exist until

he started creating them, but he became my ally to overthrow me." I run a hand through my hair, wishing that Milan had gotten me the truth about Lev. I need to know if there is a rat in my ranks. "He is here in Boston as we speak."

Malachy slams his hands on the table, standing. "Well, why don't we take that son of a bitch out once and for all?"

Niall shakes his head. "We can't. If we touch him, we declare war with Chicago."

I nod. "Quite right. Instead, we need to send Andrei a message."

"So you are proposing an alliance between the three of us?" Niall asks.

"Yes. We need to clarify that we will squash any threat to our operations before they have even gotten off the ground." I rub a hand across the back of my neck. "We have the upper hand as Andrei isn't aware that we know of his plans for Boston."

Someone clears their throat behind us. "I still think it's a stretch expecting me to work with this knucklehead," Milo says.

Malachy jumps to his feet. "That's rich considering you sent me a fucking treaty proposal the other day."

Milo's brow furrows. "What are you on about?"

"The proposal you sent me. It had your fucking sigil on it and everything."

Milo steps closer to Malachy, heightening the tension in the air. "I don't know what the fuck you are talking about, but I didn't send you a proposal."

Malachy stands and steps closer to Milo. "You're a fucking liar, lad. I'll get you the paper and prove it."

Milo crosses his arms over his chest. "Either way, it sounds like someone has duped you. I haven't sent you a proposal, and why would I when I'm winning the war?"

Malachy growls and launches himself at Milo, tackling him at the waist. The extent of his rage unleashes, and he takes it out on Milo.

I know I have to step in. If any of us will survive the storm heading our way, someone has to force peace between these two rivals.

23

SIENA

I stare into the eyes of my best friend, feeling shocked.

All I should feel is happiness to be reunited with her. Instead, it feels like Mikhail just popped the stupid bubble I've been floating around in for a week, and it was a bubble where we could be together indefinitely.

"Are you okay?" Aida asks, sitting down next to me and taking my hand.

I shrug. "I'm doing okay."

Aida's brow furrows. "Has he hurt you at all?" She shakes her head. "When your dress arrived stained in blood—"

"Blood?" I ask.

Aida nods. "Yeah, did he cut you?"

I shake my head. "No, it must be someone else's blood, as he hasn't harmed me."

She sighs. "That's a relief. Gia wanted to come, but apparently, it was a stretch to get Mikhail to agree on me attending the meeting." Her fists ball. "I'm so angry with that stupid Russian bastard."

I can't understand why I hate her talking about him like that. He kidnapped me, and I should hate him, but I don't.

She shakes her head. "Just when I'd made concrete progress with a truce between Malachy and Milo."

"Really? What changed?" I ask.

Aida nods. "Scarlett presented Malachy with a proposal I wrote, and he tentatively agreed to it. She told me hours after they kidnapped you." She places her hand on mine. "Not that it matters. How have you coped with being a prisoner?"

I swallow hard, feeling ashamed by the truth. "I don't want you to get mad at me."

Her brow furrows. "Why would I?"

I draw in a deep breath, searching her kind, dark eyes. "I think I've fallen for Mikhail."

Her eyes widen. "No way. Are you sure he hasn't just brainwashed you?" She glares across the glass to where Mikhail sits with Milo. "If that son of a bitch took advantage of you, I'll get Milo to murder him right here and now." She moves to stand, but I stop her.

"No, listen."

She sits back down, meeting my gaze. "I'm listening."

"It's not his fault, Aida." I rack my brain, trying to work out how to explain this to her. "When you told me how much of a dick Milo was to you, I could never understand it when your feelings changed. You told us you had fallen for him, despite how cruel he was."

Aida nods. "Yeah. It surprised me too. However, this is too damn fast for that to happen to you, Siena."

"It's not. Mikhail wasn't especially cruel, but the moment his hands were on me, it felt like he completed me." I shake my head. "It makes no sense saying it out loud, but it's how I feel."

A tense silence cloaks the room as Aida tries to process what I just told her. I get why she's skeptical about my feelings for Mikhail. To anyone looking in at our situation, it appears to be a classic case of Stockholm Syndrome, but I refuse to believe that's what this is.

My feelings are irrational, but then aren't all emotions irrational?

Aida flicks her hair behind her shoulder. "That's crazy, though, Siena. You realize that, right?"

"Yeah, it all happened so damn fast." I glance through the glass where Mikhail is now greeting another guy. "I don't know if he feels the same way, though."

Aida takes my hand, drawing my attention back to her. "He's a fool if he doesn't."

"You only say that because you are my best friend."

Aida laughs. "That's not true." Mikhail walks past the window of the office. "I guess he's hot if you are into that muscle-bound, inked Russian type."

We both laugh. "Milo is muscle-bound and inked."

Aida shakes her head. "Not in the same way as Mikhail. He's scary-looking."

I shrug. "Maybe I like scary."

"Gia will never believe this. Perhaps she is right. You need to have a criminal to know how damn good it is to be owned by one." Her brow furrows. "I hate thinking about her and my father together, though."

Aida had begged me to come because she dreaded spending Christmas alone with them. It's ironic how that happened, anyway. "How has it been?" I ask.

Aida smiles, but it's a wistful expression. "Better than I expected. After my mother died, I never saw my father smile anymore." She shakes her head. "Gia makes him happy, and that much is very clear." She shrugs. "Who am I to be angry that he found happiness, even if it is with my best friend?"

"I think you have every right to be angry. Both of them kept their relationship a secret for far too long." I sigh heavily. "But, you are right. They are both so happy it is hard to stay angry, isn't it?"

Aida nods. "Yeah, but I think it will take time for me to forgive my father for everything he did." Her brow furrows. "I mean, it's confusing since I was so angry he sent me over here to marry Milo, but now I wouldn't have it any other way. I'm happy."

I smile. "Happy and about to start a family." I set a hand on her arm. "How are you feeling? It's not very long now."

She smiles. "I feel like a bloated whale."

I laugh. "Any luck on choosing a name yet?"

Aida opens her mouth to reply, but a commotion down the hall interrupts her. We both jump to our feet, rushing out of the room.

Malachy lands punch after punch on Milo as Mikhail attempts to wrestle him away from Aida's husband. He pulls him away, and Milo gets to his feet. His lip is busted and bleeding, and a bruise is already forming around his eye.

Malachy tries to break free from Mikhail, eyes manic.

Aida walks right up to them. "What is going on here?" she demands, surprising me with the command in her voice. She sure as hell isn't scared to get involved.

Milo and Malachy continue to glare at each other. "This idiot is lying about a proposal I supposedly sent him," Milo says, spitting blood onto the floor.

Malachy growls. "It's not a fucking lie, lad."

I glance at Aida, whose face is pale. This is her doing, and she clears her throat, drawing both of their attention. "That would be my fault."

Milo's brow furrows as he stares at his wife. "What do you mean, angel?" he asks, walking toward her.

Aida sighs. "Scarlett and I have been meeting up regularly, attempting to mediate a truce behind your backs." I'm surprised how confidently she says it.

Milo stops dead in his tracks, face twisting with rage. "You did what?" he growls.

Aida holds her hands up. "Look. Scarlett and I both wanted an end to the war, and it's as simple as that."

Malachy shakes his head. "Bullshit. Scarlett wouldn't do this behind my back."

Aida glances at him. "Call her and verify if you want."

Malachy nods at his second in command, who pulls out a cell phone and dials a number, and he puts it on speakerphone.

"Hello?" a woman answers.

Malachy clears his throat. "Scarlett. I have a simple question for you, and I want a yes or no answer. Have you been meeting with Aida in secret?"

There are a few moments of silence before she replies. "Yes."

Malachy growls in response, and the man cancels the call. "Why?" he demands.

Aida shrugs. "Neither of us want our families caught up as collateral in something we could settle without bloodshed." Her brow furrows. "Have I missed something? Why is Malachy here anyway?"

"That would be my fault." Mikhail steps forward. "I wanted to arrange an alliance between the three of us as there is a far more dangerous threat to all of our families looming."

Aida smiles and steps toward Mikhail. "Finally, someone who sees some sense." Her brow furrows. "If you wanted an alliance, why did you kidnap my best friend?"

Mikhail's eyes find mine. "It was before I knew of the threat outside of our city." He glances at Milo. "It's fair to say you've been taking vast steps to increase your power in this city." He shrugs. "I would be a fool not to challenge you."

Milo glares at Aida angrily, still shocked at hearing his wife has been conspiring behind his back. "Yes. I guess so, but why take Aida's friend?" His attention moves to Mikhail. "I can only assume you fucked up and got the wrong woman."

Mikhail crosses his arms over his chest. "It doesn't

matter. What does matter is stopping Andrei Petrov before it is too late."

Milo nods. "Fine, but you will let Siena go right now if you want to talk."

A tense silence ensues as I stare at Mikhail, waiting for him to answer. He doesn't look at me, keeping his attention fixed on Milo. "Agreed," he says. The way he says it is as if letting me go is the easiest thing he's ever done.

The pain claws at my chest as I stare at the wicked Russian mob boss who told me this is what he'd do to me. His words repeat in my mind.

Once you return to your life, you will think of me always because no man will make you feel the way I do.

Letting me go was always his intention. He takes satisfaction in knowing he's found a way into my heart, only to tear it apart in the blink of an eye. I was stupid to think that a man like him could ever feel anything real for me. This is all one sick game to him.

Aida squeezes my hand as if she knows what I'm feeling right now. It hurts so much I don't know how to put it into words. Mikhail has ruined me, as he always promised he would.

Milo nods. "Fine. Why don't the three of us talk away from inquisitive ears?" He glares at Aida, who looks unfazed by her husband's angry expression.

Mikhail still won't look at me. "Of course." He walks away and leads Milo and Malachy into the office.

Aida glances at me. "I'm so sorry." She squeezes my hand. "Are you going to be okay?"

Tears flood my eyes, but I don't allow them to fall. It's

pathetic that I thought Mikhail felt the same way I did, and I won't allow him or anyone else to see the pain he has inflicted on me. "I'll be fine," I manage to croak out, turning away and walking toward the bathroom down the hall.

"Do you want me to come?" Aida asks.

I don't turn around, shaking my head. "No, I'll be back in a minute." I hasten my steps, knowing that all I need right now is to be alone.

Mikhail has made good on his promise. He has stolen my heart, and I know without a doubt that long after I return to Sicily, he will haunt my thoughts.

24

MIKHAIL

Success.

I can't understand why it feels more like a failure.

I have settled everything I wanted. Milo even agreed to add my company into the merger with Bionantechnic Group, which will bring both of us more power in the city. Yet, it feels like I lost everything.

Siena.

She was my price to pay. The Italian gem who found her way under my skin.

I didn't even say goodbye to her. I couldn't.

As I left the office block, the look in her eyes was one of pure anguish, but she should be thankful. Siena escaped me while she still had the chance. I open the door to the house to find Natalya on the other side.

Her brow furrows when she sees that I'm alone. "Where is Siena?"

The question is like a punch to the gut. "She had to go home."

Natalya crosses her arms over her chest. "And where is that exactly?"

I raise a brow. "I don't know Siena's address. Look her up if you are that interested." I step to one side, trying to go around her.

"You must think I'm a fucking idiot." She steps into my path. "I know she wasn't here by choice, and the Italian fucking accent was enough of a giveaway."

I study my sister, wondering if I've underestimated her. "So what?"

She shakes her head. "Who is she? You kidnapped her, so she must have been important."

I sigh heavily, pinching the bridge of my nose. "I don't want to do this right now."

"You were using her to blackmail Milo Mazzeo. Am I right?"

"Yes, now get out of my way." I glare at my sister.

She searches my eyes. "You are a fool, Mikhail. Siena cared about you, and you used her to get what you want."

I growl at being told the obvious. I feel bad enough right now without her rubbing salt into the wound. "Siena was my captive. I kidnapped her, and you think she cares about me?" I laugh. "She is ecstatic to be home, and I got what I wanted. She was a means to an end. Nothing more."

"You're a terrible liar." She tries to take my hand, but I yank it away. "I've never seen you look at a woman the way you looked at Siena."

I grab hold of my sister's shoulders and force her out of the way. "This does not concern you, Natalya." I walk away from her, struggling to contain my rage. Although, I know it's not entirely directed at my sister.

"You will regret this soon enough, Mikhail," she calls after me, winding me up more.

Doesn't she realize I already regret it?

I had no choice, as Andrei could tear down the entire Gurin Bratva if I allow him to continue making moves unchecked.

My cell phone rings, breaking my train of thought. It's Milan.

"What do you have for me?" I ask.

"It is best we speak in person. Are you home?" he asks.

I shut my eyes, knowing that the last thing I want is to deal with work right now. "Yes."

"Good. I will be there in fifteen minutes."

I cancel the call, leaning my shoulder against the wall. It feels like my world imploded when Milo told me that our negotiation would only begin if I let Siena go, but my emotions can't come first.

Instead of heading to my room, I continue to my study. As I round the corner, my stomach dips when I see Lev sitting opposite my desk.

"Lev, what are you doing here?" I ask, brow furrowing.

He stands. "Milan asked me here, sir. He said he had important news."

I stare at Lev, wondering why Milan didn't warn me

he'd already invited Lev. Perhaps I was too fast to hang up. "I see." I walk around my desk and take a seat. "He only just called me to say he was heading over."

Lev nods. "Do you know what it is about?"

I shake my head. "My guess is as good as yours," I lie, firing up my computer. "He said he will be fifteen minutes." If Lev is the rat helping Andrei, I will murder him with my bare hands. It is the only reason that he would have called him here.

Polina knocks on the door a few minutes later. "Sir, Milan is here for you."

I nod. "Thank you."

Milan enters, glancing at Lev as he does. "Sorry, sir. I was going to tell you I'd called Lev to the house too, but you canceled the call."

"Not to worry." I shake my head. "Take a seat." I can feel the violence rolling beneath the surface as I prepare for what is coming. "What is this about?" I ask.

Milan clears his throat, sitting next to Lev. "I found out who the rat is."

Lev's brow furrows. "The rat?" he asks.

Milan nods and sets a file down on my desk, flipping open the folder. "It's not what we expected, sir."

It feels like the blood drains from my body as I stare at the woman in the photo.

Yana.

My sister has always hated me, ever since we were children, but I never believed she had it in her to undermine me in this way. I run a hand across the back of my neck. "Govno," I curse.

This is the biggest blow I've had in the ten years I've served as pakhan.

"Holy shit. Is that your sister?" Lev asks.

I don't need this moron here. Milan asking him here now makes little sense. "Yes." I look at Milan. "How has she been helping him from Mexico, and why?"

Milan shakes his head. "I found out her husband, Alex, is Andrei's supplier, so they must have struck up a bargain, and Yana agreed to go ahead with it."

I clench my fist on the table, feeling torn apart by the news. Any snitch needs to die, but how can I kill my pregnant sister?

"This is a nightmare."

"Bratva code states you need to end her, family or not." Milan rubs a hand across the scruff at his chin. "But as we are the superiors in the bratva, we can overrule it." His brow furrows. "It's why I asked Lev here. So we can decide."

I loosen my tie and stand. "Yana is pregnant." I walk over to the dresser and pour myself a glass of vodka, knocking it back in one. The fiery liquid burning my throat is a welcome sensation.

"So you do not wish to kill her, sir?" Lev asks.

I glare at him. "If I'm honest, I'm torn." Yana has never cared for me, and now she's tried to dismantle our father's work from the inside out. She has no care for Natalya either to do this. "I will need to confront my sister and decide once I hear her story."

"Is that wise, sir?" Milan asks, standing too. "You realize she could warn Andrei."

I turn to face him. "I will ensure that isn't possible." I glance between him and Lev. "Do you two trust me?"

Both of them nod. "Of course, sir," they say in unison.

"Then trust me to handle this." I crack my neck. "Do not say a word to anyone. Do you understand?"

"Perfectly, sir," Lev says.

Milan approaches me and holds out his hand, and I take it. "I promise I will take this to my grave."

"Good. Now you are both excused." I wave my hand toward the door. "Take a day or two off. I'll call you if I need you." I glare at Lev, who is still seated, eager for them to leave me.

Lev and Milan follow each other out of my office without another word, leaving me alone with my chaotic thoughts. Today has been the worst day of my career as pakhan. I let Siena go, something I never wanted to do. To top it all off, my sister is a rat.

I don't know what Andrei offered her, but I need to find out why she would do this to our family.

It feels like every time I take one step forward, I'm pushed two steps back. I just never expected my family to turn on me, no matter our past. Blood is blood, and you never screw over the people with whom you share blood.

Yana sits at the dinner table across from me, blissfully unaware that I know she's a rat.

I can't comprehend how she can live with herself,

sitting here as if everything is okay while she plots my downfall. Our entire family's downfall as the bratva is Natalya's legacy.

I grab my knife and clink it against my wine glass, drawing everyone's attention. "I would like to make an announcement."

Everyone falls silent, staring at me.

I clear my throat. "Unfortunately, someone in this room has been plotting against me and the legacy of our family."

Yana sits up straighter, and her eyes flash with fear.

The click of the door locking echoes through the vast dining room. Alex stands, reaching for his gun at this waist.

I'm too fast as I point my gun at him instead. "Gun on the table, now."

"Mikhail, what are you doing?" Natalya asks, still so innocent about the world in which we operate.

"Yana has been conspiring with a man who wishes to take control of Boston." I don't take my eyes off of Alex. "Isn't that right, Yana?"

Yana trembles, glancing at Alex, who is frozen. He glares at me with a hatred I don't believe I ever earned from him. "It is true. Please, brother, put down the gun and let me explain."

I don't take my eyes off of the Mexican who my sister married. "Take any weapons off of you and place them on the table," I instruct. "Then, we can talk about this."

Alex does as I say, removing his gun from his belt and

placing it on the table before reaching under his trouser leg to pull out a large knife.

My mother speaks next. "Why do you have all these weapons, Alex?"

I still don't take my eyes off Alex, knowing he is the biggest threat in this room. "He's part of the cartel, mother."

"Is this true, Yana?" she asks.

"That is not important. Is that all of your weapons?" I ask, eyeing Alex.

"Yes."

I narrow my eyes and glance at Natalya. "Check, sister."

She stands obediently, glancing at me. "Are you sure they betrayed you?" she asks.

I glance at her out of the corner of my eye. "Check him, now," I growl.

She moves to the other side of the table and frisks him for weapons. After a thorough check, she nods. "He's clear." She returns to my side.

"I am sure that both Yana and Alex have betrayed me because my spy found photographic evidence of Yana meeting with Andrei Petrov."

"¿Qué diablos, Yana?" Alex asks, shocked at the news.

I glare at him. "Don't pretend you had nothing to do with this, Alex."

He looks me in the eye. "Andrei Petrov has been a thorn in the cartel's side for too fucking long, and I want nothing to do with him." He looks at Yana. "Why?"

Yana glances at him. "He threatened our baby."

His brow furrows. “How does he even know you are pregnant?”

Tears well in her eyes, and she shakes her head. “I don’t know. About six months ago, he contacted me while you were away on business, told me I couldn’t tell you or our baby would die before they are even born.”

“So he threatened you. That’s what this is about?” I ask.

She nods. “Yes, it’s why I agreed to come here for Christmas, as he told me I had to.”

I shake my head and lower the gun. “Why the fuck didn’t you come to me? I can protect you and your baby.” I glance at Alex. “Hell, Alex can protect you in Mexico. How did you think he would get past the cartel to you?”

“I don’t know. I was just scared.” Yana swallows. “He had footage of me in our house, and he sent it via email.” She shrugs. “I was sure his threat was real, so I didn’t risk it.”

“What is he doing in Boston right now?”

Yana glances between her husband and me before shaking her head. “He’ll kill the baby and me if I tell you.”

I slam my hand down on the table, making her jump. “Yana, don’t make me be the one who has to take both of your lives. I’m under pressure from the men who found this out to silence you the traditional way.”

My mother gasps. “You wouldn’t dare, Mikhail.”

I glance at her. “I won’t have a choice if she doesn’t tell me everything.”

Yana sobs, but I can’t find it in myself to feel sorry for

her. This is her doing, no one else's. Her husband is an important man in the cartel, and she thought Andrei Petrov could touch her. It's pathetic. "Andrei buys his fucking drugs from your husband's cartel, and you thought he would kill you and your unborn baby?" I shake my head. "Get a grip, Yana. It was all talk." I cock the gun in my hand and point it at my sister. "Now, talk."

She swallows, her neck bobbing as she does. "Okay, I'll tell you everything." She holds her hands up.

Alex glares at her, clearly angered at learning the truth. I'm surprised this didn't involve him as he's never had much love for me, but clearly, he has even less love for Andrei Petrov. "Yes, I want to hear it all too," he adds.

Yana spills every detail, and all of us listen. Andrei Petrov has one thing going for him: he knew the weakest member of my family and targeted her. It's smart, but what he didn't bank on was my spy finding it all out.

Despite Yana's lack of love for me, this wasn't her trying to hurt me. What I'm not sure about is how he kept his sudden investment in my city a secret.

"Fine. I believe you didn't do this to hurt the family purposely." I lower my gun and stow it in my holster. "Give me your phone, Yana, and you, Alex."

Alex looks uncertain, shaking his head. "What if one of my men needs to contact me?"

I shake my head. "It is merely a temporary measure, and you will have it back within two days at the latest."

He sighs and hands it over, and Yana does the same. I glare at her. "Both of you will not leave the house. Do you understand?"

Yana and Alex nod in reply.

"Good." I glance at Natalya. "Can you get security doubled at the house? This could get ugly."

Natalya nods. "I'll contact Lev to sort it."

"Thank you." I sigh heavily. "I need to contact Milo and Malachy."

Everyone looks confused at the suggestion.

"I had no choice but to agree to an alliance with our enemies. It's the only way we're going to keep hold of Boston."

A tense silence falls over the room as I turn around and leave. The stakes have never been so high for the Gurin Bratva. Andrei poses the most real threat to our legacy that we've ever faced, and, with Spartak involved, the chance of surviving this without the Irish and Italians on our side would be slim to none.

Andrei Petrov is a force to be reckoned with. However, we have the upper hand, and he doesn't know that his cover has been blown. We'll obliterate his attempts to take Boston before he's even has a chance.

25

SIENA

Nothing has ever hurt this badly, which is pathetic.

I should be ecstatic that Mikhail freed me from his capture after holding me under lock and key, keeping me from my friends. Yet, all I feel is despair.

I lie on the bed in the spare room, staring at the ceiling. I'm not sure what time it is, but it's been light outside for hours. It's hard to find the motivation to move ever since he let me go. There is one thing I'm certain of, and it's that Mikhail ruined me for all other men. He took my heart and then broke it in two as if it meant nothing at all.

I'll never see him again, and that hurts like hell.

Aida and Gia worry that I have Stockholm Syndrome, as it's not normal to fall for your captor, but they don't understand. I've never felt this way for anyone before. Our connection was real and deep, at least to me, and it meant something.

It's a shame it meant nothing to Mikhail.

It's been two days since he let me go, but it feels like an eternity. I've never felt so low in all of my life, despite Aida's and Gia's attempts to raise my spirits.

Mikhail doesn't feel the same way about me as I feel about him, and it's a truth that I am trying to come to terms with. If he cared about me, he wouldn't have let me go without another glance in my direction.

He walked out of that office block as if it was the easiest thing he's ever done. As if there was never anything between us.

All I could do was watch in despair. It's hard to comprehend how a man could be so utterly consumed by me one minute and then walk away without a glance in my direction the next.

A knock sounds at my door, and I force myself off the bed, groaning. "Who is it?" I ask.

"It's me," Aida says.

I draw in a deep breath and open the door. "What do you want?"

"That's not a very nice way to speak to your best friend." She sets her hands on her hips. "You need to snap out of this, Siena."

I narrow my eyes at her. "How would you feel if Milo just abandoned you, as if you meant nothing?"

Aida shakes her head. "Look, I'm not telling you how you should feel, but don't take it out on me. Alright?"

I sigh heavily and nod. "Yeah, I'm sorry."

She dismisses my apology with her hand. "No need to apologize. I'm going to a meeting with Milo and Mikhail this afternoon." She tilts her head. "Do you want to come?"

My heart skips a beat at the prospect of seeing him again, but my stomach churns with sickness. If he's as cold as he was toward me the last time, it will break me all over again. "I don't think that's a good idea."

Aida looks confused. "I thought you wanted to see him again." She grabs my hand and squeezes. "Maybe once he sees you again, things will be different, and he might miss you too."

I shake my head. "I doubt it, Aida. I can't deal with him giving me the cold shoulder again."

"You need closure, Siena. One way or the other. Isn't it worth trying?"

I search her dark eyes, wondering if she is right. Will I always think of what could have been if I'd taken the chance and confronted him about it? It takes guts, though, to admit feelings for a man who is broken and deranged. His wicked ways were addictive, but they could be just as destructive. "I'm not sure." My brow furrows. "Why is Milo taking you to the meeting, anyway?"

Aida looks a little guilty. "He doesn't know I'm going yet."

I sigh heavily, knowing he will not agree to take us to the meeting. Milo is a stern and no-nonsense kind of guy, and he will be angry at Aida for suggesting it. "Milo won't let us go to the meeting, Aida." I shake my head. "Thanks for trying, though."

"He doesn't need to let us. We will be in the car before he is and refuse to get out." She yanks me out of the room. "Come on. We need to be quick, as he's leaving in twenty minutes."

I pull her to a stop. "I need to change first. I'm a mess."

Her eyes roam down my crumpled clothes. "Shit. Okay, get ready quickly." She pushes me into the room. "Ten minutes, that's all you've got."

I head into the bathroom and check my hair, combing through it to make it more presentable. All I've done is fester in this room for two days, struggling to do basic things like combing my hair or dressing properly.

"I should shower," I call to Aida.

"There's no time," she calls back.

I swallow hard and fix my face as best I can before washing myself with a flannel. "I'm a mess," I murmur, glaring at myself in the mirror. No wonder Mikhail didn't think twice about leaving me. My eyes are bloodshot from crying.

I can't face him looking like this. It's pathetic.

I clean my face and put face cream around my eyes, trying to dull the redness. Hopefully, I'll look a little better by the time we see him.

"You've got less than five minutes. Move it along, Siena."

I swallow hard and put on a small amount of makeup before returning to the room. I go to the closet and grab a casual day dress.

Aida leans against the doorframe as I change. "Wonderful choice. I've always loved that dress on you."

I smile at her, despite feeling like a mess inside and out. "Okay, I'm ready once I pick what shoes to wear."

Aida enters and grabs a pair of beige pumps. "These suit the dress."

I nod in agreement and slip them on. "Okay, let's do this."

Aida smiles. "Damn, you scrub up good."

I shake my head. "I haven't even showered."

She pulls a small bottle of perfume out of her purse. "Here. You will smell as fresh as a daisy with this."

I take it and spray some on my neck and wrists. "Thanks."

Aida leads the way out of my room and down the stairs. "The car should already be out front, waiting for him."

Aida is right. When we step out of the front door, the car is waiting, and the engine is already running. "I still don't get how you are going to get him to agree to leave with you in the car."

Aida smirks as if she has a plan. "Don't underestimate me, Siena. I've got a plan." She dangles two pairs of handcuffs in my face. "He won't have the time to pick both locks, or he will be late." She smirks. "And the one thing he hates more than anything is being late for a meeting."

I laugh for the first time since Mikhail released me. "You are crazy, but that's why I love you."

She enters the large town car and slides into the seat furthest away from the door, facing opposite where Milo would sit.

I slide in next to her. "What are you going to chain our hands to?" I ask.

She signals at the door grab handle. "Those." She claps the handcuff around her wrist and then through the grab handle, forcing it closed. "Your turn." She hands me the other handcuff, and I do the same.

"You realize this is insane?"

She smiles. "Yes, but it will be worth it if you get closure."

We sit in anticipation, waiting for Milo to enter the car. "Are you ready, sir?" the driver asks.

"Yes, we can't be late." His feet crunch on the gravel drive as he walks toward the car door.

Aida and I hold our breath as he opens the door, sliding in. "What the fuck?" he asks, brow furrowing. "Aida, what are you doing in here?"

She holds her chin high and meets his irritated gaze. "We are coming with you, as Siena needs closure with Mikhail."

"Like hell you are," he growls, trying to grab Aida. It's at that moment he notices the handcuff around her wrist. "Cazzo."

"Sir, is something wrong?" the driver asks from the other side of the privacy screen.

"You could say that," he says. "Put down the screen."

He does as he says, and the driver pales when he sees both of us sitting there. "I'm so sorry, sir. I don't know how this happened." He clears his throat. "Mrs. Mazzeo, I can get you another car arranged."

Aida shakes her head. "No need, James. I am coming with Mr. Mazzeo to his meeting, and so is Siena."

Milo growls a low, feral sound. "You will pay for this later, angel."

Aida meets his gaze and smiles. "I'm counting on it, amore mio."

I'll give it to her. She has some serious balls to speak to Milo that way. The man frightens me. He's scarier than Mikhail, and that's saying something, considering Mikhail kidnapped me. Not to mention, he's larger than Milo in every way, but there's something about the way Milo looks at people that sends a chill through my body.

"Fine. You will accompany me, but I am not happy about this." He narrows his eyes. "I assume you didn't bring the keys for them." He nods at the handcuffs on her wrist.

Aida shakes her head. "No, but you are good at picking locks."

Milo grunts and moves to sit between us, pulling a small lock pick out of his inside pocket and sliding it into the lock of Aida's handcuffs. "Move, James. I don't want to be late."

"Of course, sir," he says, putting the car into gear and erecting the privacy screen between us.

"You are going to endure a very severe punishment for this, Mrs. Mazzeo," Milo murmurs.

Aida shudders before meeting his gaze. "Then so be it." She glares at him. "Siena loves Mikhail, and she has the right to see him again." The pair of handcuffs click-free, and he pulls them off her wrist.

Milo then glances at me. “You are a fool to love the Russian.”

I clench my jaw as his comment irritates me. “You can’t help who you fall for.”

He nods and turns his attention to the restraint on my wrist. “Very true.” He slides the pick into the barrel and works on removing my handcuff. Milo frees it faster this time before moving over to the opposite side of the car. “I am not impressed by this silly charade to force me to take you to the meeting.” His eyes narrow. “If I’d had a bodyguard here to babysit you two, I would leave you both in the car.”

Aida folds her arms over her chest. “Well, luckily, that’s not the case.”

I glance out of the window and ignore the married couple’s little row. All I can think about is Mikhail and seeing him again. Milo is probably right. I’m a fool to love Mikhail because he won’t reciprocate my feelings.

As I watch the world go by outside of the window, dread sets in. Dread that he will break my heart for the second time in three days. It’s a pain I know I can’t handle for the second time. Aida was wrong to give me hope because he could crush the hope as quickly as Aida ignited it.

26

MIKHAIL

My world freezes as I see her walk in behind Milo.

Siena.

She looks like a God damn angel in a beautiful casual winter day dress with a faux fur, knee-length coat clinging to her shoulders.

Why is she here?

I calm myself, making sure I don't give away my delight at seeing her again. It's ridiculous how utterly consumed my thoughts are by that woman. Lev was a fucking idiot for bringing her into my path and derailing me in ways I never saw coming.

"Milo, thank you for coming." I glance at Aida, who stands next to Siena. "I didn't realize you were bringing an audience."

Milo looks irritated as he shakes his head. "Neither did I," he says, glowering at his wife.

It's clear that despite his reputation, Aida has him

wrapped around her little finger. I can't bring myself to look Siena in the eye. The hurt I saw in them when I agreed to Milo's terms made me feel sick, and I can't handle seeing the same hurt again.

"Fine. Shall we begin?" I glance at the office where Malachy sits, tapping his fingers on the desk impatiently. "I have the perfect solution to our predicament."

Milo nods and enters the room, ignoring Malachy as he sits as far away from him as possible at the table.

I take a seat at the head of it, clasping my hands together.

It irritates me that Aida and Siena enter the room too. "This meeting is only for us three." I glare at Milo. "Ladies, please wait outside."

"No chance," Aida says, sitting down next to her husband.

Siena takes a seat next to her, keeping her eyes down.

"It's against the code of our organizations to let outsiders attend meetings. I will walk away if you don't get these women out of here, Milo."

Milo nods and grabs hold of his wife, yanking her out of the chair. "Be a good girl and wait for me outside, angel."

Aida glares at her husband, pursing her lips. "What if I refuse?"

"Then I'll drag you out and tie you to a chair," he growls.

Aida's shoulders slump. "Fine. Let's go, Siena."

Siena glances up at me, and our eyes meet for the first time since I let her go. Her expression is sorrowful, and her hazel eyes look dull and bloodshot. My stomach twists with guilt.

It's hard to believe that she could have been crying about me letting her go.

She breaks our eye contact and follows her friend with her head bowed.

I promised her I'd make sure she'd never forget me once I let her go. What I didn't bank on was me never being able to forget her. She doesn't realize that letting her go was one of the hardest things I've ever done. It's only been two days, but it feels like a part of me died the moment I stepped away from her.

The door slams behind them, breaking me from my daze. "Good, now let's get down to business, as I have a solution to our problem."

"Let's hear it then, lad," Malachy says, impatience in his tone.

"I found the rat in my operation, who has been helping Andrei and dealt with them accordingly." I rub a hand across the back of my neck. "They gave me his plan. He intends to wipe us all out at separate events at New Year. Milo, I believe you are attending a party at City Hall. Is that correct?"

Milo's brow furrows, and he nods. "Yeah."

I turn my attention to Malachy. "You are attending a party for the Irish community downtown pub called The Burren."

Malachy nods. "Aye, every damn year I go to the same party, and everyone knows that."

I nod. "And I was going to attend a party at the Four Seasons hotel."

"Was?" Milo asks.

"Yes. I'm not sure it's a good idea to walk into Andrei Petrov's trap."

Malachy runs a hand through his hair. "What is the plan to take this son of a bitch down?"

I crack my neck, wishing we could kill him. It's not possible because of his many allies and the chaos it would bring to our bratva. We wouldn't survive the aftermath. "We run him out of town and clarify that anyone who tries to fuck with Boston will be met with the wrath of three united organizations."

Milo nods. "Yes, but how?"

I smirk. "Well, Andrei intends to hit us at those parties, which means we hit him instead." I stand from the desk and pace the floor. "Andrei won't be stupid enough to be there himself, I bet, but we will take out the men he sends to kill us before they have the chance and send their hands to him in a fucking box." I glance out of the office window, staring at Siena, who has her back to me.

If she knew the violence that lurks beneath the surface, she would run the other way. She saw a snippet in that bathroom after Ivan tried to rape her. Siena doesn't know the depths of my depravity.

Despite everything that is going on with Andrei, I can't get her out of my mind. I want her still, perhaps now more than ever. I turn to face my two new allies again, tearing my eyes off of the woman who haunts my thoughts.

Malachy nods. "Fair enough. I will take some of my men to the pub and take his men out before he gets to me."

"I'll do the same. A few of my best men will be in attendance at the city council party, as well as Fabio," Milo says, his brow furrowing. "Do you believe Andrei wants to take him out too?"

"I don't know. That is the honest answer." I run a hand through my hair. "It would be wise for both of you to keep a distance from the party."

Milo shakes his head in disagreement. "No, if we don't attend, then we will raise Andrei's suspicion, and he might call his men off before we can find them."

He's right. If we aren't in attendance as expected, Andrei will know something is wrong. "True, but isn't the risk too high? His men could get to us before you find them."

Milo looks offended. "I will ensure that doesn't happen."

"Aye, me too. What do you take us for, lad? Idiots?"

I shake my head. "No, but Andrei is smart." My brow furrows. "During the night, we will level to the ground three of the empty apartment blocks he's bought in Boston. One each." I pace the breadth of the room. "Hopefully, it will send him running with his tail between his legs." I pinch my nose. "If it doesn't work, we keep moving against him until he gives up." I can hardly consider this plan not working, as it will mean we are fighting a war against a foreign entity in our city's walls.

"He won't dare try to stand against all three of us," Milo says.

I meet his gaze. "You don't know Andrei Petrov."

Milo doesn't acknowledge that warning. He stands up. "I will await instructions from you on how to proceed regarding the building. Send all the details to Piero. He will handle it."

I nod. "I will. Shall we liaise with Niall on this?" I ask Malachy.

He grinds his teeth before nodding. "Aye, lad. Get him the information. He will handle leveling the building you give us." Malachy stands and glances at Milo. "If we are going to work together, then we might as well be civil." He holds a hand out to Milo.

Milo regards it for a few seconds before taking it and shaking. "I agree," he says.

I feel thankful that their childish bickering has subsided. Hopefully, Andrei's attempt to take Boston will strengthen the city in more ways than one. In theory, there should be no more war with the Italians, Irish, and Russians working together. However, I know better than anyone that in the underbelly of Boston, alliances can be fleeting.

"I'll be in touch." I glance at my watch. "We have precisely thirty-two hours to get our plan in motion. It's going to be a tall task, but we can pull it off if we work together."

Milo nods and claps me on the shoulder. "Let's make him flee this city and wish he never came here."

Malachy nods. "Aye, see you two on the other side." He walks out first, leaving Milo and me in the room.

Milo glances at me as if he wants to say something. "I think she's pretty torn up, Mikhail."

I take a moment to realize who he's talking about. "Yeah, I gathered."

He nods. "If you care about her, don't fuck it up." He shrugs. "I'm talking from experience. If you push too hard, you will lose her forever." He walks away, leaving me pondering his words.

For ten years, my world has revolved around the Gurin Bratva. It is all I've cared about, that and my family. Siena gives me a new purpose and a reason for living other than the blood and violence of the bratva.

I walk out of the office door, feeling my eyes drawn to her. Siena is like a magnet, impossible to stay away from.

Milo and Aida are chatting on one side. Siena stands alone on the other side, glancing down at her hands clasped together. She's a vision of perfection, an angel a man like me has no right to be near. I'm black to the core, and she's as pure white as snow. We're opposites, but perhaps that's why we're so right for each other.

I never feel anxious about anything, but as I move toward her, my stomach twists.

Siena glances up as if she detects my presence. Her stunning hazel eyes meet mine, and it feels like time slows down. The sadness in them is ever-present, and it stops me in my tracks as I wonder how to speak to her.

Did I break her that badly?

As I think of it from her perspective, it looks as if I

made good on my promise. I took what I wanted from her, used her the way I said I would, and then tossed her aside once I got Milo to agree to my terms.

The only thing I didn't expect was falling for my kukolka. She's become more important to me than the bratva and more important to me than anything else on this planet.

I move toward her again, knowing with all certainty that life isn't worth living without her. I'll fight for her no matter what obstacles we have to face. She's an innocent young woman who doesn't deserve to be dragged into the darkness of my life, but I'm too selfish to give her up. Siena lives in Italy, and I live in Boston, but none of this changes anything.

We can figure out the logistics later. Right now, I need to win her back. The hungry desire that consumes me whenever we are close takes hold of me, capturing me in its trap. Nothing will stop me from having my way with her.

I need her the same way I need oxygen to breathe, water to hydrate, and food for energy. Siena has become a fundamental part of my survival.

"Siena," I murmur her name once I'm within a few feet of her. "How have you been?" I ask.

My heart is pounding in my ears as I try to work out how to tell her the truth.

I love her.

It's simple but complicated at the same time.

27

SIENA

The look in his dark brown eyes is one of starving hunger, the same hunger he's always looked at me with but amplified.

It inspires hope inside of me again: hope that there is a chance we can rekindle something between us.

"Siena?" He says my name again, breaking me from my daze.

"Sorry, what?" I ask, realizing he said something, but I didn't hear.

His brow furrows. "I asked how you've been."

I swallow hard. "Oh, not great," I reply, shuffling from one foot to the other. "You?"

He tilts his head slightly. "As well as can be."

An awkward, tense silence pulses in the air as I stare at him, longing for him to say something else. He clears his throat. "Natalya has been asking after you." He digs his cell phone out of his pocket. "She wants your number. What is it?"

I raise a brow. "It's a Sicilian number, not American."

He smiles. "That doesn't matter." He passes the cell phone into my hand. "Put it in."

I glance down to see the title of the contact on his phone as *kukolka*. I type my number in, feeling utterly pathetic. He wants my number for his sister, and Mikhail doesn't give two shits about me now that he has gotten what he wants from Milo.

"Here." I shove the phone into his hand and turn to walk away, feeling the pain ignite in my chest.

Mikhail grabs my wrist before I can escape. "Not so fast, malishka."

Tears well in my eyes as I stare into nothing, wishing the floor would swallow me whole.

"Look at me," he orders.

I take in a deep breath, trying to stop the tears from falling. Slowly, I turn to face him. "What do you want?" I ask, infusing my tone with irritation.

His dark eyes hold no emotion as he looks at me, seeing the unshed tears in my eyes. "You, malishka. I want you."

My brow furrows as I stare at him. "You had me, and you let me go."

He runs a hand across the back of his neck. "I could never truly have you that way, Siena, and you should know that."

"What do you mean?"

He sighs heavily and glances over at Milo and Aida, who linger a short distance from us. "Can we talk somewhere more private?"

I glance at Aida, who smiles at me encouragingly. "Fine. Make it quick, though."

Mikhail leads me into the office and shuts the door, keeping his back to me as he walks further into the room. "I miss you," he murmurs, barely loud enough for me to hear, but I do.

I swallow hard, wondering if this is one of his games. "Are you playing with me?"

He turns and faces me, irritation in his eyes. "No," he says, shaking his head as he moves toward me. "I couldn't keep you, Siena, because I kidnapped you." The muscles in his jaw clench. "I wanted to keep you more than anything, malishka." He takes a few steps closer to me, passionate lust blazing in his eyes. "I just couldn't like that."

I take a step back, uncertain whether he truly means what he says. "How can I trust you? You walked out of this office block as if letting me go was the easiest thing you've ever done." I shake my head. "Even today, when I arrived, you hardly looked at me."

Mikhail charges toward me and grabs hold of my hips, yanking me hard against his powerful body. "You misunderstood, malishka." He searches my eyes. "I walked out of here without looking at you because I knew if I did, I wouldn't be able to go through with it." His eyes flash with such passionate rage, it frightens me a little. "Letting you go was the hardest fucking thing I've ever done."

Mikhail melds his lips to mine forcefully, grabbing hold of my hips so hard I know he'll leave bruises. His tongue thrusts into my mouth with as much force, taking and demanding everything from me.

I feel my uncertainty ease as he kisses me. Mikhail feels the same way I feel.

When he finally breaks away from me, we're both panting for oxygen. He doesn't let go of me, holding me just as tightly. "I don't think I can leave without you today, though, malishka."

I gaze up at him, feeling a warmth radiate through me at his admission. "Then don't."

He smiles at me. "I'm not sure Milo will be too pleased, as it was a term of the agreement."

I shake my head. "It's different if I choose to go with you."

He smiles that wicked smile that makes my stomach flutter. "So, will you come home with me?"

I search his dark onyx eyes. "Freely or as your captive?" I ask.

His Adam's apple bobs as he swallows. "Freely. You will come and go as you please. I will not lock you in a room." His brow furrows. "Unless you've been a naughty girl."

I laugh at that, reveling in the musky scent of him that I'm addicted to. The warmth of his powerful body pressed against mine is a welcome sensation.

I can't help the question that enters my mind: what happens when I return to Italy? Despite my happiness that he feels the same way I do, it is too complicated.

I try to ignore the question, as I'd rather live out this

fantasy with him as long as possible. "Okay, I want to come home with you."

He moves his lips to my neck and kisses me there. "Good. I can't wait to be inside of you." He moves them lower, teasing them over my collarbone. "I've been going out of my mind since you've been gone."

I shudder at the deep baritone of his voice. "Sounds good to me."

He clears his throat and takes a step back. "Shall we break the news to them?"

"Yes," I say.

Mikhail steps away, taking my hand in his.

When we walk back out into the main entryway of the office, Aida squeals. "Thank goodness for that." She claps her hands.

I feel heat filtering through my body at her ridiculously embarrassing reaction to us holding hands. "Please don't," I mutter. Normally, I'm the embarrassing one, not Aida.

"Sorry," she mutters before taking Milo's hand. "It looks like Siena is staying with Mikhail. Shall we go home?"

Milo's brow furrows as he glances at his wife. "Why? Are you ready for your punishment, angel?"

Aida shudders and glances our way, turning red. "Call me later," she says.

Mikhail looks a little confused as the two of them walk away. "How did she know?"

I shake my head. "It was her plan, bringing me here."

He grabs my hand and pulls me against him. "I feel

duped, malishka. Maybe you need a punishment too," he whispers into my ear. "Go back into the office and lie on my desk for me."

Excitement coils through me as I turn around and head toward the office we just came out of. The office floor is empty, meaning we can do whatever the hell we want. After all, it's Mikhail's building.

I lie down over his desk on my front with my head propped up by my hands.

Mikhail walks in slowly. The predatory look in his eyes is thrilling. He turns and shuts the door behind him, twisting the lock. My heart rate picks up speed as I stare at him, waiting for his next move.

"I don't think you are prepared for what I have in store, malishka." His dark eyes find me on the desk, and he groans. "I'm going to devour you."

I can hardly contain my excitement as my thighs grow slick with arousal. I'm practically dripping for him. "I can't wait," I say.

Mikhail's laugh floods the room. The wicked, dark tone sets my soul on fire. "Be careful what you wish for." He slides a finger into his tie and undoes it, then chucks it on the floor.

I watch him from the desk as he slowly removes all of his clothes until he's standing in front of me in all his natural glory.

My stomach tightens at the sight of his cock fully hard and dripping pre-cum onto the office floor. "I've missed this," I murmur.

He tilts his head to the side and grabs the length of his huge cock, tugging it up and down. "You've missed my cock, malishka?" he asks.

I nod in response, utterly mesmerized by the man approaching me.

"Good. Then lie on your back and open your mouth for me like a good girl," he purrs.

I swallow hard before adjusting my position so that I'm lying with my head over the desk.

Mikhail approaches, and I open my mouth.

He stands at the edge of the desk and thrusts his cock into my throat hard.

I breathe through my nose, shutting my eyes as his taste overwhelms my senses. It's only been two days since I saw him last, but it felt like the longest two days of my life, even longer than the two days that he kept me locked in that basement.

I let him take my throat roughly, enjoying the feel of his dominant hands gripping my throat. Before I met Mikhail, I never felt such opposite, powerful emotions in quick succession. Utter despair quickly paves the way to blissful happiness.

"That's it, malishka. I want you to choke on my cock like a good girl," he growls, the intensity in his voice making me ache between my thighs.

I moan around his cock, knowing that there has never been a single time in my life that I've felt so needy for anything or anyone.

He groans as he picks up the pace, his cock leaking

onto my tongue as he does. "You are so naughty moaning with my cock in your mouth." He slides it out of my mouth and kneels over me, bringing his face to within an inch of mine. "Do you like choking on my cock?"

I lick my bottom lip and nod. "Fuck yes, daddy."

He growls and slides every inch back into my throat. "You are such a good girl, Siena. I'm going to give you my cum."

I whimper as he assaults my throat harder, fucking it with all his strength. His cock hardens in my throat a few seconds before he unleashes his load. Mikhail roars like an animal as he tips over the edge.

I swallow the first load, overwhelmed by the amount of cum as it spills out of my mouth and down my chin.

Mikhail continues to rock back and forth into my throat, making sure every drop is out. "Swallow every drop, malishka."

I do as he says, desperate to satisfy his every desire.

Mikhail sits on the office chair next to the desk, fisting his still rock-hard cock in his hand. "Sit on it, malishka."

My body trembles in anticipation as I slide off of the desk, slipping my panties off quickly. I'm practically dripping for him, desperate to feel every inch of him complete me.

He chuckles as I eagerly straddle him, trying to sink over his thick length.

I groan as he grabs my hips, stopping me from sitting on his cock. "Please, Mikhail," I beg.

He captures my lips, kissing me softly. "Patience. You do as I say when I say. Understand?" he asks.

I swallow hard and nod. "Yes, daddy."

He groans at me calling him that, his eyes fluttering shut. "I love it when you call me that, kukolka." He forces me down over his cock hard. "It sounds so right," he growls.

I moan as his thick length stretches me the way I long to be stretched.

He holds me still, looking into my eyes as I adapt to the sudden invasion. "How does it feel to have me inside of you again, malishka?"

"So fucking good."

He chuckles and wraps a hand around my throat, choking me. "Ride me," he orders.

I don't need to be told twice. I move my hips up and down, rising and falling on his thick cock.

Mikhail keeps his hand tightly wrapped around my throat, partially blocking my airways most tantalizingly. He moves his hips to meet my movements, thrusting his shaft harder into me with each rise and fall.

Our bodies come together in a clash of skin as our need surpasses anything we've experienced before.

"You feel like heaven," he groans into my ear, biting the shell softly. "I could spend the rest of my life balls deep in your tight little cunt," he growls.

My muscles spasm as I feel my orgasm growing close. The pressure Mikhail keeps on my throat is just right as he continues to choke me. I never thought I'd enjoy such rough sex, but it's the best sensation I've ever experienced.

Mikhail grunts with each thrust as he drives me toward the edge of no return.

"Fuck, I'm going to come," I cry, warning him that I'm close.

"Good. Come on my cock like a good girl," he purrs, letting go of my throat and moving his grip to my hips.

He digs his fingertips into my hips, hard enough to bruise.

I groan as my orgasm barrels into me with a fierce force. My body trembles as my muscles contract, tightening around his cock. I continue to rise and fall on his length as white filters into my vision.

"Fuck, malishka. So damn tight," Mikhail groans, thrusting into me over and over as he fucks me through it.

He bites my neck hard as he comes undone, breaking the skin and making me bleed.

The pain is welcome, and it only heightens the indescribable pleasure. He roars into my skin as he comes undone. The intensity of our desire for each other knows no bounds.

He continues to drive his cock into me until every drop of cum is drained before falling back in the chair. His chest rises and falls as he tries to draw oxygen into his lungs.

I remain in Mikhail's lap, still naked. Mikhail's powerful arms hold me so tightly as if he is scared of letting me go.

Gently, I trail my finger over his colorful tattoos, admiring every one of them. Mikhail is a piece of art, and my desire for him is overwhelming.

"You are mine, zhizn moya," he murmurs into my ear.

I meet his adoring gaze, knowing that he's never

looked at me that way before. Part of me wants to ask what that nickname means, but instead, I rest my head on his chest and reply, "Always."

I mean it, even if I am supposed to get on a plane to go back to Italy in four days. Mikhail has taken my heart captive, and there's no way I ever want to be free of him.

28

MIKHAIL

Tonight is the night.

The mafia bosses of Boston are going to bring the new year in with a bang. Three high-rise, empty apartment blocks Andrei purchased will be leveled to the ground by the end of the night.

We have already set the bombs up, and our men are waiting for the order. I sit next to Siena in the back of the town car, wondering if it is a bad idea to take something so precious into a war zone.

Milo and Malachy were right. We need to act naturally and attend the parties as expected. I am on my way to the Four Seasons hotel. Something tells me there is a reason Andrei chose the same hotel to stay in during his time in Boston. He will be the one trying to take me out tonight.

"What are you thinking about?" Siena asks, looking at me inquisitively.

I smile at her and grab her hand, squeezing it. "Only

work." I shake my head. "Why don't you keep my mind off of it?"

Her brow furrows. "How?"

"Why don't you tell me about your life in Sicily?"

She smiles before sighing. "Sicily is lovely, but it doesn't have many prospects." She twirls her finger in the end of her hair. "I have told no one except for my parents, but I accepted a job in Rome starting in the New Year at an interior design firm."

A job in Rome.

How can I ask her to walk away from everything and move here?

The fact is that I can't leave Boston even if I wanted to. My life is tied to this city in ways I'll never be able to break. If we are to remain together, then I need her to stay here.

I swallow my concern. "I see. Are you excited to move?"

Siena looks a little torn at the question. "Scared mostly." She falls silent as tension floods the air. I wish I hadn't asked her about her life back in Italy, as all it does is bring up the unspoken issue between us. Siena is due to fly back to Italy in three days.

We haven't spoken about what happens when she does, and I can't even think about her leaving me. I want to lock her in my room and never let her go, forcing her to stay in Boston for all eternity.

"We are here," I say as I notice the hotel ahead.

Siena cranes her neck to see the hotel, but she's too

short. "I've hardly seen any of Boston since I've been here," she muses.

I meet her gaze. "I'll make sure I take you on a tour tomorrow."

She smiles and nods. "I'd like that."

A comfortable silence falls between us as Igor, my driver, finds somewhere to park. He's under instructions to ensure we're parked somewhere for a quick getaway if anything goes wrong. Ten of my best men will be in attendance, ready to take out Andrei's assassins.

Once he stops, I get out of the car first and walk around, then open Siena's door.

She takes my hand and allows me to help her onto the sidewalk. I pull her close and murmur into her ear, "You look stunning." She looks stunning wearing anything, but the beautiful pale green evening gown she chose complements her skin and golden hair.

"Thank you," she replies, meeting my gaze. "Shall we?"

I nod and set my hand on the small of her back, guiding her into the event.

A small queue of people is waiting to enter, but I walk straight up to the door. The man at the door gives me a nod, and we slip through.

Siena jerks me to a stop. "Why did you skip the queue?"

I smile at her innocence. "Because this is my party, malishka."

Her eyes widen. "You rented The Four Seasons hotel?" she asks.

"Not exactly. I own shares in the group."

She shakes her head in disbelief. "You must be filthy rich, then."

"Hmm, and I can't wait to do filthy things to you later." I squeeze her hip, making her shudder.

"Mikhail, don't talk like that here." She glances around nervously.

I pull her tight against my side and lean down to her ear. "I will talk however the fuck I want, kukolka."

She glares at me shaking her head. "It's impolite."

I smirk. "If you keep questioning me. I'll have to punish you right here."

Her brow hitches. "You wouldn't do that in front of these people."

Siena is blissfully unaware that the underwear I told her to wear tonight are vibrating remote-controllable panties. I slide my hand into my pocket and press the button.

Siena jumps in shock, eyes widening as she looks at me. "You didn't."

I smirk at her. "Oh, believe me, I did."

She grunts in frustration as I turn it off again.

"If you are a good girl, I won't have to punish you with them, though, will I?"

She glares at me, and it's a look that makes my cock harder than it already is. "I guess not."

I glance around the room. My gaze stops dead on Andrei and his wife, Vera, standing near the back of the event hall.

"Motherfucker," I murmur.

Siena's brow hitches upward. "Is something wrong?"

I smile at her, shaking my head. "No, I just need to speak with someone."

"Do you want me to come?" she asks.

The last thing I want to do is bring Siena to Andrei's attention. "No, wait for me over there." I nod toward a plush sofa where Milan sits, knowing he will keep her safe.

She looks at the sofa reluctantly before searching my eyes. "You won't be long, will you?"

I kiss her cheek. "No, malishka. I can never stay away from you for long." I bite the lobe of her ear. "Now be a good girl, and do as I say."

She nods and walks over to the sofa, sitting on the other side of it to Milan.

I had fully expected to see Andrei here tonight since all the hotel guests are allowed into the party, as it was the requirement for me holding it here. It is disrespectful, though, that he never contacted me to confirm that he would be attending.

A woman walks past holding a tray of champagne—not my favorite, but it will have to do. Andrei notices me approaching first and gives me a nod. "Mikhail, it is good to see you."

I try to act natural, despite the fury bubbling away deep down. "Andrei, it is a surprise to see you in town. When did you arrive?"

"This morning, as we fancied a change from New York for New Year."

Liar.

His entire family was here for Christmas, including his

young children. I have it under good authority that he sent the rest of his family home this morning. "Who would want to escape New York at New Year? Isn't it the best place to be?"

Vera clears her throat. "It gets boring year after year of the same."

I turn my attention to his wife. "True. You look lovely as ever, Vera." I reach for her hand and kiss the back of it, knowing it will irritate her. "How have you been?"

It takes all my strength to remain civil. My men are on watch, monitoring us. I notice Lev circle around, watching me like a hawk.

Vera reclaims her hand. "Fine, Mikhail. This is a great party."

I laugh. "It has hardly started yet." I take a sip of the champagne in my hand, feeling ridiculous, as this isn't what I drink.

Andrei's brow furrows. "I never took you for the champagne kind of guy."

I shake my head. "No, I'm not. It was just available." I place the glass down on a nearby table. "If you will excuse me, I need to find a better drink. Enjoy the party. I'm sure we will speak again."

Andrei nods. "Yes. See you later."

I say nothing more and head toward the sofa where Siena sits patiently, waiting for me. She smiles the most angelic smile the moment she sees me.

A man like me doesn't deserve an angel like her.

I sit next to her and take her hand.

"Is everything okay?" she asks.

I nod. "Yes. At least, it will be."

Her brow furrows questioningly, but before she can ask me what I mean, I kiss her passionately.

She moans into my mouth, wrapping her fingers around the back of my neck.

I break the kiss and press my forehead to hers. "I had better get us both a drink."

Siena pouts. "Can't I come with you? I don't like sitting here alone."

I smirk at that and grab the controller out of my pocket, pressing the button.

Siena jolts against me, eyes widening.

"Now, you are not alone." I press my lips to her neck and kiss her there. "You can feel my presence even when I'm not next to you," I murmur.

Siena moans softly, a sweet sound that makes my balls ache with need. I shouldn't be indulging in such frivolous activities when my life is literally on the line at this party. Siena is a distraction I should have left at home tonight, but my obsessive nature is impossible to ignore with her.

"Now, be a good girl and stay here."

She bites her bottom lip, squeezing her thighs together as the panties vibrate. "That isn't fair," she whines, the pleasure detectable in her tone.

I kiss her lips quickly before breaking away and walking toward the bar.

Siena won't admit it, but she loves me toying with her. It's the reason she longed for me even after I released her as my prisoner.

I can't help but feel that I'm walking in the same footsteps of my father.

My mother and father didn't have a traditional relationship since he, too, captured her.

She was the daughter of his sworn enemy, and he intended to use her for his gain. Instead, he fell in love with her and fled his home country.

Perhaps it is the Gurin curse to fall in love with a woman you take captive.

The moment I set eyes on Siena, I knew she was special.

I approach the bar and rap my fingers on the hardwood counter, waiting impatiently for one of the bartenders to notice me.

One of the female bartenders does and rushes over to me. "What can I get you, sir?" she asks.

"One double vodka and a glass of champagne."

She nods. "Right away."

I glance at the men and women around the bar, wondering if any of the people are Andrei's people.

They could be anywhere, but I'm counting on Milan to notice them before they can do any harm. He knows the Petrov Bratva inside out.

"Here you go, sir." She hands me the two drinks.

"Thanks." I reach into my pocket and turn off Siena's panties, knowing she will have had enough for now. I then take the drinks and turn around, only to bump straight into a tall man.

"Fuck," I growl as the drinks spill down my suit.

The man narrows his eyes. "Watch where you are going." He has a distinctly Russian accent.

"Do you know who you are talking to?" I say, slamming the glasses down on the bar counter and grabbing his jacket roughly.

He raises a brow. "Yes, and I intend to end you right here and now."

I react fast, adrenaline kicking through my blood in a split second.

Before he can grab the gun at his waist, I twist his arm behind his back.

He howls in pain, and people glance at us. "Get the fuck off me."

"No chance." I reach for the gun myself and pull it off of him. "Intending to shoot me, were you?" I search the crowd, looking for Milan.

He is already walking this way, ready to assist me.

My heart freezes in my chest when I see three men march into the room with machine guns. "Milan, get down," I shout.

His eyes widen, and he does as I say without hesitation.

We both fall to the floor as gunshots rain down on the party. Andrei didn't go halves on his attempt to kill me. I keep the assassin who attempted to kill me in front of me, using his limp body as a shield. He has already been hit.

At that moment, as I lay on the floor, all I can think about is Siena. She's alone in this room, and these men are here for blood.

If she dies, I'll never forgive myself.

29

SIENA

Gunshots fill the room as I duck to the floor, placing my hands over my head.

Shock filters through me as I search the crowd for Mikhail, unable to find him anywhere. He went to get a drink, and then the gunmen appeared from nowhere, raining metal down on the guests.

It's carnage as people scatter away, screaming.

I can't find it in me to move at all, frozen to the spot by fear.

Mikhail is likely to be the target. My fear isn't just rooted in the fact that they could shoot me at any moment. The thing that scares me the most is losing him.

"Siena." A man says my name from behind me.

I stand and turn, noticing it's the man who drove us here. I believe Mikhail called him Igor. "Hey, do you know where Mikhail is?"

He shakes his head. "He's safe, and I have strict instructions to get you out of here."

"I can't leave him here."

Igor grabs hold of my wrist. "You can and you will, Siena. The boss will kill me if I don't do as he instructed."

My brow furrows. "Are you saying that he expected this to happen?"

Igor looks irritated. "There is no time to explain. Come on." He yanks me toward the exit of the hotel.

I search for Mikhail, uncertain about leaving him here. Then I notice his immense size heading down the hotel's corridor, dragging a woman with him.

My heart skips a beat.

What the hell is he doing?

I glance forward at Igor and slip my wrist out of his grasp, dodging the people rushing out of the exit to follow him. Mikhail is up to something, and I need to know what.

As I make my way over to the corridor, people scream and shout.

The gunmen are no longer alive, as security has shot them dead.

I believe the threat is over, so I follow him.

Mikhail turns left, and I chase him, wondering where he is going.

"In there," I hear him bark.

My stomach twists with dread as I wonder if he intends to kill the woman he is dragging around.

"Mikhail, what is this about?" another man asks.

There are a few moments of silence. "This is about your betrayal, Andrei."

I inch closer to the room they are in, stepping carefully

to make sure I'm silent. My heart is pounding so hard and fast I can hardly hear.

"I'm not sure what you are talking about," Andrei says.

"Liar," Mikhail growls, angrier than I've ever heard him. "Give me one good reason I shouldn't blow both of your heads off here and now?"

I shudder, knowing that the man I've fallen for has it in him to do that to these people. The image of blood all over his face after he beat to death the man who tried to rape me comes to the forefront of my mind.

How can I love a man who is so wicked?

It's hard to comprehend. All I should feel for Mikhail is hatred.

I inch closer to the door, wanting to get a look at the two people he is with. Andrei has a Russian accent too.

The crack of the door makes it possible to see through.

Mikhail stands with his back to me, holding the woman in front of him and pressing a gun into her neck.

Andrei is standing in front of him with his arms crossed over his chest. "You are making a grave mistake, Mikhail."

Mikhail shakes his head. "No, you made a grave mistaken when you made a move on Boston." He cocks the gun, pressing it harder into the woman's throat. "Do you take me for an idiot?"

Andrei glares at him. "Fine. I saw Boston as a lucrative addition to my empire, so I moved against you." His eyes narrow. "How did you find out?"

"I have my ways. I'll give you one thing, using Yana, I did not see coming."

Andrei smirks. "No. Did you kill your sister, Mikhail?"

"After hearing her side of the story, it was clear you blackmailed her." I shake my head. "Although, her husband and the cartel aren't too pleased."

Andrei's face pales slightly. I wonder what that means.

I glance behind me and see a man approaching. I've seen him before, but I don't know his name.

He notices me and hastens his pace.

I swallow hard, wondering if I should run or stay put. Mikhail is handling this, but it could all go wrong. The idea of losing him scares me more than anything.

The man grabs me, and I yelp, drawing Mikhail's attention.

A gun cocking follows. "Put the gun down, or I'll blow your head off first," Andrei says cooly.

Shit. I distracted Mikhail, and now he might die because of me. Panic hits as I struggle to get free from this guy.

Mikhail's attention returns to Andrei as the man drags me away, holding a hand over my mouth.

"Son of a bitch," Mikhail growls.

The man drags me, kicking back into the main events hall of the hotel, before setting me down on my feet. "I will not hurt you. My name is Milan, and I work for Mikhail." He keeps his hand over my mouth. "If I take my hand away, will you promise not to scream?"

I nod in response.

Milan takes his hand away. "You can't be here, Siena.

Mikhail wanted us to get you to safety if anything like this happened."

"Mikhail is in a room down there with a woman and a guy named Andrei." I sigh heavily. "My scream distracted Mikhail, and now Andrei is going to shoot him."

Milan shakes his head. "No, he won't. Don't underestimate Mikhail, ad he knows what he is doing. There is no way Andrei would risk Vera's life by shooting first."

My brow furrows. "Why don't you help him?"

"Boss's orders are to leave it to him. All he wanted me to do was keep you safe." Milan grabs hold of my hand. "That's what I'm going to do." He yanks me toward the exit of the hotel.

I glance down the corridor, struggling to calm my nerves.

All I want is for Mikhail to come out of this hotel alive. The thought of him getting hurt scares me. "Is anyone injured?"

Milan glances at me. "A few people got caught in the crossfire, and two of our men died."

My stomach churns as Milan leads me to safety, walking me over to the town car, where Igor sits in the driver's seat.

He opens the door to the car. "Get inside, Siena," Milan says when I don't move.

It feels wrong leaving him alone with those people. I glance back at the hotel, knowing I can't be of any help. Resigned to the fact, I slide into the back of the town car, and Milan shuts the door behind me.

He approaches the driver's side window and speaks to Igor in Russian.

My stomach sinks as he turns on the engine and pulls out of the car park. "Where are we going? What about Mikhail?" I ask.

Igor glances at me in the rearview mirror. "Mr. Gurin will be fine, as he is going to return with Milan."

A bang shakes the ground violently, and I glance back at the hotel.

My entire world feels like it shatters as I see the glass front of the hotel blow out and smoke begin billowing from the openings. "No, turn around," I shout.

Igor clenches his jaw as he stares back at the scene, but he doesn't reply. I can tell he is torn about leaving when a bomb has just exploded.

"We can't leave him here," I protest. "What kind of soldier are you if you leave your captain to die?" I shout.

Igor says something in Russian before slamming on the breaks and turning around. "He will have my head for this if he survives."

If he survives.

My heart aches at the prospect that he may no longer be alive. Mikhail is my world.

I can't live without him, and he better have survived.

Sirens flood the air as I get out of the vehicle and walk toward the carnage.

Igor grabs hold of my wrist. "No further. I agreed not to abandon him, but you can't go charging in there."

I swallow hard as Milan approaches, looking furious.

"What the fuck are you doing, Igor?"

"How can I drive away when Mikhail is in that hotel, Milan?" His eyes narrow. "Could you?"

Milan sighs heavily. "No, but he will not be happy that we disobeyed him."

Igor nods. "I'll deal with his wrath."

The emergency services arrive, and the firefighters enter the building. It feels like the longest minutes I've ever faced as I wait for them to bring him out.

The other two people must be in there unless they escaped first. I hear one firefighter through the radio request a stretcher.

My heart stutters in my chest as they wheel one to the front of the building. Two men appear, carrying Mikhail.

"It's him." I move forward, only for Milan to block me.

"Wait, Siena. They won't let anyone near him yet."

I grunt in frustration, hoping he is okay. "What is he dies?"

Igor grabs my shoulders and gives me a quick shake. "You can't think like that. You must be positive."

I nod in response and return my attention to the paramedics, who are charging a paddle. It's the most fear-inspiring thing I've ever seen as they try tirelessly to start his heart.

"Please, Mikhail," I murmur under my breath. "Please don't die." Tears flood my eyes and fall freely as the paramedics continue to work on Mikhail, trying to revive him.

Finally, they stop, and I wonder if he's dead or if it worked.

"He's stable, but we need to move him to the ICU." Someone's voice sounds through a nearby radio.

"Copy," the ambulance driver replies.

All of us let out a breath of relief at the news. I rush up to the ambulance. "Excuse me. That man is my boyfriend. Can I ride in the back with him?"

The driver regards me for a moment before nodding. "Yes. Only you, though." He glances at Igor and Milan, who stand behind me.

I turn to them. "Please let me go with him."

They nod. "Fine, we will follow in the car behind the ambulance." Milan approaches the driver. "Have they found anyone else inside?"

He shakes his head. "No, everyone else had evacuated before the blast."

Milan's brow furrows. That means that Andrei and Vera made it out before it blew. They were behind all of this.

I swallow hard, wishing I hadn't listened to Milan. He shouldn't have been alone in there.

They bring Mikhail into the back of the ambulance, and I sit next to him. He's unconscious.

It's hard to see such a powerful man so crippled. I hold his hand and squeeze. "It's going to be okay, Mikhail," I murmur.

I have to believe he will make it through this, as the alternative is too painful to consider.

30

MIKHAIL

I am a fool.

For a split second, I lost concentration. Now Andrei is pointing a gun at me. The yelp that came from outside the door was a woman who sounded a hell of a lot like Siena. If my men didn't get her out as I instructed, there would be blood.

Rage and panic mingle as I try to steady my frantic heartbeat, breathing deeply. Siena can't become collateral in my war. I'll never forgive myself or my men if they let her fall prey to this evil son of a bitch.

Andrei glares at me, holding the gun and pointing it at me and his wife, Vera.

I hold her tightly, aware of her proclivity for violence. The woman has a reputation more ruthless than Andrei's reputation. Many say her arrival in his life turned him on the path of nationwide domination.

"Let her go, Mikhail."

I push the gun against her throat tighter, shaking my

head. "You conspired with my sister to kill me and take Boston. Tell me why I shouldn't blow her head off right now."

Andrei narrows his eyes. "Because if you do, I will bring hellfire down on your entire city. What you did to my buildings will seem like nothing."

I shake my head. "How are you going to take on all three of us, Andrei?"

His brow furrows. "Three of you?"

I smirk as he hasn't gotten the message that it's not just me that knows of his plan. "Milo and Malachy have entered an alliance with me."

The bravado drops as his face pales. "An alliance within Boston. How the fuck did you get those two idiots to agree to that?"

I shrug. "It doesn't matter how. All that matters is that you back off."

Andrei searches my eyes for a few beats before holding his hands up. "Fair enough. I know when I've been beaten fair and square."

"Andrei, don't give in to him because of—"

I grab Vera's throat and squeeze hard, cutting her off. "I don't want to hear another word, or I'll choke the life out of you. Do you understand?"

Andrei's eyes flood with panic as he watches his wife fight for oxygen. "Please, Mikhail. She has nothing to do with this."

"I want her to nod if she understands."

Vera nods, and I release her throat. She gasps for air. "You fucking bastard," she says.

"I get the sense that Vera has everything to do with this, Andrei. What happened to the integrity of a pakhan's word?" I shake my head. "You agreed to be my ally and then tried to stab me in the back."

Andrei looks torn as his eyes dart between his wife and me. "I may have let success get to my head. You've made it clear you aren't a man to mess with." He holds his hands up. "I agree to back off and leave the city. Any assets within Boston which still stand, I will sign over to you, Milo, and Malachy equally."

Vera makes an irritating noise. "Why the fuck would you do that?"

I tighten my grip on her again. "Vera, think of your babies at home. Do you want them to grow up without a mother?" I snarl.

Andrei steps forward. "Don't talk about my children, Mikhail. We can solve this amicably." His gaze falls to his wife. "Back down, malishka."

Vera turns limp in my arms and nods, submitting to his will.

"Mikhail, you will let my wife go now, and we will settle this," Andrei demands.

He doesn't understand that he isn't the one doing the demanding. I'm already one step ahead of him. I narrow my eyes. "There is nothing to settle. I have a car outside ready to take you and Vera back to New York." I glance at my watch. "My men have already loaded your belongings."

Andrei's eyes narrow. "And the assets?"

"My lawyer will be in touch with yours to handle the

paperwork." I push the gun harder against Vera's head. "If any of us see you step foot in Boston again, then we will come for you."

Andrei clenches his jaw. "I'll give it to you, Mikhail. I underestimated you."

It's a lethal thing to underestimate the Gurin Bratva, but I thank my stars that Milan is my spy. "A mistake you will regret."

"Indeed." He bows his head. "We will leave now and not come back."

I nod in response and push Vera into his arms, keeping the gun trained on them both. "The car is out front."

They nod and hurry out of the room. I follow a distance behind, keeping my gun on the couple to ensure they leave.

I can't deny that I'm surprised they didn't put up more of a fight. Their eagerness to flee is odd. I watch as they hasten their footsteps the moment the exit comes into view. I notice Andrei glance at his watch before glancing over his shoulder at me.

Why is he in such a rush?

That's when I realize. They will blow the place, and it's the only explanation for why they wanted out of here fast. Their original plan was to murder my men and me and blow up the hotel, burying the evidence.

"Motherfucker," I growl, hastening my steps after them.

They slip out of the door to the hotel as I break into a sprint.

It's too late. The blast rocks the entire building. The jolt sends me to the floor, and I hit my head hard. I groan as my vision blurs and darkness pulls me down into its endless pit.

RINGING FILLS my ears as my eyes flutter open. Pain floods my irises, making me shut them.

I groan, trying to move, but my body feels too heavy.

A soft hand squeezes mine. "It's okay, Mikhail," Siena's sweet voice murmurs. "You're in the hospital."

I force my eyelids open again, squinting through blinding light. "W-what happened?" I try to recall where I was last, but my head is pounding.

"You were in a blast at the hotel." Siena's voice sounds sorrowful. "They put you in an induced coma for four days just to protect your brain from any damage."

I meet her teary-eyed gaze. "I'm sorry, malishka."

She shakes her head, tears flooding down her cheeks. "Don't apologize. I'm so glad you are alive." She stands and walks toward me, setting a kiss on my lips. "I was so scared, Mikhail."

"It's okay, malishka. I'm here."

Someone clears their throat at the door, and I glance up to see a doctor. "I'm glad to see you are awake." He walks closer. "How do you feel?"

"Like hell," I say.

He nods. "That is to be expected. You had some trauma to the head, but thankfully it has done no long-term damage." He places the clipboard at the end of my bed. "A colleague of mine will be by to do some cognitive and reflex tests with you, to be sure. A week and you should be okay to leave."

I groan. "A week?"

"Yes. You need to be monitored, and you broke a few ribs and your arm." He sighs. "A week is the minimum."

Siena smiles at the doctor. "Thank you so much for saving him."

The doctor smiles too. "You are welcome. It is my job, after all." He glances toward the door. "You have a couple of visitors waiting to see you. Shall I allow them in?"

"Who is it?"

The doctor shrugs. "No idea."

"Okay, let them in." I try to sit up, but he shakes his head.

"Stay as you are; no sitting up."

I swallow hard and nod in reply, wincing as it hurts to move my head. "Got it."

He leaves, and then the door opens. The people who enter aren't who I'm expecting.

Malachy, Scarlett, Milo, and Aida.

"Hey, lad. How are you holding up?" Malachy asks, approaching the bed. "I can't believe that son of a bitch blew up the hotel."

I grit my teeth together. "As well as expected. How did it go at the pub?" I ask.

Malachy smirks. "We killed every one of his men and sent their heads to him in New York."

"So he didn't blow up the place?"

Malachy shakes his head. "No, thankfully."

I glance at Milo. "How about you?"

Milo gives me a nod. "Same. We took out all his guys." As always, he's a man of few words.

Aida approaches Siena and wraps her arms around her. Malachy's wife also joins them.

"I am so glad you weren't in the building when it happened," she says, tears streaming down her face.

Siena hugs her back.

"Any news from Andrei?" I ask Milo and Malachy.

They shake their heads. "No, he sent the papers to our lawyers for the exchange of ownership on his properties owned here," Milo says.

"I let the bastard go thinking that was it, and then the place exploded." I wince. "I should have killed him."

"You know that wasn't an option, sir," Milan says, leaning on the doorframe.

I meet my spy's gaze. "I do, but he tried to kill me."

Milan nods. "He did, but I have tracked his every move since. Andrei has accepted defeat here." His brow furrows. "If he had been successful at taking you out, then it may have been different, but he failed."

Scarlett brings over a bouquet she is holding. "I brought you these," she says timidly, placing them in a vase next to my bed.

I force a smile. "Thanks."

I glance at the two men who used to be my enemies. I never thought I'd see them by my hospital bedside, at least not unless they were trying to assassinate me. "What's next, then?"

Milo and Malachy exchange glances. "We both agree that peace is the best option, and working together will strengthen us and protect us from threats like this in the future," Milo says.

Malachy nods. "Aye, but it doesn't mean we are going to be pals, though."

I laugh, and so does Milo. "No, but thank you both for agreeing to this. We could have all been six feet under otherwise."

Siena, Scarlett, and Aida all shake their heads. "Men."

All of us glance at them, confused, as they laugh. "Well, we best leave you to rest," Milo says.

Malachy approaches and gives me a light clap on the shoulder. "Get better, lad. We need you fighting strong soon."

I nod as they gesture for their women to follow them.

Aida gives Siena one last tight hug. "I'll see you soon. Gia apologized for not coming, but my father had to get back to Sicily for work."

Siena shakes her head. "Tell her not to worry about it. I'll talk to both of you soon."

Aida gives her one last lingering look before glancing at me. "Get better." She walks out after Milo, leaving us both alone again.

Siena sighs as she sinks into the chair next to my bed. I study her, noticing the darkness under her eyes. She looks strained and exhausted.

"You need to get some sleep, zhizn moya."

Her brow furrows. "What does that mean?"

"It means 'my life,' as that is what you are to me, Siena." I stretch my hand out toward her, and she takes it. "You are my world."

Tears flood her eyes, but she doesn't let them fall. "And you are mine."

"I love you, Siena."

Her eyes widen at the admittance of my love. I've known it for a while now. Deep down, I think I knew I would love her the moment I set eyes on her in that basement. "I love you too," she murmurs, tears now falling down her cheeks.

She stands and gets onto the side of the bed with me gently, allowing me to wrap my arms around her. "I don't think I ever want to return to Italy."

My heart skips a beat. "Ever?" I ask.

She shakes her head. "I mean to live, as I want to live with you." She meets my gaze. "Of course, I will return to visit my parents."

I smile at her. "Of course." My brow furrows. "Do you know where my jacket is?"

Siena glances over at the sofa, where it lies torn and dirty. "There."

"Can you bring it to me, malishka?"

She nods and gets up, grabbing the jacket and bringing it to me.

I reach into the pocket and sigh when I feel the small velvet box still in there. My mother gave my ancestral ring to me in the hope that I'd find a woman to marry one day, and I never thought I would until Siena came along. "Sit down, zihzn moya."

Siena does as I say, sitting on the edge of the bed.

"I have a question to ask you." I pull the box out of the jacket pocket and flip it open. "I want you to marry me. Will you do that?"

The sparkling diamond-encrusted ring sits pride of place in the center of the cushion. I don't know if it will fit her, as it may need to be resized.

Siena stares at me in shock for a long while, leaving me hanging.

"Siena?"

"Of course I'll marry you, Mikhail." She shakes her head. "Isn't this all a little crazy? We hardly know each other."

The answer to that question is certainly not. I know with all my heart that I want to spend the rest of my life with Siena. "No, it makes perfect sense." I take the ring out of the box, wincing as I try to move forward.

Siena places her hand on my chest and forces me to lie back. "Don't overexert yourself." She comes forward and holds her ring finger out for me to push it on.

It's a little loose on her. "I'll have it resized once I'm out of here."

She takes it off. "Maybe it is safer in the box, as I wouldn't want to lose it."

I dig my hand into my other jacket pocket and pull out a gold chain. "Here, put it on this and wear it around your neck. I want it on you. A symbol that you belong to me now, Siena."

She bites her bottom lip. "I think I belonged to you the moment we met, Mikhail," she murmurs.

I smile as she places the ring on the chain and does it up, then spins the chain around, so the clasp is at the back. The ring falls between her full cleavage, drawing my attention to her breasts.

I groan, shaking my head. "I can't believe I have to spend a week in here, as I'm going to go crazy if I can't fuck you during that time."

Siena shakes her head. "You almost died, and you are thinking about sex."

I hold my hand out to her, and she takes it. "With you, I can't help myself, zihzn moya." I yank her onto the side of my bed and grab the back of her neck, pulling her lips to mine.

She kisses me, opening her mouth to allow my tongue to plunder her. Our passion ignites as we kiss deeply before she finally breaks away. "You need to rest, but I will sleep with you." She adjusts herself, so she fits against me on the hospital bed.

I hold her tightly, knowing that there is no way I'm ever letting her go. From the moment I saw her in my basement, I knew she would be mine. I just never imagined I'd want to have her forever.

31

EPILOGUE

SIENA

Six months later…

The Sicilian sea sweeps in and out, dazzling as the sun's rays reflect off the perfect azure surface.

Mikhail walks from the sea, water glistening on his chiseled, tattooed body. I watch him, feeling blessed to call that man my husband. My parents are due to arrive in Sicily tonight and meet him for the first time.

I'm not sure what they will think of the wicked bratva boss who stole my heart. We will meet them at the airport and bring them back to the secluded beach villa Mikhail purchased as a wedding gift. I can come and spend time here when I get homesick and spend vacations when Mikhail wants to get out of the city.

They were a little upset with me when I married him without them there, but I insisted it was a very private affair with no one in attendance except for Aida and Gia.

Mikhail smiles when he sees me wearing his shirt on the balcony, and he hastens his steps toward me.

"Good morning, malishka. I went for a swim and didn't want to wake you." He climbs the steps and approaches me, wrapping his cold, wet arms around my waist.

"You are crazy. It's too cold in May to swim in the sea."

He chuckles. "You forget I have Russian blood. We're used to the cold." He presses a kiss on the back of my neck.

My stomach twists as something that has been bothering me comes to the forefront of my mind. Last month, I was late for my period and still haven't had one, so I took a pregnancy test, and it was positive. It should be impossible since Mikhail had a vasectomy. I know they fail sometimes, but it's very rare.

"Are you okay, malishka?" he asks, clearly noticing my shift in mood.

I prize his arms off me and turn around, shaking my head. "I don't know, Mikhail."

His brow furrows. "You can tell me what is bothering you, zhizn moya."

I don't know if I can. It makes no sense that I'm pregnant. "I was late for my period, and it never came last month." I swallow hard. "So, I took a pregnancy test, and it was positive."

Mikhail's brow furrows. "How is that possible? I had the procedure three years ago."

I shrug, shaking my head. "I don't know."

He lets go of me and paces toward the house before pacing back again. I can tell he's freaking out, but I don't know how to explain it. Mikhail never wanted children; that's why he had the vasectomy.

"You don't want me to have the child, do you?" I ask, feeling my throat close up at the mere mention of getting rid of our child. I'm not sure I can do it. My heart pounds hard against my rib cage as I wonder if this will finally break us.

Mikhail stops pacing and glances at me, muttering something in Russian. A part of me had hoped he'd changed his mind about children since we'd met, as the procedure can be reversible, but I'd never brought it up, worried it would cause problems.

However, getting pregnant after his procedure feels like fate. I want a baby, now more than ever. My two best friends both have children, and they're adorable.

"I don't know what I want, malishka." He moves closer to me and takes my hand. "I want you. That is something I'm sure of." His brow furrows. "However, I'm not sure I have it in me to be a father."

I set my hand on his tattooed chest. "Why do you say that?"

He smiles, but it's a sad smile. "I'm the pakhan of the Gurin Bratva, malishka. Criminals don't make good fathers." He pulls my hand off of his chest and paces the terrace. "I loved my father, but my childhood wasn't one most parents would wish for their child."

My brow furrows. "Just because you're a pakhan, that doesn't mean you have to follow in your father's footsteps."

I approach him and set my hand on his tense, muscular back. "You can shield our child from the bratva until he or she is old enough to understand."

He doesn't look convinced as he moves away from me again, staring out over the sea in front of us. "I am too damaged to be a father."

I bite my lip, knowing that what I'm about to say may cause serious tension. "I want the baby, Mikhail."

Mikhail turns to face me. "And I want to give you everything you want, malishka." He steps toward me. "If that is a baby, then so be it." His brow furrows. "You'll make an amazing mother, that I'm sure of."

I smile at him. "I know you'll make an amazing father, despite what you think."

Mikhail grabs my hips and pulls me against him, kissing me deeply. "I love you," he murmurs against my lips.

I smile against him. "Not as much as I love you, Daddy," I say.

He groans and lifts me off my feet, carrying me into the villa. "It's about time I fucked your pretty little cunt." His jaw clenches. "It going to be much more difficult when your parents arrive. How long are they staying?"

I chuckle at that. "Three days."

He shakes his head. "How am I going to survive?"

I search his dark eyes. "At least I brought the gag with me so you can silence me while you fuck me."

He bites my bottom lip hard. "Such a dirty girl, malishka. I'm going to do exactly that." He moves his lips to my neck and trails them lower. "First, I'm going to make you scream so loud all of Sicily will hear you."

I shudder at the promise, clutching at the back of his neck as he sets me on the sofa.

"On all fours, zhizn moya."

I eagerly get into position for him, lifting the edge of his shirt up so he can see how wet and ready I am for him.

"You dirty girl. Were you playing with your anal plug this morning while I swam?"

I glance at him over my shoulder. "Yes, Daddy. I want to be filled in both holes."

He growls and charges at me, grabbing my thighs and parting them wide. His tongue delves into my pussy, and he devours me like an animal.

I moan, arching my back.

"You're such a naughty girl, and naughty girls need to be punished."

My nipples tighten as he spanks my ass hard with his firm hand. "Yes, please punish me."

Mikhail grabs the crop off the side of the sofa and uses it on my ass, giving me three harsh strikes on each ass cheek.

I half moan and half scream at the pain that intensifies my pleasure. "Fuck," I murmur, feeling my pussy getting wetter the more he inflicts pain. "How can pain feel so good?"

Mikhail looms over me and grabs my throat, forcing me to look at him. "Because you are a dirty little masochist who can't get enough, malishka."

The dominant press of his hand around my throat is addictive. "Fuck me hard, please, daddy."

Mikhail removes his swim shorts and lines the thick head of his cock up with my aching pussy.

I feel the tip of it teasing against my soaking wet lips.

"Is this what you want?" he asks, dragging the tip through them. "My cock in your pussy and that thick plug in your ass?" he asks.

I feel my thighs shake with need. "Yes, please."

He groans as he slams his cock deep inside of me. "Then you will get what you want, dirty girl."

I grip hold of the cushions beneath me as he fucks me hard and deep. The large plug in my ass makes the sensation of his cock stretching me even more intense.

"Fuck," I cry as he digs his fingertips into my hips hard, using his powerful arms to draw me against him frantically.

Mikhail grunts as he drives into me like a man possessed.

I thought after a few months, his desire would wane, but he's more greedy than ever before.

It's as if the more we have of each other, the more we need.

"Do you love being stuffed in both holes at the same time?" he asks, his voice deep and gravelly.

I swallow hard, struggling to breathe. "Yes," I rasp.

He spanks my ass with his large hand. "So dirty. I have got a special surprise for you, Mrs. Gurin." He stops moving and slides his thick cock out of me, making me whimper.

"What is it?" I ask.

Mikhail doesn't reply, heading out of the living room toward the garage.

I wait for him to return, still on all fours.

He returns, holding a large dildo. "I think you are going to enjoy taking this and my cock at the same time."

My heart skips a beat at the thought of being that full.

"It won't fit," I protest.

He smirks his wicked smile that makes my insides churn and excites me all at the same time. "Oh, believe me, I'll make it fit, malishka."

I swallow hard. I believe him.

My thighs shudder at the thought as he moves over to the wood floor and places the dildo down. The suction cup sticks to the floor.

"Come here," he orders.

I do as he says, getting off the sofa and standing in front of him obediently, my desire to please him always winning over my fear of what is coming.

"Sit on it," he says, holding my gaze with those dark, unreadable eyes.

I do as he says, kneeling over it and allowing the thick length of it to fill me. My eyes clamp shut as it is as big as Mikhail.

To have that in my pussy and him in my ass is an overwhelming idea. "Are you sure it will fit?"

Mikhail groans and kneels behind me. "Fuck, yes." He grabs a handful of my hair and pushes me forward. "Remain at that angle," he instructs.

I feel him pull on the butt plug in my ass, gently tugging it out.

"You are already well stretched, malishka. Relax," he murmurs, squirting lube into my already stretched hole.

He adds more to his cock, and then I feel the head of his cock against the tight ring of muscles.

I breathe deeply, knowing that tensing in a moment like this never makes things better.

Mikhail applies pressure, and slowly he slides into my ass, filling me and stretching me in a way I never believed possible.

It hurts, but then I love pain. The masochist inside of me enjoys it as my pussy grows wetter. The length of his cock squeezing against the dildo deeply embedded in my pussy applies pressure to the exact spot inside of me that makes me come. I feel my body react, and before I know it, I'm hit by an intense orgasm.

Mikhail groans as his cock is deep inside of my ass. "You are such a dirty girl, coming as soon as you are filled with two cocks."

I pant for oxygen, trying to adapt to the feeling. "I never knew it could feel this good," I cry.

Mikhail digs his fingertips into my hips. "It is going to feel so much better when I fuck you, kukolka."

I shudder in anticipation, waiting for his onslaught. When he doesn't move, impatience builds. "Fuck me, then," I say.

Mikhail chuckles that wicked laugh that tells me he has no intention of following my orders. "You know who is in charge."

I whimper, desperate to feel him move.

"Do you like being so full?" Mikhail asks, drawing out my agony.

"Yes. I just want you to fuck me."

He spanks my ass, adding to my pleasurable torture. "Ask nicely, and maybe I will."

I swallow hard. "Please, fuck me, daddy," I say, trying not to sound frustrated.

Mikhail spanks my ass again before slowly moving his cock out. My nipples are hard and painful peaks, and my pussy is wetter than it has ever been.

"Faster, please," I pant.

Mikhail growls like an animal behind me, wrapping a tattooed hand around my throat from behind and squeezing. "As you wish."

He slams his cock back inside of me hard and fast, making me scream. The pain and pleasure merge as one as he takes my ass without mercy. Our bodies clash together as he thrusts into me brutally.

"That's it. Take those two cocks for me like the good girl you are, malishka," he snarls, his breath coming harder and faster as he increases the pace.

It's so damn tight and full. My brain short circuits as I try to process the sensation. I think Mikhail has finally broken me. My mind no longer functions as I'm a slave to this man.

He thrusts in and out of my ass forcefully, spanking my stinging ass cheeks now and again. It's as if he can read my mind. Mikhail is the master of my body, and he knows it better than I know it myself.

"Oh fuck, I'm going to come again," I cry, tears flooding down my cheeks as the sensation is too intense.

"Good. I want you to come with two cocks inside of you, malishka. I want to feel your ass squeezing the cum out of me."

I groan as the pleasure hits a level I've never experienced before. It feels like my soul leaves my body for a moment as if time stands still as white-hot pleasure sears every nerve ending in my body.

I scream Mikhail's name over and over, broken by the earth-shattering pleasure he has given to me.

Mikhail bites my shoulder hard enough to break the skin, roaring against it. He unloads his seed deep inside of my ass, pumping long after he's finished.

My body feels weak as I struggle to stay on my hands and knees. "Mikhail," I murmur his name.

He pulls out of me and lifts me from the floor and the dildo, carrying me over to the sofa. "You are okay, zihzn moya. Such a good girl," he purrs.

He sits on the sofa and holds me against him, running his fingers through my hair.

"I think you destroyed me," I murmur, feeling exhausted from the intensity of my orgasms.

He chuckles and presses a kiss on my forehead. "Nonsense, malishka. You are fine."

I glance up at him and shake my head. "No, I'm broken, as I want you to fuck me like that all the time."

He groans and tightens his grip on me. "Then I will."

I smile and rest my head back against his broad chest,

savoring the warmth of his body wrapped around me. We sit in blissful silence, enjoying each other's presence.

It's hard to believe one of the most frightening experiences of my life turned into the best one. Mikhail may have kidnapped me, but he took my heart in the process. I belong to him in every sense of the word, and I wouldn't have it any other way.

THANK you for reading Wicked Daddy, the last book for now in the Boston Mafia Dons series.

I hope you enjoyed following Mikhail's and Siena's story, as well as the rest of the characters in the series.

My next series moves us to Chicago in Chicago Mafia Dons. Everything starts with Maeve and Gael when their forbidden relationship catalyzes the worst mob war Chicago has seen in many years.

You can order the book now or read for FREE with a Kindle Unlimited subscription.

Cruel Savior: A Dark Forbidden Mafia Romance

I'll burn Chicago to the ground before I let her marry a Volkov.

Maeve Callaghan is my forbidden obsession. The reason I left for Europe three years ago. We were on the edge of crossing a line that could get us killed. Now I'm back and my desire returns with a vengeance.

When Ronan announces her engagement to a Russian, I know I'd die before I let her marry him. Maeve flees, taking the decision from my hands. Her father makes the grave mistake of sending me to retrieve her.

I'll betray the clan for her. Hell, I'd die for her. Maeve doesn't know the monster behind the man. I'm about to teach her how dark my soul truly is.Maeve is good and pure, but I'm rotten to the core.

I can't fight the pull any longer, no matter the consequences. I will bring the city to its knees for her. Chicago will erupt into a war like no one has ever seen. Will we survive or be a casualty of the havoc our love has caused?

Cruel Savior is the first book of the Chicago Mafia Dons Series. This book is a dark mafia romance involving bad language, dark themes, violence and scenes that may upset some people. It has no cliffhanger and a happily ever after ending and can be read as a standalone, even though all the books in the series intertwine. It features an over-the-top possessive and dark hero who wants the heroine no matter the costs.

**originally published as Merciless Defender.*

ALSO BY BIANCA COLE

Once Upon a Villian

Pride: A Dark Arranged Marriage Romance

Hook: A Dark Forced Marriage Romance

Wicked: A Dark Forbidden Mafia Romance

Unhinged: A Dark Captive Cartel Romance

Beast: A Dark Billionaire Romance

The Syndicate Academy

Corrupt Educator: A Dark Forbidden Mafia Academy Romance

Cruel Bully: A Dark Mafia Academy Romance

Sinful Lessons: A Dark Forbidden Mafia Academy Romance

Playing Dirty: A Dark Enemies to Lovers Forbidden Mafia Academy Romance

Chicago Mafia Dons

Cruel Savior: A Dark Forbidden Mafia Romance

Violent Leader: A Dark Enemies to Lovers Captive Mafia Romance

Evil Prince: A Dark Arranged Marriage Romance

Brutal Daddy: A Dark Captive Mafia Romance

Cruel Vows: A Dark Forced Marriage Mafia Romance

Dirty Secret: A Dark Enemies to Loves Mafia Romance

Dark Crown: A Dark Arranged Marriage Romance

Boston Mafia Dons Series

Empire of Carnage: A Dark Captive Mafia Romance

Cruel Obsession: A Dark Mafia Arranged Marriage Romance

Savage Bidder: A Dark Captive Mafia Romance

Ruthless King: A Dark Forbidden Mafia Romance

Vicious Bond: A Dark Brother's Best Friend Mafia Romance

Wicked Captor: A Dark Captive Mafia Romance

New York Mafia DonsSeries

Her Irish Daddy: A Dark Mafia Romance

Her Russian Daddy: A Dark Mafia Romance

Her Italian Daddy: A Dark Mafia Romance

Her Cartel Daddy: A Dark Mafia Romance

Romano Mafia Brother's Series

Her Mafia Daddy: A Dark Daddy Romance

Her Mafia Boss: A Dark Romance

Her Mafia King: A Dark Romance

New York Brotherhood Series

Bought: A Dark Mafia Romance

Captured: A Dark Mafia Romance

Claimed: A Dark Mafia Romance

Bound: A Dark Mafia Romance

Taken: A Dark Mafia Romance

Forbidden Desires Series

Bryson: An Enemies to Lovers Office Romance

Logan: A First Time Professor And Student Romance

Ryder: An Enemies to Lovers Office Romance

Dr. Fox: A Forbidden Romance

Royally Mated Series

Her Faerie King: A Faerie Royalty Paranormal Romance

Her Alpha King: A Royal Wolf Shifter Paranormal Romance

Her Dragon King: A Dragon Shifter Paranormal Romance

ABOUT THE AUTHOR

I love to write stories about over the top alpha bad boys who have heart beneath it all, fiery heroines, and happily-ever-after endings with heart and heat. My stories have twists and turns that will keep you flipping the pages and heat to set your kindle on fire.

For as long as I can remember, I've been a sucker for a good romance story. I've always loved to read. Suddenly, I realized why not combine my love of two things, books and romance?

My love of writing has grown over the past four years and I now publish on Amazon exclusively, weaving stories about dirty mafia bad boys and the women they fall head over heels in love with.

If you enjoyed this book please follow me on Amazon, Bookbub or any of the below social media platforms for alerts when more books are released.

Printed in Great Britain
by Amazon